STARTING OVER:
A TRINA RYAN NOVEL

SHERI S. LEVY

BARKING RAIN PRESS

Starting Over: A Trina Ryan Novel (Book 2)

Copyright © 2017 Sheri S. Levy (www.SheriSLevy.com)

Edited by Cindy Koepp (www.ckoepp.com)
Proofread by Ashlee Enz (www.barkingrainpress.org/ashlee-enz)

Cover artwork by: Sara Garcia Moreno (www.bitcover.net)

Barking Rain Press
PO Box 822674
Vancouver, WA 98682 USA
www.barkingrainpress.org

ISBN Trade Paperback: 1-935460-77-3
ISBN Hardcover: 1-941295-80-0
ISBN eBook: 1-935460-78-1
Library of Congress Control Number: 2017907796

First Edition: August 2017

Printed in the United States of America

DEDICATION

In memory of my mother, Lillian Shepherd.
She offered me opportunities she never had.

To Christy Smith, a talented artist
and loving friend.

To Caroline Eschenberg, my first writing
partner. I will miss your support and ideas.

Chapter 1

June

At three o'clock in the morning, I sat with my butt squished against the wall on the hard tile floor, my forehead resting on bent knees. I'd given up going back to bed and waited for Colton's next outburst.

Seconds later he whined. I lifted my head as his nose poked out of the crate, sniffing. He tilted his head and toddled toward me. His tail beat back and forth. After a quick pee on the clean newspapers, he crawled onto my lap.

He put his front paws on my shoulders, and his dark eyes flirted mischief. I smiled. "Ms. Jennifer and Mom warned me you'd be waking up all night."

Colton's ears drooped, and I stroked his velvety fur. Cradling his plump body, I buried my face in his fuzz. I inhaled his toasty puppy smell, trying hard not to think about Sydney, the first service dog I had trained. Sydney had come to me when his family had moved away from South Carolina. At six-months-old, he had been trained in his basic needs, and he'd even slept through the night. During our beach vacation, Sydney had worked his special magic with Logan, a young boy with autism. My best friend Sarah and I also met his cute older brothers, Peyton and Chase.

Sydney and I had snuggled on our last night, and I'd told him about my memories of our year together. In the morning, I'd clenched my teeth behind a fake smile and returned him to be matched to his forever companion. Minutes before leaving the facility empty-handed, large, brown puppy eyes from the nursery had connected with mine. I'd decided to train another.

Eight-week-old Colton was a blank slate. I would be his first and only foster momma until he turned eighteen months old. Colton nosed me again. He lifted his chocolate brown eyes to mine, and warmed the achy parts of my heart.

I surveyed the newspapers covering the floor, then wrinkled my nose and shook my head. If I had known how much work was involved, would I have started over again? I sucked in my cheek, nodding. *Yeah.*

I can do it. I have all summer to get him into a routine. I grabbed my frizzy hair into a quick ponytail, wadded up the messy papers, and spread new ones across the floor. "All done. Let's go outside." Before I lifted him, my puppy itched behind his ear with his right back foot. "Hmm. Fleas. They'll have to wait till later."

With no street lights, the full moon glowed like a night light and the shiny stars winked at me. An owl hooted in our forested backyard, halting Colt for a second. His ears pitched forward, and then he returned to his adventure. I gave him five more minutes with the sensor light going on and off before placing him and a handful of kibbles inside his crate. "Night-night. Pleeeeease go to sleep."

He rested his head in the opening of the crate, and fought to keep his eyes open and on me.

I tip-toed back to my temporary bedroom downstairs, grabbed a pillow, and pulled off the top sheet. Wrapping up like a mummy, I laid on the hard, wooden-floor in front of the doggy gate, and let my head sink into the pillow. Maybe being closer to him, he'll let me get some sleep. *Tomorrow's going to be a long day,* I groaned to myself.

As my eyes closed, I pictured chasing Colton in the muggy air. I'd teach him new words and then we'd snuggle together. Before long, sunlight from the laundry room window leaked under my eyelids and a whiff of coffee jolted me awake. Colton's little head hadn't moved. Feeling a bit jealous he was still snoozing, I unwound the sheet and scooted into the kitchen. I yawned and scanned the room, twisting a loose curl at my neck.

Mom crooked her head. "Rough night, Trina?"

Nodding, I rubbed the tiredness from my burning eyes. "Yep. I can't believe he's still sleeping."

Dad set his coffee cup down. "We heard you two, but we promised to stay put."

Mom grabbed her purse and headed to the door. "I've got to go. Dr. Mayer called early and needs my help with a sick dog. Since I had a spare minute, I took him out for you. You never even flinched. When he wakes, he's all yours."

I found enough energy to utter, "Thanks."

The door closed behind her.

Before I finished my cheese grits, howls pierced the silence. I rolled my eyes. "Sounds like I'm back on duty."

This is going to be harder than I thought.

In my shortie pajamas, I carried Colton outside to our fenced yard. He sniffed and bit at pine cones and chased squirrels at a tiny paw speed. His ears raised at the clunk-clunk of Mrs. Brown's golf cart driving up the path to her paddocks next door. I collapsed on the grass and leaned against a tree trunk. Colton stared toward the clatter and hunched down. He scrambled over my crossed legs and plopped into the gap.

"Mrs. B is bringing in the horses." I whispered in his ear. "You'll get to meet her soon."

He scratched his neck and crept through the trees an inch at a time. The sun simmered overhead and sent a wilted pup back to my lap. I carried him to his crate, and he crumpled into a small heap.

"Whew—finally. We'll do your bath after your nap." I bounced into the recliner to text Sarah.

Instantly, she texted. "How's Colton?"

"Adorable. Meet me in ten."

Sarah texted three smiley faces.

I grinned and wished my phone could do that.

Yesterday's clothes lay on the floor. I dressed as fast as I could then hurried to meet Sarah at the huge oak tree. My pounding heart pulsed through my arms and legs. I twisted a strand of hair and rechecked my phone for the millionth time.

Where is Sarah?

I needed to see Chancy, the barn's schooling horse I rode. Heather, the other groom, had cared for her during my week at Edisto Beach. She spent tons of time with Chancy and even gave her treats when I wasn't around. I wiped the beads of sweat off my lip and stared at the ground. What if Chancy preferred her over me? Worry bubbled up my throat. If I had to share Chancy, I couldn't pretend she was mine.

Sarah approached in crisp white shorts, a sparkly pink tee, and French-braided blond-hair. My stomach knotted, and my cheeks burned. Sarah enjoyed teasing me about my out-of-control red hair and matching freckled face. I slowed my steps to let my face cool. Then I tucked loose curls into my ragged ponytail, and smoothed out my wrinkled PAALS tee shirt.

Darby, Sarah's black and white springer spaniel, wiggled her stub of a tail as Sarah looped her arm through mine. She jabbered on about Peyton's texts without missing a beat. I nodded and smiled, tuning her out with memories of my first secret kiss with Chase, Peyton's younger brother. I considered sharing our phone conversations, but a loud noise like a cement truck grew closer and interrupted our conversation.

Sarah squinted. "What's that racket?"

"Sounds like a big diesel truck. Let's get closer." Behind a wide tree trunk, we spied a silver-gray, dually truck pulling a white, two-horse trailer. Five interlocked gray hearts decorated the sides. I clasped my hands together. "Oh, I bet that's the new boarder. I forgot she was coming today. Let's go look."

The truck slowed onto Mrs. Brown's drive. Sarah's forehead creased and she screamed over the noise. "Do you know how old she is?"

"Mrs. B said she's in the ninth grade." As the commotion lessened, I added, "And, her mother bragged to Mrs. B about all of her winnings since she started riding. Ooo! I can't wait to see her ride. Maybe, she'll even ride with me."

The engine turned off and a tall, dark-skinned man leaped from the driver's side. At the same time, a long-legged, skinny girl in black riding pants and shiny black boots stepped down from the front passenger door. The sun gleamed on her brown face, poufy bangs, and ponytail. She waved her dressage whip in the air as if it were a sword. The girl's voice boomed through the trees, "Dad, what are you doing? Look! You're too close to the fence. Pay attention!"

I turned a wide-eyed look at Sarah, whose mouth hung open. Without a word, Sarah grabbed my arm and pulled me closer.

Her father opened the trailer's top half doors and latched the panels to each side. From the rear of the trailer, a stately, black horse kicked and neighed. Standing on opposite sides of the trailer, the dad and the girl each pulled a clip out of the lock and set the ramp on the ground. The girl climbed in a side door to untie the horse. He put one hoof a couple of inches behind, and then took another step. After a frantic snort, he lurched forward.

She screamed at the horse. "Knight, walk! Get off the trailer!" Her whip slapped at the air. "What's wrong with you?"

Without warning, the horse threw his head, showing the whites of his eyes as he bolted backward down the ramp. White foam lathered his glossy chest.

Her voice raised an octave. "Dad, he's getting away!" Then she shrieked, "Move! You're no help!"

Holding my breath, I clutched Sarah's arm.

The father rushed over and pulled the whip from the girl's hands. "Morgan, quiet down! You're frightening Knight. Give him a chance."

She jerked the lead line. "Knight, you stupid horse! You *know* better."

"Oh my gawd!" My eyes widened, and I shook my head. "How could anyone treat their horse like that?" I patted my chest. "And what's she doing at *my* barn?"

Chapter 2

grabbed Sarah's arm and whirled her around. "Let's not go there now."

Sarah stopped and faced me. "Have you seen Chancy yet?"

"No. That's why I wanted to go. But now, I'll have to wait longer to know if she's still mine."

Neither of us spoke as we moved away from the barn. Further into the thick trees, I stopped. "Want to see Colton?"

Sarah's blue eyes lit. "Yes, and he can meet Darby."

We ran back to my house with Darby barking and running alongside. As we entered, Darby quieted and lifted her nose. Loud shrieks coming from the laundry room made my heart bang against my chest. "Oh no! We weren't gone long! He's supposed to be sleeping."

My legs did double time. At the baby gate, my mouth dropped open. Colton had done his business all over the floor and turned his water bowl upside down. He ducked his chin, and his eyes peered from inside the crate.

Sarah peeked over my shoulder and held her breath until she turned pink. "Ooo! Nasty." She waved her hand in front of her face. "I'm sure glad mom took care of Darby when she was a puppy. What are you going to do?"

I set my hands on my hips and stared at her. "I'm going to clean it up. I've done this with the horses, and I can do it for my pup."

Screwing her face, Sarah guzzled air and then whooshed her words out in one breath. "Do you want me to ask your dad to come help?"

"Nah. Just tell him we're back. He's in his office."

Colton's ears sagged, and his eyes begged for forgiveness. I spoke to him in a soft, happy voice. "Hey, little guy! What have you done?"

He poked his nose an inch out of his crate, his nostrils opened and closed.

"Kind of stinky in here, isn't it?" I wrinkled my nose.

He lifted his back leg and scratched a spot behind his ear.

"I'll get this cleaned up." While holding my breath, I grabbed the scooper and paper towels by the sink and cleaned until I thought I'd suffocate. My breakfast threatened to come back up. I climbed over the gate, stepped into the hallway, and sniffed a noseful of fresh air. I swallowed and inhaled twice. *Ready or not, I'm finishing this.*

Dad arrived with Sarah. "Oh!" He backed up. "I heard a commotion in here but couldn't interrupt my phone call. It looks like you've got it under control. That-a-girl."

I rolled my eyes. "Thanks, Dad."

"You're welcome." He grinned and bowed. "Just part of your training. These things happen. Get him bathed, and I'll fix lunch for you girls. I have one more call to make."

Sarah shook her head. "Ooo! Sorry, Mr. Ryan. No way I can eat after smelling this room. Trina, call me when you're going back to the barn. I'm heading home."

"Ah, come on Sarah." My shoulders straightened. "Don't you want to watch?"

She twisted her head back and forth, pinching her nose.

I used my most convincing voice. "This will be his very first bath, and you'll miss it."

Sarah's monotone nasal voice hummed. "Mom wants me to unpack, and Darby's getting bored. I'll see you later."

I ducked my head and mumbled at the floor. "Okay. Later."

Colton lay beside his crate, the tops of his ears lifted up and down at the noise of running water. Once the sink filled, I lowered him inch by inch, letting his front paws touch. His eyes widened, his body stiffened, and he tried to crawl out of my arms. I cupped my right hand with water and put it up to his nose. He sniffed, and then lapped the warm water and inched in.

Pointing the spray nozzle away from his body, I let him relax to the sound and rush of the water. "Stand. Good boy." He blinked, but didn't fight me. I sprayed him in quick, soft squirts, speaking slowly, and worked in a new lavender scented shampoo. "This will be my first scientific experiment. Let's see if the lavender smell calms you."

Colt turned white in the soapsuds. Only his black nose poked out and dead fleas floated to the top of the froth."

As I rinsed his body, every few seconds, Colt shook from his head to the tip of his pointy tail. Soap and water splattered. Dark-brown splats landed on the floor, the wall, and on me.

Using my hands as a shield didn't add any protection. Water dripped from my chin and my soaked clothes. "Okay, Colt, almost done." I rinsed him until the murky-water turned clear.

He squirmed, and fought being wrapped in a towel. But as soon as I rubbed every inch of his body, his eyes softened and closed. If he had been a cat, he would've purred. I set him on the floor, and in one second, he untangled himself from the towel.

Then he raced off. Colton ran through the hallway, leaving a trail of puddles. As I caught him, all four legs thrashed. I fought to hold him, but he slipped right through my fingers. He looked over his shoulder to see if I followed and ran smack into the wall.

"Oh, no! Are you all right?" I pressed his body to the floor. "I've got you now, you little squirm ball."

Colton rolled over as if he was a turtle on his back and kicked his legs in the air. I smiled at the sight and scratched his tummy. In the next instant, he wiggled around to his feet and escaped.

Barking echoed from the den. He jogged around the coffee table and kept his eyes on me. His mouth pulled back in a grin. I went one way, and he took off the other direction. He sprinted to my parents' bedroom, sprang onto their newly upholstered, yellow and orange ottoman. Without a pause, he launched himself onto the matching chair and shook.

Colton stood, panting. That gave me enough time to rush forward and get a tight hold. I squeezed his wet body to mine, and he twisted to get free.

Dad tried to contain his laughter. "He's certainly full of himself."

In the kitchen, I set Colt behind another baby gate and giggled. "I don't think he inhaled enough of the lavender smell."

While I helped Dad with lunch, Colton lunged at my shoe lace.

My legs tangled over his body, and I stumbled to the nearest counter. "I'm taking him outside."

Colt wound himself inside my legs, pulling on the other shoelace. As I stepped toward the sliding glass door, my foot punted him like a football an inch above the floor. He spun into the cabinet, and scrambled to his feet.

Before he charged at me again, I slid the glass door open. Colton raced across the grass and watched squirrels bounce from limb to limb. As he slowly ran down like a wind-up toy, I wrapped his purple training harness around his chest and clicked on his leash for the first time.

I swallowed my laughter as he halted, and gave me The Look as if saying, "What have you done?"

He wasn't fighting the harness. He'd worn one since he was three days old. But today I had attached a leash to the two-purple corded bands wrapped around him. He shook his entire body, inched through the trees, and shivered twice before surrendering to the new feeling.

In a few minutes, the summer heat made Colton's tongue droop, and he slunk home. Inside, I unclipped his leash and harness and he quivered once more. I massaged his back with both of my hands and his glance told me, "Thank you." I opened the baby gate to the hallway, and he toddled to his crate.

The aroma of a BLT sandwich floated through the hallway, competing with the lingering poopy odor.

During lunch Dad listened to me complain about the new girl. "Give her a chance. You don't know what happened before they got here."

I tilted my head with a puzzled look. "You think?"

He nodded and finished his lunch.

"I'll try." I released my breath at the same time I spoke. "Dad, I know I've already left Colt, but I've got to find out about Chancy. He's asleep now, and I promise, I won't stay long. Fifteen minutes, max." Grinning, I raised my eyebrows. "And I bet he's safe for a while."

Dad checked his watch. "I'll call this my lunch break. Hurry. I have more work to do."

"Thanks." I ran the whole way. Before going into the barn, I jutted my chin forward, preparing to meet the new girl. With both wooden sliding doors open at each end of the barn, the little breeze we enjoyed drifted through one door and out the other. Knight flung his head over the first stall door. He inspected my every movement, and then he snorted and neighed.

I rubbed his nose. "Hey, fella. You're awfully handsome." I glanced around and called, "Morgan?" No sound. I returned my attention to Knight. "I guess you've been left all alone on your first day here."

"Hey, Trina." Mrs. Brown called from the tack room on the opposite side of the six stalls. She walked out, smiling. "I wondered when you'd be back. Chancy's been waiting for you."

"Really? Oh, Mrs. Brown. It's so nice to see you." I hugged her. "I came to see if she's still my schooling horse."

Chancy tossed her head over the fifth stall door, blowing her lips. My pulse speeded. "Hey, Pretty Girl. I'm comin'."

One by one, the other three horses threw their heads over their stall doors. I let out a happy gasp and rushed down the row of heads, speaking to each horse and patting their necks. The last stall on the same side temporarily held Ashley's Warm Blood, Vaunted, a stocky, bright bay with three white legs. His thoroughbred mother had been bred with a draft horse. This type of horse suited riders showing in advanced events. Vaunted could jump higher with stronger legs and had a calmer disposition than a hot-blooded thoroughbred.

Mrs. Brown followed me. "First off, you don't have to worry about losing Chancy. I'll keep her for you as long as you want to ride. She enjoyed Heather riding her, but as you can see, she's excited to see you."

"What's up with the new girl? She seems kind-of spoiled."

"Morgan? I haven't met her yet. Spoken with her mother, though. It seems Morgan's only boarded at fancy stables where all the grooming and feeding was done for her. And Mrs. Hart doesn't want her daughter doing any of what she referred to as 'menial labor.'"

My eyes widened. "Really?" I snickered under my breath. "Her name's Morgan Hart? Whoo! Her last name doesn't go with her personality."

Mrs. Brown chuckled. "Hang in there, Trina. Let's not jump to any conclusions."

I stroked Chancy's smooth, round belly and listened to Ms. B's words.

"I told her mother we'd be responsible for the care of her horse when she's not here. But when she's riding, it's her job to tend to her horse's needs. We'll have to see how it goes."

"Maybe I'll meet her tomorrow. I've only got a few minutes before I have to get home. Did you hear I have a new puppy to train?"

"I did. Your mom called last night. I can't wait to meet him. Is he as cute as Sydney?"

"Almost." I stared at the floor. Every time I heard Sydney's name, my stomach ached like I'd swallowed a rock. I gulped and smiled. "He's so much younger and full of mischief. He looks and acts different than Sydney, which makes it easier to start over. Driving home, we invented new names. His nose looks like a piece of coal. And the word coal made me think of a colt. So, I decided to name him Colton."

Mrs. Brown's eyes crinkled. "Your own little colt. Very cute."

I rubbed Chancy's soft brown nose. "Sarah and I plan to do treats with the horses tonight. When's Morgan coming back?"

"I don't know, but honey, no bad attitudes are going to change our happy barn."

I bowed my head and muttered, "I hope not."

Chapter 3

While Colton slumbered deep in puppy land, I flopped on the couch and stuffed extra cushions behind me. Afraid I'd fall asleep, I turned on the TV, and texted Sarah about going to give the horses treats tonight. Without any warning, my eyes closed.

In my dreams, my toes nestled into the sand on Edisto Island. Darby chased seagulls and Sydney chased her. Chase stood so close to me I could hear his breath. We watched the sparkling waves ripple in the sun and when they broke, white foam swished over our feet, making us laugh. Sydney patted the bubbles and looked up at me with his golden eyes and then...Colt's pitiful barks snapped me awake. I popped up. "I'm coming, Colt."

He met me at the doggy gate. His pointy, black tail whipped back and forth as he strained to set his front feet at the top. Like a prize fighter, he tried again and again until he collapsed on the floor, whining.

"Hey, baby." I squinted. "What's wrong?"

He sat. His mouth stretched across his teeth like a grin and his dark eyes grew larger.

I giggled at his response. "You little stinker. I bet you just want some attention."

Mom's sentences played in my head. After every nap, he must be taken outside. Once he can tell you he needs to go out, things will get easier.

"Maybe you're telling me you have to go potty?" I bent over the gate, picked him up, and placed him on my shoulder. In seconds, his needle-sharp teeth nibbled on my neck and ear.

"Ouch!" I gently clamped his mouth with my hand.

Before we reached the sliding glass door, my shirt grew warm, soggy, and vinegary. "NO! No. No." I jogged, bobbling him in my arms and set him on the grass. "Darn it, Colt. This is my favorite shirt."

He sniffed the ground as he turned in circles and then squatted.

I told him, "Do business," as he pottied, teaching him to connect the words to the action.

In a cheery voice, I said, "Good boy!" And to myself I said, *I'm going to have to be quicker.*

His treat disappeared in one gulp, and then he raced to the house. He panted and his tongue flopped sideways. He'd already learned about air-conditioning.

Upstairs in my real bedroom, I changed and read Sarah's text. "Have soccer practice — 6:00. Be home by 8. Ok?"

"Perfect. Hope it's cooler. Have lots of treats."

The rest of my first day romped by. Colt slept, woke to potty, ate biscuits, chewed or tugged on anything that could fit into his mouth, and repeated everything in that order. While he slept, I read a few chapters of The Ins and Outs of Puppy Raising and ate snacks. Keeping up with a puppy made me hungry, too.

After dinner, Mom volunteered to keep Colton awake, hoping he'd sleep longer through the night.

As I filled my backpack with apples and carrots, my stomach flip-flopped. Then the adrenalin rush kicked in, and I couldn't wait any longer. I caught a few short breaths and raced down the path.

The moon hid behind the pine tree branches as the sun slipped away, giving a yellow tinge to the night sky. Knickers and whinnying floated through the still, damp air. Sticky sweat trickled down my back, even though it was close to eight-thirty. After sunset, maybe, we'd be lucky and catch a cooler wind. Not likely in June in South Carolina, but I could always wish.

Sarah met me on the path, and we chatted toward the barn.

"How was practice?" I asked.

She widened her eyes and snickered. "Good. I'll be ready for soccer camp."

"And to see Peyton?"

Sarah bobbed her head, vibrating with enthusiasm. "That's the plan. In two weeks. He texted twice yesterday. I hate that they live an hour and a half away. It's going to be sooo hard to see each other. Have you heard from Chase?"

I walked backwards, raised my shoulders to my ears, and grinned. "Yep. He texted me late last night and called me early this morning, checking on Colton. He promised to call every evening, but I have to shoot him a quick text to tell him I'm in for the night. The best part is he's riding up with Peyton. He's going to visit with me all day while his dad drives you and Peyton to camp."

She crossed her hands on her heart and smirked. "Wow! I thought you didn't care about guys." Sarah's eyebrows arched. "What are you going to do while he's here?"

My face stretched into a grin. "We'll have plenty to do with Colton, the pool, and the horses. He loves riding."

I halted and gave Sarah my serious face. "Since you finally told me at the beach about not knowing how to swim, do you want me to teach you?" I met her gaze. "Just in case you're asked to swim at camp."

"You think?" She put her finger up to her cheek and squinted at the sky. "Hmm!"

I giggled. "Sarah, you're so dramatic."

She laughed and grabbed my arm. "I could try. I like Mrs. Brown's pool. When?"

"You know me and the water. Anytime. Well, almost anytime. When I'm not working with Colton."

Sarah sucked in her cheek. "I'll think about it. Have you seen Knight?"

"Yep. This afternoon. He's really nice. You can feed him tonight."

The paddocks were cut into six spaces in three rows. The two largest were further away on lower ground shaded by clumps of hardwood trees. The natural shelter was the perfect place for protection from bad weather.

During the summer, Mrs. B or I walked the horses out to their paddocks. They anticipated spending their evenings nibbling grass in the cooler air. In the morning, they anxiously waited to leave the broiling sun and rest inside their stalls.

Tonight Mrs. B beat me. She had already moved the horses to their paddocks. I counted two heads in the right front paddock. The small, chestnut mare by the fence had a matching mane and a white star on her forehead. I knew my Chancy anywhere. The other thoroughbred mare eating grass was Dove, a tall, dark-brown bay with black socks, mane, and tail.

The left front paddock held Sonny, a stocky black quarter horse with a thick black mane and a long blaze down his face. He roamed along the fence rails, peering into the woods. Rapp, a white paint gelding with patches of brown, walked toward us. Vaunted roamed by himself in the middle-right paddock, using the junction of his paddock to socialize with the rest of the horses.

"Morgan must have kept Knight inside," I said. "We'll check on him before we leave." I dropped the backpack. "Help yourself."

I spent the most time feeding and talking to Chancy. Each horse ate three pieces of apple and one whole carrot in small chomps. Stroking their noses made their fur scratchy going up and smooth going down like corduroy. As I rubbed their foreheads, they leaned into my hand.

Before leaving, I sprayed them with an orange-smelling bug repellant as their tails swished at the irritating flies.

I grabbed Sarah's hand. "Let's find Knight."

Chancy neighed as I walked away. I returned for one more belly rub. "Hey, pretty girl. I'll try to come back tomorrow. Sleep tight."

Snorts came from inside the barn. "Come on, Sarah. Knight's in there all by himself. Poor guy."

At his stall, Sarah put her hands on her hips and pouted. "That's mean. Here, Knight. We'll make you feel better."

We took turns feeding him, patting his neck, and talking to him. When I stopped, he nosed my shoulder.

"Look Sarah, he's showing his appreciation. He certainly doesn't have Morgan's personality."

Reaching deep into my pocket, I found one more piece of apple. As he chewed, I rubbed the side of his face. "Knight. You're a true prince."

I brushed my hands back and forth. "All gone. See you in the morning."

As we walked away, he forced a blast of air from his lips, and pawed his floor.

Twisting around, I raced back to him and patted his long neck. "I'm so sorry. I know you're not happy. Morgan sure needs a lesson on caring for you. Maybe two or three."

He nodded his head and pushed me with his nose.

"So you agree." I laughed. "I'll see what I can do. I promise."

Chapter 4

On my puppy's second day before I had finished his morning exercises, he collapsed under a tree, curled his paws under his chin, and dozed.

I carried his limp body to the house and whispered. "It's okay, baby boy. I'll go see Chancy, and we'll train when I get back."

Colton curved into a ball on the laundry room's cool floor, panting. I changed into my makeshift riding clothes—jeans, a purple and pink tie-dyed tee, and brown ankle boots—and headed to Dad's office. I wrote on his memo pad. "Colt's tired. He'll sleep for a while."

Dad eyed me, read my note, and shook his head, while listening to whoever was on the other end of the phone. He scribbled, "Can't. Have C-call. Take phone. Will call if he wakes."

I waved and practically ran out the door. I'd have to hurry through my morning jobs. With my heart bouncing inside my chest, I floated along the path, inhaling the sweet-smelling honeysuckle growing wild in the woods. "I'm coming, Chancy."

She nickered to me. As I approached, she paced back and forth and met me at the fence. I slipped the halter over her neck, fed her a carrot, and walked her into the barn.

The aroma of manure, hay, and horses made me sigh. One day, I'd have a great-paying job, and have my own barn, my own horse, and lots of dogs. Until then, I'd be happy helping. After walking each horse into their stall, I cleaned everyone's water buckets and filled their hay racks.

Knight watched me and snorted. "Do you need some attention?" He nodded like he understood. "Since you're new here, I'll make sure you're comfortable. I'm sorry you've been stuck in here all night."

After repeating the same chores for him, I grabbed the pick to clean his stall. He nibbled at my shirt and tried to pull a carrot from my back pocket. "Oh, you're playful, aren't you? And maybe you feel a little neglected." I broke off a piece and let him nuzzle my hand.

He blinked his dark eyes at me and chomped.

I stole a glance through his window at Ashley, a top-competitive rider boarding for a month. In the riding stadium, she soared over four-foot jumps and cantered around the ring, doing flying lead changes. Her horse's strides changed from the right front leg to the left front leg while in canter, a 1-2-3 rhythm. Her long honey-colored hair flapped in the wind under her helmet, and I imagined myself out there.

Mrs. Brown wordlessly put her arm around my shoulders. "She looks good, doesn't she?"

I turned my head to her and smiled. "I sure hope one day I'll be doing that on the Clemson Riding Team."

"Come on. I'll help you tack up." Mrs. B took me by the hand to Chancy's stall. "Chancy needs you to ride her. Just pick her feet and groom her after. Ashley can watch you while she's training here. I'll finish with the horses."

I stared at my feet. My conscience said NO! I pictured Colton waking and me not there. But my heart fluttered. My stomach flipped over. I gulped. "Okay. For just a few minutes." *This is wrong, but I so want to ride.* "Dad's going to call if Colton wakes. I'll take a quick ride around the stadium."

Mrs. Brown inserted the bit, and then pulled the bridle over Chancy's head. I hauled her heavy English saddle up the mounting block. It hung to my knees. I climbed up one step at a time, pulling the saddle with me. On the top step, I used all my strength and heaved it over Chancy's back. She remained still. "What a good girl! We're almost ready."

I stepped down to the ground and reached under her stomach for the girth. Once I had hold, I pulled the two straps through the buckles, yanking hard. After they were clasped, my silly horse always let her air out, loosening the buckles.

Mrs. Brown ran her hand under the girth. "Not snug enough. Try again."

Once more I tugged each strap.

"That's better." She smiled.

Standing again on the mounting block, I placed my left leg in the stirrup, and swung my right leg over the saddle. Sitting straight, neck stretching tall, legs hanging loosely, my smile grew to a silly grin and spread, showing every tooth all the way back to my molars.

After Mrs. Brown readjusted the stirrups, I slid my feet into them and pressed my heels into Chancy's side. Her right ear pointed forward like an antenna. I rocked back and forth with her walking gait, careful to keep my hands still and at waist level.

Mrs. B stood at the fence. "I want you to ride close to the fence line. Look straight ahead. That's it. Trot for a while, and then go down the diagonal." She walked away, but continued talking. "Have fun. I'll listen for a call. When you're tired, Ashley will help you untack."

"Thanks, Mrs. Brown. This is wonderful. I could stay out here forever."

After fifteen minutes, my legs bounced away from Chancy's side. My back slumped and my hands were uneven. I pulled back on the reins. "I've got to do better than this."

I pressed my bottom into the saddle, getting a tighter seat, caught my breath, and rearranged my feet. "Let's try again."

Ashley sat on the fence, grinning and giving me the thumbs-up.

I only lasted another ten minutes before Chancy and I plodded to the barn. I brushed her using slow, circular strokes with her curry comb, loosening dirt and sweat. That helped her shed during the summer months. Before I had curried her right side, the old-style phone rang from a wooden ledge in the middle of the barn. My breath caught, and I dashed to answer before another ring.

The call was for Mrs. B, who never bothered with her cell phone, and I wrote down the message. Returning to Chancy light-hearted, I walked her into the stall. I returned with grain for her purple bucket. As she nuzzled it in circles, I tore off a four-inch chunk of hay from the square bale in the feed room, and placed it into her rack.

"Here's a flake of hay to nibble when you're finished playing in your food, silly girl."

She nibbled, ignoring the loud diesel truck chugging up the gravel road. The noise interrupted my thoughts. I expected voices, but heard nothing except the truck grumbling away.

I finished brushing Chancy's mane. My pulse slowed, and once again, my mind pictured me racing over jumps and winning ribbons. I stroked her bulging side, letting my hand slide across her shiny satin coat. I longed for more time. "I have to get home, pretty girl. See you tonight."

Boots clicked inside the barn across the cement floor and stopped outside the stall where I worked. Chancy's head shifted to the door, and I looked up.

Morgan glared at me for an instant through the stall door, and then she snapped her head around and marched to Knight's stall. She never said one word to him. Likewise, he didn't snort or whinny as she arrived.

Before leaving, I peeked in Knight's stall with a big welcoming smile. "Hey, I'm Trina. Welcome to our barn.'"

She lifted her chin, curled her lip, and growled. "Barn? Ugh! You mean 'shed' Are you the grunt that works here?"

All the blood rushed to my face. I balled my fists. I stiffened and stared at her. In my mind, lots of thoughts spilled out. *You have a lot of nerve. Who are you to bash our barn?*

But what came out was, "Excuse me?"

Her evil eyes bored through me. "Well, what I should have said is, my stall's not clean, and I'm ready to ride."

I stood face to face with her. The anger inside of me was so new. My words surprised me as I let them fly. "There's the pick, and there's the wheelbarrow. I'm finished for the day. And, you're on your own."

Chapter 5

I clenched my fists and ran, keeping all the boiling fury inside. My head shook, and I growled out loud. "How can anyone be so mean? She has her own horse and can ride every day."

Proud that I had gotten a word in, I stomped my way home. Before I stepped into the house, I calmed myself by breathing slower, wiped the fugitive tears from my cheeks, and changed my mind. I needed to see Sarah. Not Dad. I'd interrupted him too many times, and he'd say the same thing. "Give it time. She's new."

Rushing up to my bedroom, I waited for Colton to wake, and tried to relax by sketching my own nesting loggerhead turtle. Each stroke of the pencil brought warm memories of Chase's drawing in our Edisto beach house. Colt whimpered, and I rushed downstairs to carry him outside. While he wandered and played, I called Sarah, instead of texting. That was our code for urgent.

On the third ring, Sarah answered. "What's up?"

"Meet me on the road. Colt needs a walk, and I'll fill you in on Morgan."

Living in the country, our houses were a good distance apart. Ten neighbors had barns with pasture land and other neighbors had acres of wild grass. I lived on eight acres covered in hardwoods and pine trees with a small manicured grassy area around the house. Sarah and I rode our bikes, roller-bladed, or used our scooters to travel back and forth to each other's houses.

Colt saw me lift the leash off the hook and hid behind his crate. "Walk?" I held the treat in front of his nose, giving him the option to choose. I wanted to hurry him but knew I'd cause him to react, and I'd lose ground. I closed my eyes, inhaled, and let my frustration out as a slow breeze. "Come on, Colt. Walk."

He leaned his head, keeping his eyes on me. After several puppy steps, he stood in front of me. I clicked the clicker and fed him a cookie before I attached his leash to his harness. "Good boy. Walk."

He took one step, waited and then took another. The longer we walked, the more he relaxed and jogged along.

"That-a-boy."

Sarah buzzed toward us on her electric scooter. I smiled and my shoulders relaxed for a moment. I couldn't wait to share my awful experience. And then Colton's body slouched. He squinted and froze. I said, "Sit." When he glanced calmly at the scooter heading toward us, I clicked, and gave him a treat. But Sarah came closer. Colt hid behind me and peeked through my legs, safely curious about the motor's roar.

"Sarah, you may want to leave the scooter. We'll have another practice session, later."

When Sarah set her scooter on the side of the road, he darted toward her. She bent face to face with him, "Hi, Colt. It's me."

His tail swung as she petted his back and spoke in baby tones. When she looked at me, she took a step backward. "Ooo. Something's got to be bad when your eyes turn olive green. All right. I'm all ears. Tell."

With my arms crossed, I huffed out all my air in one big breath. "I just met that awful girl boarding with Mrs. Brown." I paused to breathe and started again. "She's horrible. She insulted me, and I never want to be at the barn with her. Never, ever again!"

Sarah's mouth gaped open. "What'd she say?"

I told Sarah everything, including how I told Morgan off and raced home. "Poor Mrs. Brown. I know she needs another boarder, but that girl can't stay." I hiked my shoulders to my neck and tensed every part of my body until I shuddered. "She just can't."

Sarah hadn't made a sound. Squinting her eyes, she pointed. "To the barn. I want to meet this girl."

"I don't know, Sarah. Maybe we should wait until Mrs. Brown has a chance with her."

"Nah. Let's go. I'll protect you."

At the barn, we walked past Morgan jumping Knight in the ring. Inside, Mrs. Brown swept the barn floor. "Hey, girls. Trina, did you have a good ride?"

Colt stood next to me, checking out the barn. "Kind of. I've got a lot to work on, and then I met the grumpy Ms. Princess."

Mrs. Brown's eyes challenged me. "I spoke to Morgan when she arrived. She seemed to be in a good mood before I disappeared to the paddocks. When I returned, you were leaving in a huff."

"Ah. She must have known you were gone." I stood nose to nose with Mrs. B and smiled. "She's sneaky. She called this barn 'a dump' and me 'a grunt.' She expected me to have her horse ready to ride. Mrs. B, she's a real pain."

"Well. I'll have none of that going on in my barn." Mrs. Brown put her hands on her hips. "We'll have a little discussion on the rules before she rides again. And if she doesn't like the way our barn's run, she'll have to find another place to board."

Sarah, being almost a head taller than me, plopped her arm over my shoulder. "See? Mrs. B may be small, but she's a power to be reckoned with. I knew she wouldn't let Morgan act that way."

All the tension left my body. "Whew! Knight's such a nice horse. I feel sorry for him. He doesn't seem to be the problem. I wonder why she's so angry."

Mrs. Brown clasped both of my hands. "Hang in there. I know you well enough, and I bet it won't take long for you to figure out why she's so irritating."

Sarah chuckled. "I have an idea. How about using your training methods on her? Maybe she needs some positive reinforcement."

"That's hilarious, Sarah." I laughed, which let some of my anger escape. "But—but your idea might work. "I glanced around the barn, thinking. "I'd have to figure out her problem, first." Then I caught Mrs. Brown staring at me. "Mrs. B, I did clean her stall before she came this morning."

"I know you did, honey." Mrs. Brown squatted to look at Colton. "Can I pick him up?"

"Certainly." I grinned. "But, be careful. His sharp baby teeth really hurt."

She cooed to Colt, and nosed him. "You're just gorgeous." She glanced up with a frown. "Trina, promise me you'll be careful with him around the horses. It just takes one kick and he'll be hurt."

Nodding, I locked eyes with her. "I know. I'd never let him loose in here."

"And Sarah," Mrs. Brown turned and grinned. "When are you coming to ride?"

She snickered. "You know I like my feet on the ground."

Mrs. Brown set Colt down and smiled at Sarah. "Maybe one day, I'll get you on a horse."

Sarah slapped her leg and giggled. "Yeah. And maybe one day I'll fly."

Then we all froze as Morgan's voice rang through the barn. She was yelling awful things at Knight. Words I'd never say out loud.

Mrs. Brown ran outside. We followed. We saw Morgan jerk Knight's harness and her crop flew high in the air, ready to come down on his rear.

Rushing into the stadium, Mrs. B. stood between Knight and Morgan. "Back up, young lady. Now! You will not treat your horse that way on my property."

She screamed at Mrs. Brown.

Before more insults rolled out, Mrs. Brown grabbed Knight's reins and pointed. "Go to the barn. I'm in charge of Knight right now. Get yourself under control."

Sarah and I clamped our mouths shut.

Morgan stormed to the barn, kicking at the dirt and sending sandy dust clouds into the air.

Mrs. Brown looked at us. "It might be better if you leave. Don't you worry. Things will work out."

"Ok," we said in unison.

I added, "See you tomorrow, Mrs. B." I looked at Sarah. "Let's go to my house and do something."

"Yeah. I'm ready for air conditioning."

The rest of the afternoon, we went in and out with Colton. Sarah and I attempted to play a computer game, but every time Colt seemed restless, I rushed him outside.

Sarah moaned. "We'll never finish this game, and I have to leave in a few minutes."

"Well, Sarah. This is what you do with a puppy. He'll be easier in a few more weeks."

She shrugged. "Not to change the subject, but I've been thinking about your offer."

My eyebrows raised. "Which offer?"

Sarah gave me a hesitant smile. "Whenever you have time." She paused and stared off.

"Sarah." I waved my hand in front of her face. "Come on. Spit it out."

"I—I want you to teach me to swim before I go to soccer camp."

"Really?"

She nodded, twisting her hands together.

My arm shot up like Clemson had made a touchdown. "Yay! Thursday's good. Right after Colton's trainer leaves. That'll give us the next two weeks before you go. You'll be a swimming pro in no time."

Chapter 6

Wednesday morning, Colton showed a new kind of energy. We sprinted through the backyard until I collapsed against a tree trunk, but he kept going. As I threw three miniature tennis balls from the shade, Colt chased them and chewed on each one, but he wouldn't bring any back. He fixed his eager gaze on me and woofed. His pointy tail whipped back and forth as he bowed.

Since I had to teach him not to bark, I trailed behind him retrieving balls and tossing them before he made his demand. Like a panther, he zoomed through the grass, never slowing down. The fiery-yellow sun made me sticky, wet, and thirsty, but I laughed at his antics until I cried, "Enough! Time to go in and rest."

Throughout the day, I followed the same schedule with Colton: potty, feed, exercise, and rest. When he collapsed for a long nap, I followed his cue. A young puppy took more energy than I'd ever expected.

On Thursday, I had no time for the barn. I wanted Colt to be exercised and have a short nap before our first session with the volunteer trainer. Wide awake now, he made shrill yips, and pranced back and forth in front of the dining room window. A car pulled into the driveway.

I lifted him close to my chest and opened the front door. Ms. Sue caressed Colton, and spoke to him before we moved to the couch. I settled him next to my feet with a frozen chew bone filled with cheese.

She opened her laptop and explained about the reports. "Ms. Jennifer told me you've already trained one dog, so this is probably familiar."

I glanced at her screen. "Yep. I used those forms for Sydney. The only thing that's different is that Sydney came to me when he was six months old, and he already knew a lot of commands. Even though I've earned my handling privileges, I would appreciate it if you could give me some tips on how to teach Colt his first commands. When I started training to be a puppy raiser, I worked with four and five month old puppies, and they already had the first commands down, too."

"Yes, we'll get to that today. At the kennel, Colton seemed to have a mind of his own." Ms. Sue chuckled. "I'm hoping it's because he's young. We'll know as he progresses. But you did such a good job with Sydney, I expect you'll be able to handle a willful pup."

My pulse raced, and I straightened. "Oh, that makes me feel better. I can't wait. What're we doing today?"

"First, let me ask you some questions about his toilet training, crating, walking on leash, etc. Once I can check off his skills as of this date, we'll start some new training. He's still very young, so we'll go slowly."

After I shared our routine, Ms. Sue asked me to dress Colton in his harness. I struggled to buckle the clasp on his purple harness he'd worn since he arrived. "Oh my. I've loosened it as far as I can. It was a bit tight yesterday." Throwing back my shoulders, I smiled. "It doesn't fit anymore."

Ms. Sue grinned and pulled a new cape style from her bag. "Here. Try this one on. Our seamstress, Ms. Adrianna, makes all sizes for growing boys."

This cape had purple material in a triangular shape like a scarf bound by purple cording, and room for the letters PAALS across the top. Colton looked over his shoulder and back to me with an expression of surprise, and then tried to shake it off. "Wow! Look at you!" He seemed pleased with my attention and stopped shaking. We strolled to the laundry room and I gave the command, "Crate." I threw a cookie inside, Colt jogged in, and came out licking his lips.

Ms. Sue's eyes narrowed as she smiled. "That's super, Trina. Show me how he does with a leash?"

"We're working on it. It's not his favorite thing." I grabbed the leash and held it in front of me. "Colt, leash."

He hid inside his crate and peeked out. I held another cookie to him. He looked from the cookie to the leash and took a minute to decide. Then he slinked out and stood in front of me. I clicked and hooked his leash.

"Great! I like the way you only said the command one time, and waited patiently for him to comprehend your command. It's good you're already using the clicker, too. Okay, now show me how he walks outside on the leash. Will he Do Business on leash?"

"No. He doesn't go on command yet, only by accident while we're walking around the yard. I always say, 'Do Business,' when he does. I click with a perky 'Yes,' and give him a treat."

"You're doing all the right things. He's only nine weeks old, right?"

I nodded.

Ms. Sue scooted forward on the couch. "He has a few weeks to go before he can control his body. Everything he does needs to be fun. We don't want him to get confused or frustrated. That'd slow the process. Today I'll show you how to get him to Sit, and later do Wait and Down. I want you to groom him every day. Brush his teeth with the rubber finger pad and touch every part of his body. And here is a CD of noises. Put it on when he is playing in his room. He must get used to every sound possible. Don't hesitate to startle him."

I chuckled at remembering Sarah's scooter. "That'll be fun. I already know one sound we need to work on."

Ms. Sue's eyes twinkled. "Wonderful! These are the most important things he can learn right now. You will be desensitizing him and creating a calm service dog."

When we finished the questions, Ms. Sue gave me three more pages of things Colt needed to learn during the months to come. He would walk on different surfaces, go to various places with all kinds of people, and use all of his senses.

I had used the same list with Sydney and knew what I had ahead of me. We'd start slow and by the time he was eighteen months old, he'd be ready.

Ms. Sue climbed into her car and opened her window. "Remember, playing is part of training."

I cuddled little Colton in my arms. "Okay."

She waved. "See you next week."

As she drove away, my thoughts raced back to Sydney playing Tug-of-War and Fetch. The memory of him visiting Logan's parents at Edisto Beach caught me off guard. I had asked Sydney to Fetch the juice box from the refrigerator. He had wandered into their kitchen, tugged the refrigerator door open, and retrieved the carton. Sydney had returned to the living room and expected to hand it to Logan's mother, but she was so frightened of dogs she hadn't been able to take the box.

I'd had to give him a new command. "Sydney, give to Logan."

Because of his autism, Logan could only speak one or two words, but when Sydney had come closer, he had grabbed the juice box. In seconds, Logan had the straw poked into the hole and had slurped the juice. His face had beamed like he'd won the prize.

I drew in a big sigh and closed my eyes. The warm air sailed through my lungs, and as I exhaled, relaxation took over my body. I saw myself doing all this with Colt. We would accomplish these tasks, and he'd be another wonderful, happy service dog. Though the memory of returning Sydney still hurt, I had no time to think about that.

"Come on Colt. Let's play and then while you sleep, I'll teach Sarah how to swim." I shook my head. "She may be tougher to train than you."

Chapter 7

Mornings during the next two weeks were intense. Once the sun rose, I popped out of bed to care for Colton's needs. Since he tired easily, I raced to the barn to care for the horses while he took his morning nap. After barn chores and another long puppy session, Colton and I snuggled before his longest afternoon nap.

Next came Sarah's swimming lessons. We met every day to practice. Training and grooming Colton gobbled up the rest of my time. I missed riding Chancy more than once each week, but watching my puppy learn was all the reward I needed. And he learned so fast.

Today I swam laps, relaxed on the lounge chair, and waited for Sarah's arrival.

Her boisterous entrance brought me to attention before I actually saw her. "Ok, Trina. I'm ready for my last lesson."

I lay on my chair, watching her wave her big toe in the water, and then step down to the first step. She eventually worked her way down the three steps to the shallow water.

I sat up. "Go ahead. I'll watch from here."

"Oh no. I'm not swimming without you being close." Sarah stiffened. "What if I go under?"

I didn't move but shook my head. "No, Sarah, you need to do this on your own. It's time."

Looking at the water, Sarah froze. Only her chest moved up and down. "What if I start to drown?"

"There's no way." I chuckled to myself. "Your feet can touch the bottom of the pool, silly. It's shallow there, remember?"

"Ok. It'll be your fault if I drown." She exaggerated opening her mouth, inhaling a large breath, and puffing her cheeks. She pretended to dive, but only her arms went into the water and her chin pointed in the air.

Laughing, I tossed my legs over the lounge chair. "Tread water, goofy. That's it. See. You're doing great. Now try using your arms. That's it. Put your face in the water and swim toward me."

I jumped in and Sarah swam to me.

"Wow. You stroked four times. You really swam. Before summer's over, you'll be ready for the swim team."

Once again we heard snickering and looked up. Sarah forgot she was in the middle of the pool and screamed. I grabbed her arm and pulled her to the shallow water.

Morgan cackled. "Wow! What a champion swimmer!"

Sarah slapped the water, her face flaming-red. She walked over to the steps and rushed out, ignoring Morgan. "Trina, I'm heading home. See you around eight." She dried her face and wrapped-up in her towel.

"Ask your mom if you can have dinner with me, and then we'll go."

"All right. I'll text you." Sarah never looked at Morgan.

I dried with my back to her and slipped on my flip flops. Hearing a splash, I sighed, and headed toward the barn.

Mrs. Brown hustled from place to place, fixing the horses grain with supplements.

I hollered ahead. "Do you want a hand?"

"Well, what a nice surprise." Mrs. B carried a bucket in each hand toward the hungry horses. "I thought you were swimming with Sarah."

Taking one pail from her, I followed. "We were until Miss Snooty came over to insult Sarah. We've decided to ignore her."

"Trina, I know she's being difficult, but give her a chance. It's easy to see she's not a happy girl."

I flashed her The Look and hooked the bucket in Sonny's stall. "It might be easier to pretend she's invisible."

"She never talks about her family." Mrs. Brown moved into Dove's stall and continued. "I know someone drops her off and doesn't come back for hours. Some days I bring her snacks. She can be very pleasant and witty when she's not stressed."

Dove swished her tail, anxious for dinner.

"Maybe it'd be better if I stayed away when she's here. Does she have a schedule?"

Ms. B walked out and closed the half door. "Every day's different. After swimming she'll return here and wait for a ride home. Let me show you this." She pointed at the wall. "I've put up an erasable whiteboard calendar and left colored markers for everyone to write their names and schedules for each week.

This'll help me know when riders'll be here, who's having a lesson, and so on. I'll ask her to write on it."

"Great idea." I added my name in purple magic marker and jotted down my riding lesson the next Wednesday at 9:00, and morning chores on Sunday, Tuesday and Friday of next week. Walking toward Chancy's stall, I called to Mrs. B. now in the tack room. "I'll check with Heather and see if that schedule works for her. I never know when I'll have time to ride."

She poked her head out the door. "Thanks, Trina. That works. Are you coming back tonight?"

I stopped in front of her. "Yep. With Sarah and Colton."

"I'll ask Morgan to write her schedule on the board and you'll see it tonight." Then she disappeared into another stall.

At dinner, Dad and Mom listened to Sarah and me complain about Morgan. Dad's face broke into a giant grin. "Let her have her fun. She obviously has some kind of a problem with making friends."

"That's for sure." Sarah and I cackled together.

I stopped to catch my breath. "We've tried pretending she's invisible. Not sure that did anything? And we've tried talking with her. Whew! She's really bizarre. I think the best thing for me is to see her schedule on the board, and try to stay far away."

Sarah bobbed her head. "Sounds good to me."

"Come on, Sarah. Treat time at the barn."

We carried our plates to the sink and promised to be back in an hour or so.

Colt's little legs moved faster now that he'd grown a couple inches, but Sarah carried him as I walked each horse out to the paddocks. Once all the horses had enjoyed their treats and were settled, we ran inside to check the chalkboard.

Morgan's name was written in black. Just like her dark mood. And, she hadn't added anything else.

Chapter 8

The next morning, dew on the grass twinkled. I tiptoed to the laundry room. Colton lay on the floor with his head on his soft bed as if it were his pillow. His eyes seemed to be staring at the wall. I stood waiting and watching. My brow furrowed. Is he sick?

Nope. A second later, he spotted me out of the corner of his eye and dashed to the gate.

"Hey, baby boy. Are you ready for another bright and sunny morning?"

He squealed and wiggled. I opened the gate, lifted his firm body, and gave him a bear hug. "Wow. Only a couple of wet papers. Let's hurry outside."

At the end of breakfast, Dad cleared his throat and stared at me.

My stomach hit the floor. "What's wrong?"

"T, I had a call late last night about an appointment. I've got to go out of town for a couple of days. You're doing a great job with Colton on your own, and I know you'll be fine."

I felt safer having him around when Mom was working. I groaned, and let my chin fall to my chest. Playing with a droopy curl, my brain whirled on a solution. *How can I go to the barn without leaving Colton at home, alone?* I straightened my shoulders and smiled. "I've got it! Since Colt still sleeps a lot, I bet he'd be okay in the empty stall. He can't get hurt in there, and I can keep an eye on him while I work."

Dad pushed his chair under the table. "Sounds like a great plan."

I let Colt walk almost to the barn. He went from a run to a walk and then he sat and stared at me, panting. I carried him the rest of the way. He settled into the vacant stall with a water bowl, a squishy ball, and squeaky rubber mouse. I closed the half-door and peeked over the top.

He inched toward each corner of the room and dug at the straw with a front paw. When he sniffed, he flinched backward. In another second, he explored the same spot, hunching down like he was on the attack, taking itty bitty steps to sniff it again. I stifled my laugh and wanted to watch longer, but I needed to pick the stalls.

I started on my morning barn chores. Mrs. B had convinced Morgan to let Knight spend his nights under the stars. He seemed to be relaxing in his new home, and he was more comfortable around me. I couldn't say the same thing about his relationship with Morgan.

The sun rolled overhead and the dew evaporated. The horses swished their tails like fans, shooing the flies away. I grabbed a halter from the fence post, and walked one horse at a time into a stall while I patted its neck and carried on a happy, one-sided dialogue.

Inside each horse lapped at their fresh water. Daytime was nap time and each horse alternated taking weight off one leg at a time. I looked in on Colton, still sleeping soundly. Relieved, I could stay longer, I started back to work. My light-hearted feeling seeped away as the diesel engine rumbled closer. Trouble was on the way, early today.

I drew in a deep breath and let it out slowly. Ready or not, here she comes.

Only one truck door slammed. Whoever brought her in the morning never stayed. Her hurried and forceful steps echoed. I braced myself for her harsh words but continued working.

Knight stood in his clean stall and watched Morgan approach. He never neighed or snorted, just stared out the back window.

My heart hurt for him. I wondered how they competed together without being a team. I'd give anything to compete with Chancy.

Then Morgan hollered, "I see you put Knight in his stall. Has he been brushed?"

I breathed through my nose, sealed my lips, and moved toward her. Each word I spoke showed control. "I know you've been told that's your job. Heather or I clean the stalls and feed the horses. If we're not here, Mrs. Brown cares for them. Everyone grooms their own horse."

She narrowed her dark gaze, and then she let out a hiss. "I've never boarded at such a second-rate barn. There's no way I can do my own grooming and such tedious work."

"Then I guess, it's time for you to learn."

"Well." She scowled. "If you weren't wasting your time training a stupid puppy, you'd have more time to be here." She stared coldly at me. "I could hire you to groom Knight. You could earn more money and have more lessons."

I put the palm of my hand in her face, stopping her from saying another word. I hated the feeling of having no control over my heated face and my freckles multiplying. I swallowed. "Stop. Don't say another word. I'm training my puppy to help someone else." Through the slits of my eyes, I glared fire. My head swiveled side to side. "There's no way I'd ever be your groom."

Morgan stammered. "Well, there are no other barns close and my parents refuse to drive any further."

"The deal is, Knight's your horse. He needs your attention. How in the world do you compete without being friends?"

"He's new. Just got him before we moved here. He's not my friend. He's my ticket for a scholarship to a prestigious college and their riding team."

My jaw dropped. *We want the same thing?* I swallowed. "But if you're not friends, he'll never trust you."

"He'll learn. With my last horse, I won at all the shows. Knight has to win or my parents will freak. I have my first lesson with him in two weeks."

"Who took care of your other horse?"

"My groom, Mr. Grumbly. An old man who lived at the barn."

"Well. You missed out, letting someone else care for your horse." I paused, deciding if I should say more. With a surge of courage, I went ahead. "I love brushing and cleaning Chancy. I tell her all my secrets, and she lets me know what she's thinking."

Morgan studied the floor and rubbed the toe of her boot in circles.

Colt whimpered, and I rushed to the stall. His front paws flinched and his little nose twitched in his dreams. As I looked in, Morgan's warm breath brushed my neck. She peeked over my shoulder. Out of the corner of my eye, I noticed a crack of a smile break across her face, but it disappeared in seconds. I pretended not to notice.

Is she being nasty to me to keep me from getting to know her? What is she hiding?

At that moment, Mrs. Brown's cheerful chatter filled the barn and the horses responded like a classroom of happy children.

Morgan silently backed away.

Mrs. B spoke to Morgan like she was glad to see her. And then she guided Morgan through the process of currying Knight and checking his shoes before adding the saddle. As a rider, she should have known these things a long time ago.

She was nice enough to Mrs. B, but to me Morgan was a rude, selfish, real live diva.

I shook my head side to side. *I'm out of here.*

Chapter 9
July

With Colton one week from turning three months old, he slept later, and didn't need me in the middle of the night. Feeling light as air, I packed my belongings to the beat of my favorite song, "I Have a Heart Full of Rhythm," and floated up to my bedroom to get ready for company.

The rest of the day moved in slow motion. Anticipating Chase's visit the next morning hyped every nerve in my body. Instead of falling asleep, I planned the order of activities we'd do together, reversed my ideas, and then rearranged them. Finally, I decided Chase needed to choose what he wanted to do first. Since I wasn't sleeping, I walked downstairs to say hello to my snuggle buddy. Maybe he'd relax me.

Hearing my steps while half asleep, Colton trudged to the gate. "I know you're sleepy, little guy, but would you like to Go Outside?" His tail wiggled his whole bottom.

We wandered around the backyard, and the humid air soothed my lively brain. "All right. Back to bed." I rubbed my nose in his warm neck. "Ooo. You smell like my sweaty socks. Cool down and sleep tight! See you when the sun comes up."

I tip-toed up the stairs, slid under my sheet, and closed my eyes. I made myself think of one thing, Chase's green eyes staring into mine. Well, maybe two, his playful smile. And I fell asleep.

In the middle of my romantic dream, Mom shook me awake. "Honey, time to get up. Chase is on his way."

I shot up in bed. "What?"

"Chase's dad just called. They'll be here in a few minutes."

I put a hand on each cheek and screamed. "Oh no! I need to get dressed. Last night I worried about what we were going to do today, but I never figured out what I was going to wear."

Mom smiled. "Honey, anything you wear will be perfect. I'll be downstairs and get the door."

My eyes flew to the pile of clothes in the corner and my breath caught. I jumped out of bed and pulled open my dresser. Woo! One pair of white shorts lay folded and neat. In the top drawer, my favorite purple tee shirt with the PAALS symbol above the front pocket looked wrinkle free. I flew into the bathroom and tackled my out of control, sun-bleached hair. Brushing the curls frantically, I swept them into one ponytail and brushed my teeth. Once I was as ready as I could be, I stood back, examining myself.

Ugh! I look like a frizz ball. I scrunched my nose. *Once I go swimming or horseback riding my hair won't matter.*

The doorbell jolted me out of my thoughts. Colton barked, and Mom's voice carried upstairs. I bounced down the steps, and there he stood. Neither of us moved. We stared at each other without saying a word.

Mom broke the silence. "Come on in, Chase. Have you had breakfast?"

He nodded. "Dad stopped at Mc Donald's. We had a biscuit before we got on the freeway."

"Well, I can't imagine that filled you up. Let's go into the kitchen. I need coffee, and Trina hasn't eaten yet. Would you two like some pancakes?"

I frowned. "Mom, aren't you going to work today?"

Her eyes lifted with a startled expression. "Yes, but I don't have to be there this early. How about a big batch and some bacon?"

"That sounds great." Chase smiled at Mom and then turned to me. "So Trina, what are we doing today?"

Mom shooed us out of the kitchen. "Go. I'll call you when it's ready."

"All right. Follow me, Chase. I need to take Colton outside."

He followed me to the laundry room, cleared his throat, and whispered, "I—I can't wait to meet your new guy." Then he forced himself to speak louder. "The first pictures you sent, he was so little. How's he doing?"

I hiked my shoulders, beaming. "He's adorable but tons of work. Once he's potty trained, life will be a lot easier. He does wear out quickly, and then I get a break when he naps."

Colton met us at the baby gate, turned in circles, and yapped. I lifted him swiftly.

"Can I hold him?" Chase put his arms out.

I chuckled. "That could be dangerous." I told him about my experience, and he dropped his arms as we hurried outside.

Colton ran through the trees, barking at the birds.

As he slowed down, I asked him, "Do you want Breakfast?"

He halted and ran to the house.

Chase tucked his chin and flashed me a surprised look. "He certainly is smart. He knew exactly what you said."

"Yep, I'm always amazed at the number of words our dogs learn. That's why they make such good service dogs."

When we walked into the kitchen, the aroma of bacon and pancakes made my stomach rumble. "Thanks, Mom. I'm starving."

"Yes, thank you, Mrs. Ryan." Chase's eyes glistened, seeing the platter of pancakes. "That biscuit was a long time ago."

In between mouthfuls, I politely swallowed and then shared. "We really should go horseback riding as soon as I finish Colton's training. It's going to get major hot wearing jeans."

Chase glanced at Mom standing at the sink and Dad reading behind the newspaper. He leaned in close to whisper in my ear. "And then we can swim. Later, we can listen to music and draw."

I stayed close, feeling his warm breath on my neck, and then I murmured in his ear. "Sounds perfect."

As Dad dropped his newspaper, Chase bounced back in his seat.

Dad glanced at me and then at Chase. "I just want you two to know I'll be in and out of my office, but mostly in."

Mom walked over to the table and took our dishes. "I'll be back early with groceries. Chase's dad will join us for dinner around six o'clock."

I grinned at Chase.

He winked.

We'd have most of the day to ourselves.

Caring for Colton would definitely keep us busy, but we had so much else to do.

One day wasn't going to be long enough. Every part of my body buzzed. And these new sensations took my breath away, making me weak and shaky.

———

Chase sat, ready to be a spectator. I attached Colton's cape and started his commands. "Walk! Wait! Hurry! Let's go!" Grooming came next.

Chase helped brush Colt's teeth. I put my hand on top of his, guiding the brush back and forth. He lifted his face to mine and his twinkling green eyes smirked with mischief.

My stomach did a flip flop. I smiled back. *Ooo! I think this will be a day to remember.*

"All right, done. Let's pack a lunch and some drinks for a picnic in the woods."

Colton's head tilted at the word "woods." He twirled in circles.

His excitement rubbed off on us, and we mimicked his behavior, giggling, and talking while packing lunch into two backpacks.

Chase raced into the downstairs bathroom to put on his jeans. I darted upstairs to change, and then stuck my head in Dad's office to tell him we were off.

———

Inside the barn, Colton dashed into his stall and sniffed each new toy I placed on the straw. He'd be asleep in a few minutes, and we'd be back from our trail ride before he woke.

Mrs. Brown poked her head out of the tack room for a second and smiled. A couple minutes later, she came out with a broom and kept her back to us while sweeping the straw that escaped from each stall. I walked over and tapped her shoulder. She flinched and smiled.

"Oh, Hey T. You two having fun?

I beamed at her. "We are just beginning our day. Come over and meet Chase."

Chase approached with his handsome smile.

He put out his hand to shake hers. "It's nice to meet you."

She chatted, and we fidgeted, answering her many questions. After a quiet giggle, she turned and spoke over her shoulder. "I've kept you long enough. Go have some fun. I'll play with Colt if he wakes. Just stay safe out there. And pay attention to what you need to be doing. Okay?"

I caught her eyes. "We'll be fine. Nothing can happen on the trail."

Chapter 10

Chase patted and spoke to each horse, then he chuckled. "I've only ridden once at a riding park. They gave me the oldest and slowest horse in the barn. She didn't want to walk, and I had to keep kicking her sides. It wasn't very much fun."

Smiling, I headed over to Sonny. "I have the perfect horse for you. I'm going to tack our horses which means 'put on their gear.' You can watch me get them ready, and I'll let you help put on Sonny's saddle."

I walked him through tacking Sonny then gave Chase a few instructions on steering. He followed me out, or Sonny maybe did. We plodded into the woods and up the grassy field between the houses with our backpacks. The comfortable morning breeze rustled the tree limbs and lifted the scent of honeysuckle into the air. Squawking geese flew in formation, and squirrels dashed back and forth. The horses' ears pitched forward like antennae and their heads turned to find the cause. A long distance from any homes, deer stands had been built in the trees, but thankfully, it wasn't hunting season.

Once Chase started talking about Logan, his younger brother with autism, he couldn't stop smiling. Every time he spoke, he'd let go of one rein and fling his hand in the air, and Sonny would stop walking. "You wouldn't believe the change in Logan since he met Sydney and you. His speech improves every day and he's so funny. He tells himself, 'Look, Logan.' And he makes himself lift his eyes. He's happier, but he really misses Sydney. He asks, 'See, Sydney?' I can't answer that question because we don't know if Sydney will be his service dog. But we're sure hoping."

As he paused for air, I answered. "Me, too. I'm so happy to hear he's doing well."

And then I shared Colton's funny antics and the work involved in his training. I started to mention Morgan and her horrible behavior but didn't want to change our carefree mood. After thirty minutes of wandering around in the woods, the heat and humidity melted us. Chase picked a quiet place under the trees next to the stream.

The horses' necks relaxed and bent toward the water, lazily drinking. A minute later, their mouths lifted a couple inches from the water, and their eyes darted. Soon, their necks flew upward and their heads lurched to the right. Once again, their ears twitched different directions, concentrating on something.

I paid attention, too. Maybe deer had wandered close. Since they had lost interest in drinking, and I didn't want them darting off, I walked both horses to the trees, and threw their reins over branches. What could be bothering them? They gazed through the trees to the right, making me alert. And then the sharp twitter of birds came alive from the trees. Were they alarmed, also?

Shivers crept up my arms. *I hope it's a deer.*

Chase caught my expression. "What's wrong, Trina?"

I shrugged. "Probably nothing, but the horses are spooked. It could be the breeze has picked up. I ride out here all the time, and I've never had a problem."

"Well then, let's not worry about it." He took out our beach towels, and laid them on the grass.

I unzipped my backpack, and Chase snickered. "I know you're always hungry. And I am, too, but let's go for a walk, first."

"Sounds good, but I'm thirsty." I opened my water bottle, took a long swallow, and held it out for Chase. "Here, have a drink. The weather is major hot, and we need water." I put the other bottle back, and as soon as I turned around, he grabbed my empty hand.

"I've waited all morning for this." He held both of our hands in the air.

My heart rocked and rolled. *Is that what I hear? My heart thumping?*

After a while, my regular breathing returned, and holding hands was perfectly normal. We walked deeper into the woods and talked about anything that came to mind. Suddenly, a different snort echoed to the right somewhere hidden in the woods. Chase stared at me. He'd heard it, too.

I stiffened. "That didn't come from Chancy or Sonny. We've got to check on the horses." Holding hands, we jogged back. In a distance through the trees, I spotted a large black horse nibbling grass.

I squinted and looked harder. "I know who it is." I threw my elbows back and my hands clenched. My heart pounded so fast I couldn't say another word.

Chase looked like a boxer, ready for a fight. He held his fists close to his chest and tossed his head side to side. "Who?"

My eyes narrowed. "I haven't told you about the new girl at the barn. She's spying on us. Watch what happens when I call her name."

"Hey, Morgan," I screamed. "I see Knight. Did you come to join us?"

Chase pulled on my hand and spoke loudly. "Don't invite her to join us. I want to be with you. Only you."

Surprised by Chase's outburst, I stared at him. "Really?"

"Yes, I've waited a long time for our one day together. Please don't invite her."

And that's all it took for Morgan. She rode through the woods, eager to ruin our day.

As she approached I whispered to Chase. "I have a plan. Just follow along. She won't stay."

He frowned and shook his head.

"Morgan, come meet Chase. He's a friend from Edisto Beach."

Knight plodded along and stopped just outside the tree line. Morgan sat straight in her saddle and stared at us. "Why are you here all alone?"

"We're having a picnic." I inhaled twice and calmed my voice. "Do you want to join us?"

Morgan pulled on Knight's reins and grumbled. "Nope. I heard voices. I ride out here every day to warm up Knight. You've messed up my training routine. Now, I've wasted too much time, and I'm behind on my schedule. I'm going back and telling Mrs. Brown what you're doing."

We walked away, and I called over my shoulder. "Thanks. She'll be happy to know we're safe. See you back at the barn."

Morgan turned Knight around and kicked his sides. "Get moving, Knight. We don't have all day!"

Chase turned to me. "Oh boy! She's a mess. Thanks for getting her to disappear! Now back to what we were doing."

Hearing my stomach growl, I snickered, "I think it's time for lunch. Are you hungry?

"Yep, and I know you are." He released my hand so we could eat. After lunch, we pulled off our shoes, rolled our loose jeans up to our knees, and waded in the stream. Chase splashed me with his foot. We giggled and splashed, getting closer and closer, making our wet and muddy clothes cling to our skin.

Standing face to face with water dripping down our chins, Chase leaned forward and kissed me on the lips. My eyes flickered, and I froze. Suddenly uncomfortable, we stood staring at each other.

Chase blinked. "Are you okay with me kissing you? We didn't get much practice at Edisto, and I've waited as long as I could."

I smiled, knowing he couldn't detect my flush under the mud.

I lowered my head. "Yes." I muttered. In a second, I made eye contact and mumbled a little louder. "I think I've been waiting all day for you to try. That-that was nice."

His eyes narrowed, questioning me. He nodded, grabbed his towel, dried his face, and tenderly wiped the mud from my cheek. "Okay, a real kiss." We leaned forward, and touched each other's lips without retreating. When we finally parted, we stood, eyeing each other, and grinning.

Chase spoke first. "Wow! I'm ready for a swim. How about you?"

I nodded. "Time for the pool."

We climbed on our horses and rode.

Everything around me intensified. The slight breeze tickled my skin. The green leaves shined under our blue sky. I covered my stomach with both hands, hoping to stop my insides from vibrating.

Comfortable again, we talked and laughed about our Edisto adventures all the way back.

On entering the barn, Chase held the horses' reins while I peeked in on Colton, still asleep. I then explained the next process of brushing and hosing the horses, and scraping off the excess water.

Finished with cooling down our horses, Chase walked Sonny into his stall, and I did the same with Chancy. They were ready for their afternoon nap.

Colton heard my voice and barked. He walked on leash most of the way home. Halfway there, he pawed Chase's leg, begging to be carried.

Chase scooped him up and huddled him close to his chest. He grinned. "When Logan gets his service dog, I hope I'll be able to enjoy him, too."

"I need to tell you." I halted and puckered my face. "You'll be able do things for the dog when he's not working with Logan, but you can't get attached. The dog must only make a connection with Logan."

Chase straightened. "When Mom filled the application for Logan to get a service dog, she had to name one parent and one sibling who would help with the dog care. Since Logan's so young, she chose herself and me. Then she went to the bookstore on Edisto looking for books on how to care for dogs. She even bought some psychology books to help overcome her anxieties. She's getting herself ready for Logan's dog."

"Wow! That's awesome your Mom is overcoming her fear of dogs. She has months to learn. Since you live close to PAALS, you could always take a dog class. Maybe we could meet at a class."

Chase's eyes brightened and his smile widened. "I'm going to look into that."

Dad met us in the kitchen. "So, how was your ride?" He saw the mud on our wet clothes. "Are you two okay? What happened?"

Laughing at Dad's reaction, I continued to stack the leftover food in the refrigerator.

"Oh, sir." Chase's voice deepened, sounding serious. "We stepped into the stream to cool off." Chase cleared his throat. There was a short pause as he rallied with a clever word. "Um, and before we thought about it, we had a water fight. We got muddy and wet. But we're okay."

Dad chuckled. "Well, I'm glad you had a good time." And then he made his voice stern. "What's next?"

I grinned over my shoulder. "We're going swimming."

"Sounds like a good idea." Dad headed to the hall. "I'm going back to work. You might want to clean up before—"

"Yep, we planned on that. By the way, Dad, there's sandwiches left over in the frig. Help yourself."

Chapter 11

Before going to the pool, Colton caught sticks or a ball and chased us in the backyard. His little body slowed down like a battery running out of juice, but I encouraged him to walk to the barn until his little legs wore out. Long naps were good for both of us.

Along the way, Chase picked up my little guy and held him snuggly on his shoulder. He set Colton down in his stall, never waking him.

Mrs. B watched Chase with my puppy and did a thumbs up.

Before she started another conversation, I waved. "Thanks, Mrs. B for letting us swim in your pool. I'll get Colton in an hour."

Chase grabbed my hand, and we giggled all the way to the pool.

He dropped our supplies on the chair and dove in. While he was under water, I pulled off my green cover up and hurried into the cold water. We had spent hours together on the beach in bathing suits, but this time I was embarrassed. I stepped gingerly down one step at a time, goose bumps blooming, but the warmth on my cheeks made me aware my freckles were racing to be seen. I bent over and splashed cold water on my cheeks.

Chase treaded and slapped the water. "Get in, silly. It feels great once you get wet."

The chill made me gasp. I sucked in a lungful of air and dove through the water straight into his stomach as he treaded in the deep end of the pool. He reached down and pulled me up. As I inhaled and closed my mouth, he placed a quick kiss on my lips. Once again I treaded water and stared at him while I caught my breath.

He smiled. "Let's race."

I dared him with my eyes. "Okay. Which stroke first?"

"What's your best one?"

"Breaststroke."

"Me, too. Let's go!

Smiling, I poked him on his shoulder. "No cheating. We go on three. Ready?"

He nodded.

"One, two, three."

I didn't think, just swam. Only turning my head on one breath, I swam ahead by a hand. I kicked harder, and kept my face down until I smacked the edge of the pool. I won by an inch.

Chase swept his black hair out of his eyes. "Ok, you got me that time. Now backstroke. And I count this time."

My worst stroke!

Again, we blasted away. I kicked hard, but my legs didn't keep me afloat. I leaned my head farther back, got a face full of water, and didn't swim in a straight line. I treaded water, caught my breath, and tried again.

Chase waited for me at the edge. "Ah, I beat you good this time."

Panting, I signaled to the chairs.

Chase chuckled. "Are you saying, 'Let's go to the lounge chairs?'"

I nodded, breathing fast.

He dipped into the water and swam toward the stairs. "Are you going back to Edisto next summer?"

I dog-paddled to the steps. "Sarah and I keep talking about Edisto. We hope so."

"Me too." Chase splashed back in the water and free-styled to the other end. He grabbed the side of the pool, shook the water out of his hair, and pulled himself onto the deck. We met at the lounge chairs and stretched out on our towels. Before long the sun baked us. Chase popped up and did a cannonball into the pool. I chose to enjoy the warmth of the sun on my eyelids.

His soggy footsteps slapped the decking before he shook his wet hair over me. My eyes popped open.

He laughed out loud, and then crinkled his face. "You're getting sunburned. Did you put on sun lotion?"

I squinted up at him. "I don't think so."

"Okay, Red, roll over. Let me rub some on your back and shoulders. You can't reach those places."

Dive bombers crashed in my stomach. As he rubbed lotion on my shoulders and back, my heart thumped so fast I had to inhale in small bursts. Suddenly, we heard snickering. I lifted my head toward the bushes. Morgan's face showed between the branches. She cackled and made kissy noises.

I bolted straight up. My muscles quivered, and my eyes shot poison darts at her. "What is your problem?"

She walked out, still in her riding clothes. "I heard you two were at the pool and thought you might need a chaperone."

Chase swallowed, his beet red face contorted, but he controlled his voice to a mild screech. "You already bothered us in the woods. Can't you find something better to do?"

She raised her finger like she was going to lecture us, changed her mind, and stomped away.

I clapped. "Good job, Chase. Good job!"

We went for another swim, cooling our frustrations, and then dried off and headed back to the barn, hand in hand.

I grinned. "We can go back later, if you want."

"Okay." He stopped walking and faced me. "We need to make this day last. What's next?"

"Mr. Colton has an afternoon training session. He should be wide awake by now."

———

By late afternoon, Chase and I collapsed on the love seat and couch in the den. After we'd recharged for a few minutes, he pulled out a CD he had made with my favorite tunes. We listened and drew pictures at the kitchen table. When a bouncy song came on, we danced. Since Colton needed to go outside often, we moved to the porch and talked.

After dinner, Chase's dad lingered for an extra hour. Not knowing when we'd to see each other again, we grew quiet and sad.

Colton whined, and pawed my leg.

Playtime, huh?

Chase and I wandered into the woods, hand in hand, tossing a ball for Colton and waited for his dad's words.

"Chase, time to go!"

Chapter 12

The day after Sarah returned from her week at Soccer Camp, she joined me to play computer games. A brief mention of her upcoming trip to Disney World with her friend April hurt, but I had made my decision about not going on the trip the day I adopted Colton.

Colton continued to interrupt for his potty breaks. We rushed in and out the door for hours. Each time he did his business, he got a cookie, and we dashed inside for air conditioning. This time, as I closed the door, before I even took a step, he pawed me and glued his eyes to mine.

I squinted at him and opened the door. He rushed to a tree, lifted his leg, waited for a teeny-tiny drip to fall, and raced back for a treat. His mouth slid over his teeth like a grin, and he blinked his warm brown eyes at me.

Dipping my chin, I chuckled. "Oh. You've got to be kidding! You little stinker. I've caught on to you. You've figured how to get a treat whenever you want. Who's training whom?"

Sarah laughed so hard she sat on the carpet and slapped the floor. "Duh! He's known all day. I kept waiting for you to figure it out."

As soon as we ran out of air, I pointed at Colton. He stared up at me.

"Okay, Mister. There will be no more potty breaks until Sarah and I finish this game."

Settling in to concentrate on the game, Sarah groaned. "Now we can talk." She started with Day One at soccer camp, mentioning all of the hours they practiced, and of course, every minute she had with Peyton. "After dinner, if we could fit a visit into our schedule, we'd meet in a—" Sarah giggled. "—a secluded spot. Especially the night they had a fireworks show." She gazed at me, waiting for my reaction.

"Are you waiting for me to ask for more or to be alarmed?"

Sarah shrugged her shoulders, crinkling her nose. "He was always a gentleman. We talked and held hands, and I got a few kisses. Those made me bubbly inside. On the fourth, we had the most amazing the fireworks show. As they exploded way up high, Peyton wrapped his arm around my shoulder and held me tight." Sarah closed her eyes and inhaled a deep breath. Seconds passed before she reopened her eyes and cooed. "Gosh, I miss him, already. How was your visit with Chase?"

"Awesome!" I wiggled my shoulders and smiled. I briefly told her how we spent the day together. My cheeks flushed as I added more details on how Chase had asked his parents for a free day without Logan.

"Wow! That's special."

"Yes, it was. Chase told me that Logan talks about Sydney every day. It sure would be nice if Logan got to have Syd as his service dog."

Sarah's eyes lit. "When will they know?"

"I'm not really sure. But the teams start training together a few weeks before the graduation ceremony. And that's usually in November or December. Wouldn't that be a cool Christmas present?"

"Yes, that would be neat. But Trina, you've changed the subject. I told you about Peyton and me. What about you and Chase?"

"Well—" I stood and paced. "I guess we did the same things you did. Except, I watched the fireworks with Mom and Dad in the street. Umm. I almost forgot to ask. Did you go swimming?"

Sarah grinned. "Unfortunately, we had no time for swimming."

"Oh, that's too bad. You could have shown off your skills."

"Nah, I was relieved. We worked out so hard I was exhausted. There you just did it again. Trina, don't you want to tell me *anything* about you and Chase?"

"I don't know. It feels pretty weird talking about it. We're both kind of shy, and we only had one day. Chase loved being with Colt."

Keeping her chin down, Sarah lifted only her eyeballs at me. "So you're not telling me anything."

I blinked. "Okay. How about this? At the pool, I let him rub lotion on my back. At the same time, Morgan snickered at us from behind the bushes. Chase told her to go away, and she did. After she disappeared, I rubbed lotion on his back. The best part is, he's calling every night."

"That's better." Sarah pressed her lips together. "I'm sorry you have to deal with her."

I shrugged. "I've been thinking. Sarah, what if we don't react to Morgan? I tried being nice when she met us in the woods. She got flustered. My other friends at school last year mentioned the same problems with their brothers or sisters. They say that refusing to respond makes them change their behavior or go away. It's kind of like how I train Colton."

"Oh. She's so hard to ignore." Sarah's eyes widened. "Maybe you can do that, but I'm not sure I can."

"Maybe it'll help if I try talking with her. Maybe she needs a friend. She's so unhappy. Maybe something bad's happening in her life. I read in one of my books about a girl who lived with relatives who treated her so badly, she acted ticked-off all the time. It was her way of keeping anyone from knowing her."

I stopped talking and let my thoughts sink in.

Sarah held her head in her hands and moaned. "Not *again,* Trina. You can't fix everyone. Do you remember when you felt sorry for that guy everyone believed had cooties? I almost stopped breathing when you asked him to dance last year."

I squinted "Really? He was standing all alone with no one speaking to him."

"Well." Sarah shook her head. "All the kids in the cafeteria whispered back and forth and stared at you. It was embarrassing."

"Did you see his face when I asked him to dance? That was worth all the questions I got later." My heart pounded. "You never said anything about it."

"I didn't want to hurt your feelings. I know how you always rescue helpless animals and thought it was the same kind of thing. But *this* girl, Morgan, she's hateful."

"But there's a reason. I just need to find out why." I stared at the ceiling. "That's the answer. The next time she starts harassing me at the barn, I'll turn the conversation back on her instead of getting mad."

"Whoa. You're asking for it!" Sarah turned off the computer, stood, and paced. She turned her head side to side and clucked her tongue. "It's your life. So, what should we do now? It's too hot to do anything outside."

Colton's head had switched back and forth as Sarah and I took turns talking. He was like a spectator in the stands watching a tennis match. Sitting next to him, I cupped his little face and giggled. "You're so funny. I bet you even understand what we've said. How would you like to go swimming?"

His ears shifted forward, showing he recognized the word "swim."

I glanced at Sarah. "Go put on your suit and we can take Colton. Mrs. B told me I could bring him any time if he was potty trained. I'd say today he proved he's trained. He loves splashing in his kiddie pool and it will help him be a water dog like Sydney."

We met on the path, and Colton walked like a pro. At the pool, we laid our towels on the lounges, and I carried my little guy to the pool steps.

He bent his head and licked. I lifted him higher, "No water."

Sarah's eyes quizzed me.

"I'm teaching him to not sip this water. It will be easier when I take him to the beach next summer. Remember how sick Sydney got from drinking the ocean water? I don't want Colton to go through that."

Colton jerked his head toward the bushes and fidgeted in my arms.

Morgan paraded out in a royal blue bikini, looking gorgeous, her curly hair loose about her round face, making her large eyes stand out.

He wiggled and waggled. "Hey, Morgan. Come over and meet Colton. He wants to meet you."

Sarah gave me The Look. Under her breath, she whispered, "What are you doing?"

Morgan halted and lost her confident look. I guessed she didn't have a clue on what to do or say.

I whispered back. "I'm trying my new technique."

Morgan hadn't moved.

In a friendly voice, I called. "Morgan, come join us in the water. It's hot out there."

She sat on the other side of the pool, kicking her feet in the water. "Where's your little boyfriend?"

"Sadly, he's in Columbia. Too far away to visit."

After a minute of silence, she tried again. "I'm going to tell Mrs. B you have Colton in the pool. I can't swim with his hair and pee in the water."

After inhaling and letting it out, I swallowed my irritation. "First off, Mrs. Brown knows. Colt's already pottied, and he's got really short hair that goes into the filter. I'm trying to be friendly, but I'm not going to beg you to join us."

She flashed daggers at me with a nasty look. "I'll get in when I'm ready."

"Good. I've got to take Colton home for a nap. You can have the pool all to yourself." I lifted Colton to my chest. "By the way, Knight looked good out in the ring this morning."

Morgan snapped at me. "So, it was your turn to spy on me?"

"Ah ha! I didn't know you were spying on me." I let out a sarcastic snicker. "Well, there's not much to watch when I'm riding." I waited a couple of seconds to let that sink in her mean brain. "But just so you know, I've never spied on you. When I'm working, it's hard not to see you in the ring. And you and Knight are looking good."

Whew! I had stayed positive.

Sarah and I stepped out of the pool and rushed to our flip flops.

"Yikes! The cement's too hot for you, Mr. Colt." I set him on the grass next to the pool and didn't take my eyes off him while I dried.

"Bye, Morgan." Sarah picked up the cooler and threw her towel over her shoulder.

I lifted Colton in my arms, and Sarah and I shared a satisfied grin. "Yeah, Morgan. See you later."

We heard a giant splash. I turned to Sarah. "That's her way of not having to answer us. Isn't she something?"

Chapter 13

After months of saving my earnings, I had enough money for my first pair of chaps. Over the weekend Dad drove me to The Tack Shop. I tried on a number of pairs and decided on the softest and best brown suede leather I could afford. I stashed the box under the bed and waited for my once-a-month lesson.

Wednesday morning couldn't come fast enough. I lay on the bed, waiting for the sun to flicker through the open blinds. And of course, this morning Colton slept later. I tossed and turned until I gave up and dressed in shorts and a tee. It would be my turn to wake Colt.

He started whining before he saw me. Knowing my footsteps or my scent, he turned in circles as I approached, and then stretched his front paws over the top of the gate.

"Good morning, little guy! Are you ready for another day?" He squealed and his nails scrambled across the floor. "Time to go outside." I picked him up, nuzzled my nose into his fur, and inhaled his sweet puppy scent. I squeezed him tight. We each needed our snuggle after being separated all night.

Finished with his morning needs and breakfast, Colt followed me up to my bedroom. I pulled the baby blue box from under my bed and stared at the navy blue lettering. THE TACK SHOP. My heart flip-flopped. I unfolded the tissue paper and gazed at my new chaps.

Colt jammed his nose in the box, sniffed, and raised his eyes to me.

"Yep. This is my prize for working so hard. I get another lesson today, and you can come to the barn."

Colton marched next to my legs, playing a game of tagging the back of my flip flops. Each rubber shoe had teeth marks, and it was time to teach him to walk without playing. In the kitchen, I opened the doggie cookie jar and broke the treats into tiny pieces. He smelled them and watched my hand go into my pocket. I grabbed my clicker. Now he had to figure out what the trick was for the day. I walked to the glass doors. He lost interest in my shoes, and stared at my pocket. I teased him, jiggling the heel of my shoe. He looked down, forgot about the treat, and lunged at the foam. The second he stopped and looked at me, I clicked and gave him a treat.

"Yes!" I jiggled my foot again, and he lunged at the heel of my shoe. I didn't say anything. He bit. When he looked up, I clicked. "Yes!" And fed him.

We repeated this process. After a couple minutes, he stopped attacking my shoe. I jiggled the back of my flip flop, he looked at the shoe, and then stared at me, anticipating the click and a treat.

"Yes! Good boy! I patted his head, and we moved outside.

He raced to the trees and found a ball hidden under a gardenia bush full of pearly white buds popping open. But he got distracted by the fragrance, sniffed at a few blooms, and then remembered the ball. We played catch and tug-a-rope until he finally ran out of gas. I carried him inside for a quick rest.

Dad sat at the kitchen table, reading the paper and drinking coffee. He lowered the paper under his chin. "So, what time is your lesson?"

"Mr. Simon will be ready for me at nine. I'll go early and do some chores, and then get Chancy ready. And, I'm wearing my chaps today."

Dad set his cup down. "I wish I had time to watch. I have a conference call at the same time."

I stood and patted Dad's shoulder. "That's okay. I'm not riding enough to improve, but I enjoy trying."

Colton walked all the way to the barn and into the stall. He watched me set new toys on the straw. I added a metal mixer-beater, a stiff potato brush, and a hard plastic jingle bell for his mouth's sensory exploration. One day he'd need to pull on things that weren't soft. But first he did his routine of exploring.

Closing the half door, I looked over. "Be right back." He glanced up quickly and returned to his search for new smells.

After all the horses stood happily in their stalls with fresh hay and water, I had enough time to brush Chancy and pick the dirt from her hooves. Excited to wear my chaps for the first time, I trotted into the tack room and slid them over my shorts. I saddled Chancy and double checked the girth before I led her out to the rectangular riding ring to warm up. My legs stayed cooler without my tight riding pants.

Mr. Simon parked his shiny red truck and headed over to meet me. "Howdy, young lady. Are you ready?"

I continued swaying on Chancy's back. "Yep I'm excited. I've been riding when I can. It hasn't been much, but I'll do my best."

"Come over here and let me check her girth." He tightened it one more notch. "That's better. "Go around the ring a couple more times." He retrieved his silver thermos from his truck and poured himself a cup. After a couple of sips, he set the steaming brew on the fence post.

I walked Chancy, allowing her to stretch her muscles and letting me feel her rhythm.

Mr. Simon stood in the middle of the ring. "Push your heels down. That's it. Now keep them there. Do you feel it?"

"Yes, my muscles are screaming, 'No more!'" I chuckled. "My legs feel like Jell-O."

Mr. Simon smiled with a nod. "Keep at it. They'll get stronger."

Straightening my back, I focused straight ahead, and grasped the reins, struggling to keep them from moving up and down.

"Steady your hands. Pretend there's a pin in your head and someone is pulling you up." I straightened again. "Okay. That's better. Now give her some leg, go around one more time and then ask her to trot."

I bounced up and down and couldn't contain my grin.

"Good job, Trina." Mr. Simon clapped his hands. "Keep it going. More leg. Don't let her quit. Come on. Press hard with your legs. More. Put your heels down. Farther. That's it. Okay a couple more times. Now, let's see you canter."

Chancy's ears twitched, telling me she was listening. Every movement I made while on her back translated into a command. I was the driver, and if she didn't do what I wanted her to do, it was usually my fault.

After a few minutes, my legs turned to pudding. I lost my seat. My legs had stopped communicating with Chancy, and I had no ability to direct her. Mr. Simon called, "Okay. Walk. Good job."

As I walked the stadium, I caught Dad out of the corner of my eye, standing by the fence with Colton asleep in his arms. He gave me a thumbs up, waved, and headed home. I smiled and continued riding without moving my head.

Back in the barn, I hosed my warm horse with cold water and used the sweat scraper to remove the excess. Then I led Chancy into her stall and fed her apple chunks before brushing her saddle marks off her back. She lowered her head and nudged me to stroke her muzzle.

Muffled crying came from somewhere nearby.

I poked my head into the hallway. Sobbing and a low soothing voice floated from Knight's stall.

I held my breath. *I know I shouldn't. But, how can I not listen?*

After a moment, I tip-toed to the tack room, carrying Mrs. Brown's grooming supplies. As I stood outside the door holding my breath, the details drifted to me. My radar ears tuned-in to every word from Morgan.

Then Sarah walked in the shady barn and called. "Trina. Are you still here?"

My heart leaped in my chest like I'd been prodded with a hot branding iron.

I backed into the tack room, wiped away a loose tear, and stepped out for a second. "Sarah, I'm in the tack room."

Mrs. Brown and Morgan stopped talking.

Sarah walked in, her eyes examining me. I had my finger to my lips.

As soon as Mrs. Brown's boots clunked toward us, I spoke louder. "Well, hi, Sarah. You just missed my lesson."

Mrs. Brown entered the room, and I tried to look innocent.

"Hi, Mrs. B. I was just putting your grooming tools away. I had a great lesson."

Her focused eyes zoomed into my soul. "Hon, if you heard anything, please remember Morgan's feelings."

A surprised expression sprouted on my face, and I hoped the green in my eyes didn't give me away. "I only heard crying as I walked into the tack room. I need to clean my tack." That was almost the truth. I smiled and released my breath.

"You know, Trina. It might be best if you leave your tack for later."

I locked arms with Sarah. "Okay. We'll head out to the pond. Is everything all right?"

Mrs. Brown avoided my question. "I had planned to see your lesson. I'll try to watch next time."

Heading toward the door, I called back. "That's okay. I've got to ride more often to make any progress. I'm so busy with Colton's training, I barely have time to practice."

Almost out the door, I turned. "I'll be back in the morning. Heather has something to do tomorrow, so it'll be just me. Thanks for letting me bring Colton. He loves coming to the stall."

Mrs. Brown approached even closer. Her voice softened and her eyes pleaded with me. "Please, Trina. Give Morgan some time. We're working on a few things." She smiled and patted my arm before heading toward Knight's stall.

Chapter 14

Far away from the barn, Mrs. Brown's statement hit me as funny. Out of the blue, I bent over, cracking-up with laughter and patting my knees. "Morgan's feelings? Those two words do not go together." I gulped some air and burst out loud. "Be careful not to hurt her feelings! Hmm. Really? After all her insults."

Sarah's head bobbled with a stunned expression. "Did you really hear anything?"

"Yeah, but I don't want to talk about it right now." I looked at my feet and swallowed my moment of pleasure.

She stopped in her tracks. "Why not?"

I shrugged. "I need to think about what she said."

Sarah looked at me sideways. "How long are you going to need?"

"I don't know. She's really hurting, and I shouldn't be laughing." I took a long breath and blew it out. "But I've been so angry, it felt good to let loose. Now, I've got to think about her situation."

Clutching my arm, Sarah smirked. "Want to spend the night at my house tonight? I don't have soccer practice."

"Uh-huh. So you can get me to talk?"

"That wasn't the reason." She huffed.

I leaned my head, questioning her with a squint. "All right. If you promise not to bug me with questions. Let's go ask."

Mom sat in the kitchen drinking tea, and Colton slept next to her chair until we barged into the room and spoke.

Mom's puzzled face stared. "And who is going to take care of Colton?"

"Oh. My. Gawd! I got so caught up in Morgan's problems, I actually forgot about him." I turned to Sarah. "What was I thinking? I have to stay here. And be up early with him. You could stay here, Sarah. I won't wake you when I get up."

Sarah pulled out her phone and texted her mom. She answered. "Fine." Sarah scurried home to get her pillow, her tablet, and a flashlight.

After dinner, we reverted back to our old days of playing Ghost in the Graveyard, using it as a game to desensitize Colt. I made Colt stay as Sarah hid behind a tree. Colton chased me, looking for her. When he got close enough, Sarah jumped out, screaming. Then we switched. Colt had to find me. When he tired, his tongue drooped sideways. We rested on the grass and in seconds, Colton crawled across my lap. The cicadas sang to us as we watched for falling stars.

I stroked his head. "Isn't he the cutest?" I pulled him up to my face and kissed the top of his nose. "Maybe you'll sleep longer since I'm keeping you up."

"That'd be nice." Sarah smiled and rubbed Colton's back. "Are you ready to go to the barn?"

"Yep. Let's get our flashlights, and I'll leash Colt."

The horses neighed and whinnied from their paddocks as we approached. Colt stayed by my side and lifted his nose at the fence. Rapp, the gentle paint, stuck his head between a lower rail, to sniff at Colton.

Colton planted his front paws on the lowest fence rail and they bumped noses.

"That a boy." I patted Rapp's nose. "Horse."

I split the treats in my pocket with Sarah, and we distributed them to the horses. When all the treats had disappeared, I brushed my hands together. The horses knew what that action meant.

"All gone." I turned to Sarah. "Okay. Time to go home."

Colton had learned the word "home" and headed that direction. Knight rushed over to his fence and blew a trumpet sound, announcing he wanted one more nose rub. I darted over and gave him one last pat.

As we walked home, the wind picked up, and gathered all the dark clouds. Little by little every star disappeared. July was noted for noisy thunderstorms that sometimes brought tornadoes.

Sarah grew nervous, and we hurried inside moments before the downpour. Colton watched the flash through the window, and before the thunder roared, I grabbed leftover treats in my pocket. I wanted him to expect something special when the noise boomed. After two bursts, his eyes went to my hand, and he licked his lips.

Upstairs, the timing was perfect to continue desensitizing Colton to noises. I had already slammed doors, clanged pots and pans, let the tea pot whistle, and dropped a tennis shoe in the dryer while he played in his room. Tonight, I dropped the blinds to hide the lightning from Sarah and startle Colton.

"It's great that our summer storms blow through quickly."

Sarah grinned and stared at the blinds. "Later, when the lightening is gone, let's go for a walk in the woods. I love the smell of our pine trees after a storm."

"Me too. And I bet we'll see fireflies flickering through the wet leaves."

Sarah and I waited out the storm, listening to her favorite tunes on her phone. The music blared for a couple of minutes, and then she turned the volume down. My bullet proof puppy yawned and thumped his tail on the floor.

Since we needed to occupy ourselves while listening to the music, I pulled out my beach puzzle. We searched for pieces to three dolphins leaping behind a shrimp boat and Colton lay next to my chair.

Sarah leaned closer. "All right. Enough ignoring the subject. You know I'm dying for you to spill the beans. Are you waiting for me to beg?"

"Hmm—I'm just not sure I should tell." I never looked up.

Sarah twisted around. "What did you just say?"

"When you found me in the barn, I had heard Morgan. And I've been thinking about everything she said. But you can't share anything. If I tell you."

"Of course. You know I won't."

I glanced at her over my right shoulder and clicked my tongue. "Well, you tell me secrets from other friends that I'm not supposed to know. Why would my information be any different to you?"

"Well—" Sarah got serious for a whole minute. "—I'm thinking." She paced the room, and then plopped across the edge of the bed on her stomach, leaned on her elbows, and held her chin up with her hands.

Colton followed. He stretched his body next to Sarah's, tuning-in to her expressions.

In her position, Sarah purposely made the words come out missing their beginning sounds, but I understood. "This is really personal to you, so I promise on our friendship to keep my lips sealed. How's that?"

I fell across the other side of the bed and caught her devious eyes. "It's great. But do you really mean it? And, can you really do it?"

Sarah didn't back down. She stared right back at me.

"All right, I'm going to trust you." I blew out all my breath. "Morgan cried for a while. I heard only bits and pieces in between her sobs. She said that she was always by herself. And something about having two brothers. It sounded like one is far away, like maybe in the service. And the other one is away at school, a college somewhere. I didn't hear clearly, but she mentioned that when he's around, he carts her back and forth. Otherwise she calls a taxi."

"Okay. So now she's like the only child. That's like us. We do fine."

"Yeah, but we have parents who are involved with us." I stared at her.

"So..."

"The only other thing that made me really sad for her was when she angrily shared, 'My parents are never around. My dad travels, and Mother is always working and going to school.' I don't know what any of that means, but it's enough information to see she is by herself. All the time. She may really need a friend."

"Oh, no!" Sarah bounced into an upright position and sat crossed legged with her back stiff and straight, looking like a mannequin. Her blank face told me her brain was spinning. After a moment, she spit out, "Trina, she'll chop you into small pieces and throw you out in the manure pile."

I laughed so hard, I snorted. "That's the funniest thing you've ever said. Very descriptive! And scary. Wooo!"

Colton lay across the tops of my thighs using what he'd learn later was called a hug. I wasn't upset, but one day he'd know to use use this skill to relax me. I stroked his head.

Attempting to stay serious, Sarah gave me a stern face. "She's vicious. She'll hurt your feelings."

Colton stayed on my lap. "Well, hurt feelings can't kill me. I want to try and help. It could be my good deed for the rest of the year. Maybe for the rest of my life."

Sarah's eyebrows hiked. She clasped her hands and squealed. "Oh My Gawd! That's the truth."

I glared. "Now that you know, if you say bad things about her, I'll find out."

"Okay. Okay." She nodded. "It's a pinky-finger-promise."

We crossed our right pinky fingers and shook them. "Secrets forever."

An awkward silence fell.

Colton leaped off the bed and went to the door. He whined.

"Oh, Colton wants out. And now that the storm is over, let's go explore."

We ran outside and inhaled the wet, woodsy smell. Tiny specs of yellow blinking lights flashed off and on in the trees. We caught Colton's reaction to the flashing specs and had a good laugh.

I dashed to the deck and grabbed two jars. "Here Sarah. Let's catch some fireflies."

Sarah caught six and I caught four. Their flashing lights brightened our faces, and as I held the jar closer for Colton to see, he put his nose to the jar.

When they twinkled, he backed away. He watched from a distance, and then stepped closer and closer, not moving his eyes.

After a few minutes, we unscrewed our lids and flicked the jars forward, saying, "Fly away. Fly away, home."

With my parents in bed on the other side of the house, Sarah and I had the kitchen to ourselves. We scooped giant blobs of ice cream into a bowl, poured salted caramel syrup on top, and squirted whipped cream. I added three maraschino cherries to mine.

We walked Colt to his room, and I gave him a command, "Touch." He nosed my hand, and I put a small treat inside his crate.

"Night—night, baby boy. See you in the morning!"

Sarah and I headed upstairs.

My alarm beeped way too soon. I wasn't used to staying up late, but it was worth it. Silently, I eased from the room, letting Sarah get her beauty sleep.

Colton turned in circles as I approached. Our typical fun morning began with running outside and dog grooming, but my mind worried about my decision to help Morgan.

Determined to start changing her, I told myself. "Today's the day." But every time I thought about what I was planning to do, my hands shook and my guts turned all jittery. I swallowed, trying to keep the waves down.

Finished with puppy duties, Sarah and I had breakfast before she scurried home for her soccer practice, and I headed to the barn. Colton raced into his stall. I took my old phone out of my pocket and started to call Chase. I'd run out of texting minutes. He'd tell me if I was doing the right thing.

Of course, on this morning, for the first time, Morgan arrived before I started chores. She disappeared into Knight's stall. Silence. Not even Knight made a sound.

That's not a happy pair. Maybe I should hit cancel? I am on my own. What to do? What to do? And no time to talk with Chase.

Walking toward her stall, I sucked-in warm barn air, but my heart galloped and seized my next breath. I turned around and paced in the hallway, trying to calm myself. *What could she do to me except be rude. Come on Trina. You can do this!*

Gasping, I pranced directly to her stall and stuck my head in her door. "Hi, Morgan. How's Knight?"

Morgan's horrid glare burned a hole right through me. "He's fine. Why?"

I inhaled a deep breath. I think it came all the way from my toes, but I kept my promise to myself. I held my chin high and answered. "No reason. Just a way to say, hey." I stopped talking and waited for a response. Nothing. So I started jabbering anything that came into my head. "Sarah and I feed the horses treats at night. Knight sure loves getting attention and eating apples and dog biscuits."

She didn't even flinch before she fired back at me. "Why are you giving him apples or dog stuff? What if he's allergic to those? You could've made him sick."

"Morgan, I work here. Remember?" My eyes never wavered from her. "I know about every horse. Mrs. B would have told me if there were any problems."

We continued our stare down. "Well, he's my horse, and you should ask me if you can feed him something else."

I yanked on a few strands of hair on my neck and twirled them around and around to sooth my anxiety. I kept her stare. "Okay. Now you know he's had treats every night since he's been here, and he's not allergic to them. But, I'll go ahead and ask." I swallowed. "Morgan, may I give Knight treats with the other horses?"

She threw her head sideways and walked away. "I'll talk with Mrs. B about it."

I couldn't move. I pressed my lips, locking the words inside. But after a second had passed, I pushed the thought aside and flew out her stall door.

Chapter 15

Reeling after my conversation with Morgan, I peeked over Colton's stall door. Older now, he needed more interaction, and being with him always relaxed me. "Mr. Colton. We're going for a walk."

He lifted his head, and his whole body wiggled.

Going from a walk to a jog, we circled the horses' swimming pond. Colt's ears perked. Three brownish green-mallard ducks paddled in the middle. Occasionally, their heads went under the water and their bottoms pointed to the sky as they searched for food. Colton froze, and then charged, pulling on his leash, barking, and wanting to race into the water. I kicked off my orange clogs, and let him wade up to his chest in the brown water.

The ducks ruffled their feathers, flapped their wings, and quacked so loudly, the horses snorted in the barn. After a quick huddle, the birds quacked again and then rose to the sky, one at a time. Colton lifted his head higher and higher, watching them fly away, until he flopped onto his bottom in the water.

"Okay, Mister. Enough adventure for you. Now it's my turn."

As I reentered the barn, Morgan stood next to Knight in the main hall. He tossed his head upward, and refused to take the bit while she put on the bridle. Her leathers hung by her side and her other hand held onto his halter. Morgan grumbled and stomped her foot.

No way I'll offer help. She was going to have to ask. I only had so much time at the barn. I couldn't bring Chancy out of her stall while Knight stood in the middle of the barn. I deposited Colt in his playroom, prepped Chancy in her stall, and waltzed past Morgan to the tack room for my saddle. Morgan continued to struggle with Knight. I'd give her a few more minutes before I'd ask her to put Knight back in his stall.

Knight snorted and pawed the floor. I wanted to do the same thing. I chickened-out about confronting Morgan and led Chancy toward her back door.

Morgan cleared her throat. "Umm..."

I stopped.

In an agitated voice, Morgan stood in Chancy's doorway. "So where's Mrs. Brown?"

"She doesn't usually come this early if I'm here."

Morgan looked at the floor, and tossed a small clump of straw with the toe of her boot. "Umm. I need help. You're here, so I'm asking."

That had to be painful to say. I waited to respond, just like she did with me. The silence grew louder. After another minute, I gave in. "What do you need?"

She lifted Knight's leathers. "He won't let me put on his bridle."

I backed Chancy into her stall and closed the door. Then I pulled the reins over her head and tucked them under the stirrup irons. I followed Morgan to Knight. My eyes went to the bridle, and then to her. "Have you put the bridle on him before?"

She shifted her face from place to place, refusing to make eye contact. "Mrs. Brown's been showing me, but Knight doesn't like me trying."

As I approached, Knight bowed his head and blinked his melting chocolate eyes. He neighed and rubbed his nose on my shoulder.

Morgan gasped and scowled at Knight.

I slid my hand across his shiny back, inspecting him. "I'll need the step stool. He's a big horse." Without looking at her, I said "Morgan, please go to the tack room and get the box of dog biscuits on the shelf and break them into small pieces. Then you can give him one piece at a time and talk to him in a soothing voice. You need him to relax."

She stared, narrowing her eyes before she stomped away.

I held Knight's halter while speaking to him with a happy jabber and stroking his soft nose. His gentle eyes flickered at me and his head relaxed in a down position.

Morgan returned. Knight's head flew up with wide eyes. Morgan held her hand flat with a piece of biscuit up to Knight's nose. He sniffed it sideways, but didn't attempt taking it.

I hiked my shoulders. "All right. The first thing that needs to happen is to get the two of you communicating. You've got to earn his trust."

Morgan glared. "Trina. I'm not asking for a psychology lesson. I just want to put on the stupid bridle."

"You're not going to get him to do anything, if you're not friends. You must have been kind to your first horse. What kind of horse did you have?"

"Look, Trina." Morgan straightened, poked out her chin, and then spoke without any emotion. "I only have a couple hours today. I don't want to waste the time talking about my first horse or to Knight. My brother is picking me up at 11:30. I have my first show this weekend and I'm running out of time to practice."

"I'll help you, but only if you can get him to relax. He'll never let you put on the bridle, and I'm not doing it for you." I headed for the tack room. "I'm getting the stool, and then we'll start."

Taking my time, I listened. In a grouchy tone, Morgan told Knight how she needed him to help her. I crept closer, not wanting her to know I was on my way. She held her hand up to Knight's lips. After a few seconds, he lifted his top lip and let the biscuit slip into his mouth, carefully, never taking his eyes from her. While he crunched it, Morgan watched him chew. His eyes flitted back and forth, and she repeated feeding the biscuits a couple more times. When she took one finger and trailed it down his nose, Knight actually made eye contact. Morgan spoke directly to him in a gentle voice. "Good boy!"

I moved forward. "Progress! He looks better already. That's great. Now here we go." I placed the stool next to Knight. "I'm going to show you what to do, and then you're going to do it."

Morgan exhaled a blast of air. "Mrs. B has done the same thing. I understand what to do, but Knight refuses to let me put in the bit."

"Oh." I moved the stool. "That's why I'm having you give him treats. He'll start thinking you have something yummy for him."

"That's bribing." Morgan huffed. "He's supposed to do what I ask him to do."

"Well, I don't think he knows what you expect, yet. Just like you don't know what to expect from him. It takes time to know each other. Are you ready?"

She stared at the floor and grumbled. "I guess." She hesitated, and then shoved her shoulders upward and let them fall with a forceful huff. "If I want to have any time to ride, we need to hurry this up."

"Okay. I'm going to talk you through each step. Right now, give him another biscuit and talk to him in a soft, calm voice. And then start telling Knight what you're going to do. You're going to give him a treat each time he listens to you."

Nodding her head, and out of the side of her mouth came, "And how am I supposed to know he's listening to me?"

"He'll look at you. His ears will move, or you'll see his muscles relax. Just like when you're riding. Now tell him what you're getting ready to do and give him a biscuit."

"This is ridiculous."

I didn't say another word and waited for her cooperation.

The seconds ticked by, and then she held her hand under his mouth. He nibbled the treat and made eye contact. Morgan caught his look and whispered, "Good Boy." She even patted his neck. She placed the bridle against his head. "Okay, Knight. I'm going to slide the reins over your head."

His eyes went to her face and he moved his lips. Morgan gave him a cookie. "Okay. Now I'm moving the nose band so you won't bite the leather straps." She waited for him to respond and gave him another pat and a treat. "Okay. Knight, here comes the hard part." She glanced at me and shook her head. "I can't believe I'm doing this."

I smiled. "You can't believe you're getting the bridle on, or you can't believe you're talking to your horse?"

"Both."

"Okay. Morgan. Now lay the reins over his neck and put the bit in your left hand. Look in Knight's eyes and tell him how good he's behaving and slide your thumb into the corner of his mouth until he opens. The magic trick is to push his lip in under your thumb. He can't bite you because his lip will be in the way."

Her hands shook slightly as she followed my directions.

"That's it! Good job, Morgan. Tell him how happy you are with a pat."

Morgan glanced sideways at me blinking, bulging eyes.

She stroked Knight and proceeded to tell him about putting each ear in its loop. As she pushed his forelocks away, she looked in his eyes, "Well, aren't you smart. We did it!" And she let him nibble two more treats.

"That was great, Morgan."

She smiled at Knight, untied him from the clips, and began walking him out of the barn to the stadium.

My shoulders slumped, and I bit my lip to stop them from quivering.

Never once did she make eye contact with me.

I watched her leave and mumbled under my breath. "You're welcome." My body tensed and I clamped my mouth. But I couldn't stop myself from twitching and mouthing angry words. "You ungrateful, rude brat."

She hadn't changed.

But at the last minute before she left the barn, Morgan turned her body halfway around and in a muted voice called, "Thanks, Trina."

I straightened and my heart quickened as I called after her. "You're welcome."

Minutes later Chancy and I walked to the stadium. Jumps were set up in the middle, but the horses needed to warm up. Morgan had already changed

STARTING OVER — 63

to a trot, while we walked along the fence line. The flow went well until she decided to canter on the diagonals and almost ran us over. "Morgan, unless we divide the stadium, you're going to have to call your moves or take turns."

She tugged her reins with such force, she made Knight halt smack in front of me. "Why don't you come back and ride later. You live here and can ride whenever you want."

"Wrong, Morgan. I have a puppy to train and other chores to do."

"I really need to practice some jumps. If I don't do well this weekend, my mother gets...Well, she gets upset."

If I'm going to try to be a friend, I'll back down. This time. "All right. I'll give you time to ride. At least let me trot and canter, and then I'll leave."

Morgan rode Knight to the far corner, and sat straight in her saddle, observing. I practiced putting Chancy into a trot, slowing down, and halting.

Morgan surprised me by her attention. "Check your body position and your hands."

Smiling inside, I straightened in the saddle, and squared my hands. After twenty minutes of riding, I headed Chancy toward the barn. Over my shoulder, I hollered, "Thanks for the tips. Morgan. The ring's all yours."

Standing in the shower rack, I hosed and scraped off the excess water from my frisky horse. She bumped me with her nose to knock me off balance and swished her tail in my face as I walked around her.

I played along, fussing at her and tickling around her ears. Once back in her stall, she munched on hay and stared out her window. Before I finished cleaning my tack and checking on the other horses, Morgan walked Knight into the shower area to hose him down and actually spoke kindly.

I walked over. "So, where's your show this weekend?"

She lifted her head but didn't say anything.

I didn't move.

From behind Knight she stood taller than Knights body and briefly made eye contact. "In Aiken, about two hours away."

I waited as long as she had done to respond. "I bet that's a lot of fun."

This time Morgan answered as if we were having a real conversation. "Well, this'll be my first show with Knight. I don't think we're ready, but of course, it's a must-do for my parents. They'll drop us off at the barn, unhook the truck, and go to a hotel to work."

Morgan moved to my side of Knight, but kept her back to me. She murmured, "Sometimes they show up for my events and other times, not." Louder she grumbled. "Tomorrow, I hope it's a NOT." She moved around to the other side of Knight again.

I forced my face to show no emotion. I blinked. "Where do you stay?"

Morgan stayed hidden while drying Knight's legs. "I camp out in the trailer. It's usually close to my stall. I'll visit with Knight. Actually, this may help us get more acquainted. I'll take some treats and try talking a little more with him. He does seem to relax with the attention."

I stared at Knight's face. "Aren't you scared being by yourself?"

She walked around Knight, patting his side with her back to me again. "No, I'm used to it. My show coach stays in her trailer close to mine and checks on me before I fall asleep and again in the morning." Morgan lifted her head over her shoulder, watching me. "My mother says she's trying to make me independent."

I added a strained smile. "Well. You're certainly braver than I'd ever be." I turned, swallowed my shock and waved. "See ya later. I'm off to train Mr. Colton."

Chapter 16

My summer days melted away under the heat and humidity. Throughout the week, the barn was almost mine. Morgan and I must have been on different schedules, which created a happy, hassle-free zone.

After Heather and I finished doing morning chores on Sunday, she rode the other schooling horse, Rapp. I studied the two of them together in the ring. Jealousy spiked its ugly head. Heather, who was two years younger and had been riding for only one year, performed the same level of skills I had practiced for three.

Being in a hurry, I only had time to exercise Chancy on a long lunge line in the arena. She followed my commands doing trots, canters, walks, and stops in a circle. Then I had her go the other direction. Lunging helped her skills but didn't help mine.

After working Chancy, I stroked her neck, enjoying the roughness as my hand went up and the smoothness as my hand glided down. "I'll see you later. Colton's trainer is coming early tomorrow, and I have lots to do before the weather gets too hot."

Heather rushed over. Her long pony tail swayed like Rapp's tail. "Do you want me to ride her today? I have time to ride both horses."

I started to say, "No, she'll be fine." But Chancy gave me a sideways look and made me feel guilty. The words leaked out. "I guess."

Heather stood to Chancy's left side and stroked her soft cheek. "I had fun riding her while you were at the beach. She's a great horse."

Glancing at each face, a lump of concern grew in my stomach. "Thanks, Heather. That'll be a big help. She's not getting enough riding time with me."

The week after the horse show, Mrs. B marveled at Morgan's change of attitude. "Trina what did you do?"

"Really?" I wrinkled my nose. "At the beginning of the week, you weren't here, and she needed help with her bridle. I suggested using treats and showed her how to get Knight to relax."

"Well, hon, there's definitely a change taking place. Even Knight seems quite happy."

"Oh, that's good to hear." I grinned. "How did her show go?"

Mrs. B twisted her head. "She never said anything, but I saw a yellow ribbon on Knight's inside ledge. Third place is wonderful for her first show with Knight, and I thought she was going to hang it, but it's gone now."

The following week, we had an unusual cloudy day with lower temperatures. Sarah, Colton, and I hiked in the open pasture, enjoying the cool the breeze.

Colton had learned the command Come on his six-foot leash in our back-yard. The challenge today was to attach a twenty-foot extendable leash. As he perfected the command from farther away, I added another twenty feet of rope. This allowed him to run forty-six feet in front, enjoying his freedom before I called, "Colton, Come."

He turned, jogged to me, and did a Front command. He sat, facing me, waiting for his treat. He gobbled teeny pieces of hot dogs, apples, or thin slices of string cheese. The harder the command, the more delicious the treats needed to be. After thirty minutes, Colt raced ahead, jerking me, and almost caught a cotton-tailed rabbit before it scurried down a hole at the edge of the woods. He poked his nose in, sniffed and dug.

"Nope. You can't get the bunny!" Before going any further, I untied the extra rope length, undid the extendable leash, and kept him closer on his six-foot leash. I didn't want him to wrap himself around a tree.

We made teams, Sarah and Colt and me and Colt. Sarah or I hid behind tree trunks, and let Colt use his sense of smell to search for the other. The search began after we counted to ten out loud. Colton sat motionless while he and his partner hid, except for his tail, swishing back and forth across the leaves. He learned the words Stay and Wait, and we worked on counting to ten. Then during his turn to search, he used his nose.

During my solo search for them, I let my ears lead me. Things in the woods rustled and snapped and I ran that direction. My heart raced as I stumbled. I caught myself on another tree and turned. Morgan sat against the tree with her knees pulled to her chest. "Whoa!" My heart sputtered. "Morgan, you scared me. What are you doing out here?"

She whispered, "I-I needed to get away." Morgan swallowed her sobs, bowed her head, and wiped her cheeks with both hands. She sniffed and lifted her tear stained face to me. "What are you two doing?"

Sarah came out of her hiding place. Our eyes questioned each other. When we looked back, Morgan was standing there, staring at us. She wiped her eyes with the back of each hand.

I shrugged. "Sarah and I are just running around in the woods."

Morgan narrowed her eyes.

I licked my lips, pressed them together, and made my voice perky with a little giggle. "Actually, we're being silly. Colton's favorite game is to search for one of us. It teaches him to smell and listen, and it wears him out. And it's cooler here. Why aren't you riding?"

"I don't feel like it right now." She stared off through the trees.

I didn't know what to say. "Do you want to join us?" I asked.

"I guess." While never looking at us, she spoke in a soft monotone voice. "My parents will never know."

What an eerie comment! All the fight had gone out of her. Something was terribly wrong. We stood silent, and slowly her eyes drifted to mine.

I broke the silence. "Okay. This is what we'll do. Two girls hide, and then we'll switch off with Colton."

Focusing straight ahead, she wrinkled her forehead.

"Morgan, we're pretending to be in the wilderness."

She pulled out a tissue from the waistband of her riding pants and wiped her nose. "Well, this'll be a first."

Sarah flipped her head away from Morgan. Her eyes bulged, and showed more white than blue.

I ignored Sarah's glare. "Okay. The more people, the better. That'll tire Colt even faster."

"I- I- I don't want to get close to him." Morgan looked down at Colton. "I'll just watch."

"You're not afraid of Colt, are you?"

She kicked at pine cones. "No. I'm, um, allergic to dogs. I don't want to get close to him."

Sarah blurted, "You're allergic to dogs, but not horses?"

"Yep. If that's a problem?" She threw her head, ready to leave. "I'll go back to the barn."

"No, stay." I touched her arm. "We'll work it out. Colton can stay with us."

Groaning, Sarah caved in. We took turns holding Colt, hiding and searching. He wanted to run and bark at the squirrels and the leaves fluttering across the ground. Morgan eyed Colton's every movement and her face softened.

The wind gusted through the trees as we approached the creek. I stopped and put my finger to my mouth. "Shh. Listen. The breeze sounds like a waterfall."

"It's just the trees." Sarah covered her mouth. "Oops! Forgot. We're supposed to be pretending. She glanced at Morgan. "I'm getting a little old to be playing this game."

Morgan hadn't spoken in minutes, just followed. Now she halted, and a small smile appeared across her face. "Well, it's a neat sound. It does sound like water rushing." Her silence erupted into giddy laughter. Her brown eyes grew, her eyebrows arched, and in between breaths she started to speak. "I'm, I'm actually forgetting about—" and she glanced at the ground and drew in a long breath. A second later, she added. "This is so different than what I'd be doing in Atlanta."

I took a step back and stared. "Why?"

"I haven't played since my brothers moved away. I've never had time to make friends. I'm always at the barn, training." Morgan flicked her bangs.

I turned the palms of my hands to the sky. "Why?"

Morgan pretended to check her boots. She lifted her head and gave Sarah a funny look. "This is—I shouldn't be talking about this stuff."

Sarah caught her expression. "I guess I'll head home now. You need..."

"It's okay. Maybe this is good to do." Morgan touched Sarah's arm. "You guys have tried to be nice to me. Maybe it's time for me to try, too."

A slow, tiny, smile bloomed on Sarah's face. "Okay."

We stood, waiting for the nasty Morgan to appear.

Morgan rocked back and forth for a couple of seconds. "All I can say is—My parents expect me to be the top student at school and hang with—" She used air quotes. "'—the popular group.' The girls who rode at my barn were super competitive." Morgan hung her head and muttered, "Not very friendly." After a moment she looked out at the trees. "Every parent wanted—" She wobbled her head. "No, expected their kid to win every event. It always made the parents look good." Morgan's eyes leaked, drip by drip. "And of course, I believed we all pretended to be happy. I know *I* did. What else could I do?"

"Wow!" Sarah put both hands on her chest "That sounds awful."

I was at a loss on what to say. "How-how do you do it all? I'm having trouble keeping up with a puppy, barn chores, and riding."

"I never have." Morgan's eyes zeroed in on mine. "I can't believe I'm telling you this." She bowed her head, stood quietly for what seemed a long minute, and then abruptly turned and walked away.

Sarah and I looked at each other and shrugged. Just as we thought she was leaving, she spun around and marched toward us with a purpose. "You know, this feels really good." She drew in a deep breath. "And you've helped me stop thinking about—" She dabbed at a tear and hesitated. Her face sagged as she waved away what she started to say. "I can't talk about it. But I will tell you my grades are only average, and I've never had any close friends, let alone any popular ones."

When I caught her eyes, mine softened. "Morgan. This year will be better. Which school are you going to?"

"The new Sterling Charter High School. New town. New school, new grade, new horse, new friends." Her eyes glimmered. "Where do you guys go?"

I smiled at Sarah, and then at Morgan. "We're in the eighth grade at Bethel Middle. But, I'll be fourteen in September and Sarah in November. What grade are you?"

"I'll be a freshman."

"Morgan, you're in luck. You can tell your parents you hang out with Sarah. They don't have to know she's in the eighth grade. She's popular and running for president of our class. If she wins, you can say you're friends with the school president. Sarah's involved in lots of clubs and soccer. I'm kind of a nobody 'cause I'm always hanging out at the barn or training my dog."

Sarah laughed, punched my shoulder, and smiled at Morgan. "She is *not* a nobody. At school she's everyone's helper. And I mean everyone. She works in the special classes, and she's the person the office calls if there's a new student."

"Oh." Morgan frowned at me. "So that's why you're helping me?" Her shoulders jerked to the right.

"Please don't go." I stepped in front of her. "That has nothing—"

Before I had a chance to soothe Morgan, Rapp and Sonny caught my attention, playing tag in their paddock. "I guess Mrs. B let them have extra time outside since it's cooler. It wasn't my day to go over and help."

The horses whinnied and lunged at each other, galloping back and forth. Dove and Chancy were in the adjacent paddock and snorted at the fun. Suddenly, all four horses raced to meet in the middle where Knight stood, watching but not interacting. Their feet were pounding the ground like ceremonial drumbeats.

Colt's ears perked, and he looked their direction. In a split second, he snapped the short leash out of my hand and sprinted toward the ruckus. My heart dropped into a pit of quick sand and sunk fast. I struggled to get air.

I gasped and tried to sound calm, "Colt. Come here!"

He looked back for a moment, and then changed his mind.

My breath caught again. I struggled for enough air to holler. "NOOO! He's heading to the paddocks!"

Chapter 17

I raced behind Colton. His four legs carried his little body faster than my two could run. "Colt, come!" I screamed, but he didn't respond. I tried again, clapping my hands. "Colton. Come here."

He halted and sat, panting. Relief swelled through my lungs. I pulled treats from my pouch, grabbed my clicker, and waited for him to turn all the way around. He eyed me for another second, but the horses nickered and charged the other direction. Spinning his head back to the horses, he zoomed off in a racing gear I'd never seen.

Gaining distance, he paused close to the fence. I squatted and made my PUP-PUP-PUP noise. Over his shoulder, his eyes narrowed at me. He knew what I expected him to do and ignored my command. He turned his head and nodded in beat with each hoof stomping the ground. He wanted to play, too.

He scrunched down to crawl under the bottom rail, but his small body didn't fit. His front paws slung the soft, sandy dirt every which way. Then he glimpsed the next section of fence where the rail rested higher. Panic pulsed through my heart. His twenty-inch height slid under the railing as he did the Limbo dance on his tummy.

I could hardly speak. "No, no! The horses! You'll get kicked." I found my voice and squealed. "Colton, NO!"

Morgan froze at the fence and watched. Sarah stood next to me, clapping her hands, and screaming. "Colt, Colt. Here!"

He made eye contact with me as if to say, "Look what I can do!"

In seconds, the trouble began. In the right paddock, he charged at Knight, nipping at his hooves.

Barking and hunching down, he pointed his bottom in the air and wagged his tail, Colton maneuvered in and out of Knight's tall, sturdy legs. The startled horse neighed and bolted to the other side of the fence, looking for a safe place to flee.

Colt only chased and lunged faster, but his little legs couldn't keep up. Knight kicked a back leg into the air, just missing Colton's head. Then Colt chased Sonny. Lucky for my pup, Sonny was too old to move fast, and my puppy dashed to the next paddock.

I yelled. "Sarah, run! Get Mrs. Brown. We need help."

Morgan backed up and covered her eyes. No one was able to help. I squeezed between the middle rails, fell to the sandy ground, and bounced to my feet. Standing at the side of the paddock, I waited to see which direction Colton chose. Animals can sense fear, so I swallowed, and told myself to speak calmly. "Colton." Sealing my lips, my breath came out as a whisper. "Please come here." In my head the words played over and over. *He's so tiny. One kick, and he'll be a goner.* I wanted to cry, but that wasn't going to help.

Chancy snorted as I strolled closer. Trying to keep her calm, I called. "Here, Chancy. Come here, girl." She stopped, looked for the puppy, shook her head, and made a noise we called raspberries. I approached her, stroked her nose, and walked her to the side of the paddock, out of Colton's path. She pawed the ground and nickered.

Just as I guzzled some air, Colton leaped at Rapp's long tail.

"Oh no!" My heart stammered and my voice shook, "Rapp. Hey Rapp. Come here, sweet boy." When he heard my voice, he sauntered right over to me.

Colton dashed in a straight line under Rapp's stomach between all four legs. I had hold of his halter and watched Colt running forward. I sighed. He would be safe from Rapp's legs. But as soon as relief whizzed through my lungs, Rapp put his nose under Colt's body and flung him into orbit.

I shrieked the entire time Colt sailed into the air, which seemed to be a mile off the ground and across the paddock. Seconds later, he landed in a sandy spot, thick with grass, but he hit the ground with a thump and a yelp.

My heart stopped beating. It was being squeezed like an exercise ball. I moved without thinking. Each step took an eternity before I was next to his body. I fell to the ground and examined my little guy.

Mrs. Brown called to me. I glanced up for a split second and noticed she had Rapp by his mane. Her words didn't register. "Trina, do...him...breathing. See...okay."

Sarah showed up, sobbing. "Did you hear Mrs. B?

I shook my head.

"She said, 'Do not to move him. Check his breathing. Is he okay?'"

Colton lay perfectly still. I couldn't tell if he was breathing and laid my head on his chest. It barely moved. I straightened, drew in a long breath. And spoke in a soft voice. "Oh, Colton. Please open your eyes." I stroked his side.

Mrs. B hadn't moved. "Is he all right?"

My fingers brushed his soft fur, checking for injuries. My eyes leaked onto his frail body. Maybe my tears would heal him like in the movies. "His eyes are closed. And-and he seems to be breathing, but really slowly. I don't see any blood or broken bones."

I looked up at her, and then to Sarah.

She was crying.

Mrs. Brown moved Rapp to the fence, attached a lead rope to his halter and wrapped the other end around the top railing. Chancy had not moved and seemed to know to stand without being restrained.

"Trina, you must keep Colton on a leash whenever he's around the horses. I have some expensive horses out here that aren't mine. If anything happened to them." Mrs. Brown bit her lip. "Well, you know all that. And, I know you feel bad enough. I'm sorry, honey." She blew out all of her frustration. "Trina, if Colt wakes, don't let him move."

"I feel awful, Mrs. B." I bowed my head and spoke to the ground. "Colton has never jerked the leash out of my hand before." I looked back up hoping to see her eyes. "He totally surprised me." I inhaled deeply and cried. "And then he took off at a run, and I couldn't catch him."

Sarah stood over me, silent. I sobbed while trying to speak and get myself under control. Mrs. Brown returned from checking the fences and squatted next to me. She rubbed my arm up and down. "All the rails are fine. The horses are fine, and now we need to make sure Colton's fine."

"I'm sorry, Mrs. Brown." I sobbed one more time. "I had no idea he could cause so much trouble."

"I know, Trina." She rubbed my back in circles. "He's a puppy. And puppies always find new ways to test you. You both have a lot to learn."

Sounds came from the next paddock. Mrs. Brown and I both glanced over, and then looked at each other. Morgan had come out of her trance and called Knight. He galloped toward her, and she met him in the middle of his paddock. With both hands, she examined his sleek body and each leg, and then lifted each back hoof. With a slap on his rear, Morgan spoke in happy voice, "Knight, you're okay. Go play." She called to us. "I'll check the fences over here."

Once again we heard running and yelling coming from the woods. I recognized Mom's voice before she appeared. "What's going on? I was reading on the back porch and heard screaming and horses whinnying." Her eyes searched the area. "What was all the—?"

The rest of what she started to say caught in her throat as she spotted me on the ground next to Colton's still body. And Sarah standing over me. Mom covered her mouth.

"Mom, Colt pulled the leash right out of my hand and ran to play with the horses. I don't know if Rapp didn't like being chased or was playing with Colt, but he got tossed into the air."

"Oh my! Is he okay?" Mom glanced at Mrs. Brown.

She nodded. "He seems like he's waking. He may be sore, and I bet he never comes close to a horse again."

Squatting and leaning over him, Mom spouted instructions. "Trina. Run home and call Dr. Mayer. I don't have my phone. That'll give Colton an extra few minutes to recover, and then I'll carry him home. Give her a heads up. We may need to bring him in." Then she spoke to Mrs. Brown. "If there are any damages, just let us know."

"No harm here. Trina, go use the barn phone. It'll be a lot quicker.

Sarah pulled her phone from her pocket. "Here, use mine."

I stood and traded places with Mom. She cradled Colton in her arms like a newborn baby and whispered in his ear. "Hey, little guy. You have to be okay. There you go. I see a little piece of your brown eyes. Now, let's open all the way."

His eyes closed again. He lay like a ragdoll and struggled to breathe in little puffs.

I couldn't stop staring at his limp body. What if something happened and he couldn't be a service dog? It'd be all my fault.

Colton started to fidget in Mom's arms. She looked at me. "He's waking, honey. Go ahead and call. I might feel better if we take him in."

Sarah and I moved away from the disaster area to speak. After explaining everything that happened with my head down, I looked up. Morgan had joined us.

I returned to Mom. "Dr. Mayer said for you to take a deep breath. You know all the signs. But I'm supposed to tell you, 'Give him a few minutes to recover. Check his pupils to see if they're dilated. If he seems confused, throws up, or seems to be in pain bring him in.' She'll be waiting to hear."

"All right. I'm carrying him home. You girls run on ahead. I'm going to walk slowly."

Morgan backed away with an uncomfortable expression. I picked up on the awkward moment. If we were friends, I would have looped my arm through hers. I didn't know Morgan well enough. Would she get angry at being touched?

Oh go for it. You decided to be her friend.

Instead of being too close, I touched her wrist. She looked down at my hand like she had been stung, and before she protested, I pulled her forward. "Come on over to my house. There's no way you feel like riding right now. We'll have a snack and then come back to the barn."

She walked with us, and I dropped my hand. Once inside the house, she glanced around but didn't speak. Mom arrived a few minutes after we had popped open a can of orange soda.

Colton lay awake, but not moving in Mom's arms. She set him on the carpet and all four of us kneeled around him. No one spoke. I whispered a quiet prayer. A full minute went by. It seemed forever. Then Colton lifted his head and pushed himself into a sitting position. He scanned the room, stood, and shook his whole body, starting from his head all the way down to the tip of his long tail.

Air filled my lungs, and I stroked his head. "Are you okay, Colton?"

He looked straight at me and barked. He walked to the sliding glass door and pawed the door. Mom cleared her throat. "Don't let him out. I want to keep an eye on him for a few more minutes."

I stood. "Colt. Come here." He walked to me and sat. After scratching his ear with his back foot, he put the paw into his mouth for a quick chew. He scratched his ear again, and as if he'd just thought about it, popped up and ran to his water bowl. "I'd say he's okay." I chuckled for a second, and then tears streamed down my face. "But I need to sit down."

In unison, Sarah and Morgan said, "Me, too." And we all crashed on the couch.

"By the way, Mom." I glanced at her and pointed. "This is Morgan."

Chapter 18

After Colton's scary experience, if he spotted a horse even in the distance, he slinked across the ground, making himself invisible—which was perfectly okay with me. He ran loose in the woods and never returned to the pasture. He swam in the pond and chased the ducks until they zoomed to the sky.

During his weekly home visit with Ms. Sue, I complained to her about his antics. "He never seems to run out of energy."

She smiled and glanced at Mr. Colton sitting next to my legs. "He's still very young and some Labs need a ton of exercise, physically and mentally. Let me see his birth date. Yep. He'll be officially four months old, and he's had all of his immunizations. Let's get him started in the next service puppy class next week. His brother and sister will be there. The others are a couple weeks older. The class will be in Columbia, once a week."

As Ms. Sue continued speaking, my thoughts got hung up with the word "Columbia." Where Chase and Peyton lived. Then I heard parts of her last sentence. "—learn about socializing and following more commands. That will make it safer for him to go on more outings."

After Ms. Sue drove away, I made an urgent call to Sarah.

She answered. "What's up?"

"For the next six weeks on Tuesday nights, I'm going to have puppy classes in Columbia. Colton is ready for outings. Maybe we can work out a way to go early, and see the guys, and then I'll go to class."

"Mmm. We'd need to go to their house or maybe meet at the Mall? But then they'd have to take us to class. What would I do while you're in class?"

"I don't know if either of our parents would drive us back and forth. Talk with your mom. She's home during the summer. Maybe my Dad'll need to go to Columbia for a meeting? I'll call Chase, and we'll toss ideas around."

As it worked out, Mrs. Neal offered to take Sarah and me to the Columbia Mall. We'd meet the guys at four o'clock, giving us two hours to hang out with

Chase and Peyton while she shopped. Their mom would drop them off, return at six o'clock, and deliver me to my puppy class at six-thirty. Mrs. Neal would meet Sarah at six o'clock in the mall. They'd grab dinner at the food court and shop some more, then pick me up at eight o'clock p.m. Then we'd return home.

A month seemed like a long time since we hadn't seen the guys. Chase and I talked or texted as often as possible. I realized Chase did a better job at calling than Peyton, and I didn't dare tell Sarah, or I'd make her jealous.

Finally, the next Tuesday arrived. Neither Sarah nor I could sit still, or be quiet in Mrs. Neal's car. "Okay, you two. One hour and we'll be there. But I need you to calm down." She turned on the radio.

I held a harnessed Colton on my lap in the back seat of Sarah's car. Before we drove onto the highway, I let him sniff through the half open window and enjoy the scents. By this point in his training, he rode in the car, comfortable in his seatbelt. But every time we went for a drive, the memory of his first car ride coming home from the beach played like a movie in my mind.

Colton had gurgled as he slept on my lap, still as a stuffed animal. He'd caught me off guard when his head popped up. He'd placed his paws on my chest, and locked eyes with me. In seconds, his mouth had opened, and he'd vomited wet goo all over me and in my hair.

I'd had to hold my breath until we stopped at the nearest rest stop, afraid I'd return the favor on him.

Now, I looked at my fella, with his nose dripping from the rush of air, and a pang of warmth filled my heart. We had each learned a lot in two months.

I whispered in his ear. "Wait until you see where we're going!"

Mrs. Neal parked. Sarah and I strutted from the parking lot to the mall. "Girls. Walk! We'll get there in the same amount of time but gracefully."

We met at the Food Works, and then we were on our own for two hours. Well, almost on our own. I had Colton.

I couldn't ask for a better place for Colton to experience people, food, and noise. I had filled my pouch full of treats for the trip. I carried a soft cooler over my shoulder with one baggie of dog food for his dinner and some rewards in class.

The four of us stayed together, laughing and talking about nothing.

Chase reached over and grabbed my hand. "This way I won't lose you."

Peyton smiled at Sarah and did the same with her. But he pulled her off to a quiet corner. Chase and I pretended to window shop, but drifts of Peyton apologizing to Sarah floated out.

I guess they worked it out, because they returned with big grins across their faces.

We wandered up and down each side of the Mall, peeking in a few stores. Two hours wasn't enough time. Before we knew it, we had to deliver Sarah to her mom. Peyton hugged her and said he'd "try to do a better job of calling." We hurried to meet their mom, who paced in front of the exit door.

Mrs. Manning smiled at me, and then down at Colton. "Hello, there! You are a cutie! Trina, there's a blanket on the backseat for him to sit on."

"Got it. Thanks. He's nice and clean." I sat in the middle to be next to Chase and buckled Colton on the blanket next to the window.

In the training facility's parking lot, Chase hopped out so I could follow him on his side of the car. He took my hand, and tugged me behind the car. Without any hesitation, he wrapped his arms around me in a firm hug and whispered in my ear.

"I'll call later."

We pulled apart, and his shining green eyes stared into mine.

I caught my breath and made myself move to open Colton's door. I put my hand in front of Colt's face, "Wait." I counted to ten in my head. "Okay." He jumped down and lifted his nose. "Do you recognize this place?"

His ears perked at the sounds of other dogs. He stiffened, folded his ears tight and gazed every direction. I walked backward, staring at Chase.

He hollered and waved. "I'll call later."

I nodded, and moved my mouth. "Byee!"

This new feeling made my heart ache as if it had been ripped into small pieces, and I had to pull myself together. Looking into Colton's face helped. "Come, Colt. You're going to school."

He walked, looking side to side as I coaxed him with each step. The minute my hand went into the pouch, his tongue wiped his lips from corner to corner. I made him walk two more steps, before I gave him a command. "Sit." I clicked, and he received his special school-night treat: teeny, cut up hotdogs.

We entered through the side door and walked into the familiar playroom. Colton panted and his eyes flashed from corner to corner. His first days of training had taken place in this large room, and off to the side were the gated spaces where the puppies had slept and eaten until they were eight weeks old.

I walked Colton to that area, letting him explore. He darted to his previous crate, stuck his nose inside, and wagged his tail. Backing out, he looked up at me with glowing eyes.

One by one, other puppy trainers entered the building. Colton's entire body trembled with excitement, whipping his tail back and forth. In the middle of the room, Colton prodded his sister, a small yellow Lab named Lucy. Her trainer, Patrick, had adopted her on the same day I'd chosen to train Colton.

Jessica slowly approached with Tanner, Colt's brother, a chocolate Lab. She had decided only two weeks ago to take over his training. Tanner seemed to be growing larger than Colt, and his amber eyes skirted the room. The puppies turned in circles, wagging, and nosing each other. If I had had a tail, mine would have been wiggling, too.

We'd be working together again.

My ears rang from all the chatter and barking. Two new puppy raisers stood back, against the wall, watching. I walked over and introduced myself and Colton. The tall girl with almond shaped-eyes stood, glancing from person to person. As I approached, her small smile lasted long enough for me to notice her pink-colored braces before she sealed her lips. She pushed her straight, black hair behind each ear, and tucked her chin.

She spoke softly. "Nice to meet you, Trina and Colton. I'm Annie, and this is Sasha."

Sasha, a small yellow Labradoodle, backed up for a second, and then rolled over on her back. Colton proceeded to sniff her, which in doggy language gave her permission to stand.

The curly, blond-headed boy standing next to Annie puffed his chest and made himself an inch taller than me. He slid the leash handle over his left wrist, blinked his silver-blue eyes, and offered me a handshake.

The minute my hand touched his, a buzz tingled up my arm.

He held my clammy hand firmly, placed his other hand on top like he was keeping me from moving, and stared. "Wow! Those are some green eyes."

My face overheated, and I pictured my freckles poking out two at a time. He stroked the top of my hand. "Hi, I'm Wesley, and this is Kaiser." He winked and grinned.

Every red hair on my body lifted as if he was full of electricity. I slid my hand away and looked at him sideways as if he had lost his mind. The laugh inside of me wanted to explode, but I swallowed the impulse. For a long second, I pictured Chase's happy face changing to confused.

I wiped my hand on my shorts and moved toward Jessica and Patrick, but Kaiser, Wesley's lanky, black and tan German shepherd, stood inches taller than Colt and beat his tail back and forth in Colton's face. They spent a moment catching a whiff of each other's behinds, and decided to be friends. Wanting to escape, I flagged Jessica and Patrick. "Come over here. I'll introduce you."

They headed over and minutes later, we all knew each other's names and the dogs played freely in the room.

Annie flushed and coaxed Sasha to play. But Sasha pushed herself between Annie's knees, and shoved her head out. Only her hazel eyes followed the other dogs.

Ms. Sue called the class to attention, clapping her hands. "Okay, gang. Round up your puppy, and let's begin."

Colton had changed into a domineering puppy. His independent nature seemed a bit much with the shyer dogs. If another puppy moved too close, Colton gave a low snarl. I gave him a look and he caught my expression and sat. Once again, my cheeks flushed.

Ms. Sue instructed us. "Let's keep a distance between each dog while we practice. From this day forward, there won't be social time until after class. Playtime will be outside. Today they needed a little time to meet and get acquainted."

Even though Colton knew his basic commands, being in class with other distractions made them seem brand new. He looked at each dog before he attempted to follow my commands. I held his treat above his nose, and he leapt to steal it from my fingers. Ms. Sue watched each of us practicing. "Trina, use your clicker and do the choice method."

I put the hot dog pieces in my left hand and the clicker in the right. Colt smelled the treats in my closed fist. If he sat and didn't nudge my hand, I'd open it and retrieve one piece. He had to stay seated until I chose to give him the yummy prize. "That's better, Colt. Let's try again."

Other puppies were having similar problems. Sasha lay on the floor, refusing every command. Annie glanced at me with sad eyes and shrugged her shoulders.

I smiled at her and tried again with Colt. I gave him the command for Down.

Ms. Sue wandered around the room and caught Colton behaving. "Good job, Trina."

Colton lifted his chin, spread his lips across his teeth in his silly grin. The minute Ms. Sue walked away, he popped up like a Jack in the Box. We repeated the command a number of times, and I made him stay until I said, "Okay!"

Wesley stomped the floor and fussed at his dog. "You know all this. What's the matter with you?"

Poor Kaiser squatted and peed on the floor.

Ms. Sue held Kaiser's leash while Wesley stiffly retrieved the mop from the corner of the room. He huffed loudly, jerking his head and pushing the mop angrily across the floor. Ms. Sue approached him and whispered, "You need to show your dog patience." With a pink face, he returned the mop to its bucket with a flourish and bowed to us.

———

After forty-five minutes of training, it was show time. Mrs. Neal and Sarah joined the other parents at the side of the room. One at a time, we were called to the middle of the floor to give the commands.

I stood confident, smiling at Colton, believing he would show off to the class. I used my hand signal for Sit. He sat with his chin held squarely and looked me in the eyes.

I took a long breath and let it out. "Stay." After I used the hand signal and put my hand in front of his face, he blinked and stayed. Then I dropped my arm and stepped back four steps. After thirty seconds, I smiled at him, and moved forward. "Okay."

He bounced at me, and I patted him.

"Good boy."

Colton performed some of the commands as asked without mistakes, but others we had to redo.

He yawned and looked around at the other pups.

I called his name in a firmer voice to regain his attention.

He blinked at me and tilted his head then moved first into a Sit, then a Down.

His eyes twinkled.

My heart sank. I sensed trouble.

He lowered his shoulders and pointed his rear end in the air. I didn't react. He stared at me and slowly stretched across the floor to a Down.

"Good boy." And I gave him a treat. I held my hand in front of his face. "Stay." I stepped back.

As soon as he swallowed and licked his lips, he stayed in the down position but scooted across the floor with his hind legs and wiggled up to me for another treat.

Ms. Sue walked over and patted my shoulder. "Good job, Trina. We both know he knows how to do this at home. Don't be discouraged."

The familiar hot sensation climbed my neck and over my ears.

Ms. Sue looked at the crowd. "Now your puppies are safe to be in public places and around other dogs. Have fun, practicing your new commands wherever you go."

Then she looked straight at me. "Trina, chin up. He'll do better next time."

Chapter 19
August

Sitting on the den couch, the bright sun burned over the tops of the trees and filtered between the branches. Colton, now five months old, slept by my feet after an exhausting romp at the barn. I stared at his almost grown body and my heart melted. *Where did our summer go?*

In two weeks, my fun-filled, carefree-days would be replaced by time schedules, homework, and tons of stress. But the biggest problem Sarah and I faced was still ahead. We needed to see Chase and Peyton one more time.

While giving the horses treats last night, we knew the only solution would be to meet the guys at their mall. I was supposed to ask my mom, and Sarah planned to beg hers. Around noon, Mom surprised me by coming home for lunch. I sat down at the kitchen table as she hummed her favorite tune and pulled out baked beans, coleslaw, and two sandwiches from a large bag. The sweet and spicy barbeque sauce made my mouth water.

Mom sat across from me and crossed her arms on the table. "I understand you and Sarah want to go back to the Columbia Mall?

My eyes popped open as if she'd handed me a hundred-dollar bill. Little bubbles popped one at a time inside my stomach.

"I doubt this trip is about clothes shopping, since you asked to go to the Columbia Mall." Mom leaned forward with a twinkle in her eye. "Do you want to tell me what you two have cooked up?"

Ready to convince her of the importance to see Chase I whined, "Mom, once school starts we'll never see each other again. We need one more visit. Please?"

Mom sat back in her chair, and after a long drawn out moment, she laughed. "How about tomorrow? I work a half day, and Carol starts teaching next week. We'll all go for lunch."

I did a little jig and screamed. "Yes! Thank you. Thank you. That's perfect. I've got to text Sarah." My heart raced at high speed. I squinted at Mom. "She knows doesn't she?"

Mom's face beamed like a child seeing a Christmas tree light up for the first time. "I believe she does by now."

We met the guys in front of the Food Works and got lost in conversation.

Mom tapped my shoulder. "Let's meet right here in three hours. We're going to a restaurant."

The four of us ate at the Food Works, laughed, and talked about the weeks in between our last visit. Colton sat under the table and popped up only once. After lunch we chose to go our separate ways.

Chase held my hand, but we didn't talk. Colton's head rotated, looking at the crowds. We wandered up and down the row of shops on the top level. Before we took the stairs down to the lower level, I pulled Chase over to an empty corner. "Chase, this is crazy. This is our last time together, and we need to make it fun."

He blinked and his shoulders slumped. "I don't know what to say. What if we can't be friends anymore? The phone helps, but it's not the same as being together. What are we going to do?"

Colton sat and watched us talk.

I shrugged. "I have no other ideas, except if Logan gets a service dog, we'll see each other at PAALS events. If we want to stay close, we'll have to work at it. And we have Skype."

Chase lifted his handsome face and shared his smile. "Okay. Let's liven things up." We jogged down the stairs and flew into a music store where Chase chose a CD. He tugged me to a chair and we shared the ear phones. His eyes twinkled as he mouthed. "What do you think?"

"I really like it."

He purchased the CD and looked at his watch.

"Come on. I'm going to find something that makes you think of me when we're apart."

He wrapped his arm around my shoulders, and I sunk into his side. We wandered around the lower level and giggled at the wild things we saw in the windows.

Chase pointed out. "How about that pink lizard? You like the color pink."

I giggled. "Naw, I like purple better." Then I pointed. "How about I get you that green tie? It matches both of our eyes."

Chase moaned. "Please, no ties. And I want something that is just about you."

"I remember the perfect thing I saw for you earlier." I pulled away. "Let's meet back here."

He squinted at me. "How long do you need?"

"Give me fifteen minutes. I know where I'm going."

"Okay. Hurry! We're almost out of time."

I watched him head down the aisle and go left. He had something in mind, too. I had spotted a carved, wooden turtle in a gift shop upstairs. I raced up the stairs. Colton looked up at me, happy to be jogging, again.

I rushed back and beat Chase. Colton followed me as I paced. Something poked the middle of my back and I twisted around.

Chase jumped in front of me, threw his hands in the air, and roared in a deep voice. "Boo!"

Colton barked.

"Shh! Quiet, Colton" I fussed at Chase but smiled. "You scared me!" But I focused on the bag waving in his hand. I handed Chase my small white box. "Here's my surprise."

He shook his head. "No. Ladies, first." He held out a bag with purple tissue paper sticking up.

"Wow, this is pretty." I reached into the bag and lifted out a soft, stuffed turtle.

She was lavender all over, except her shell was a deep purple, and she had two brown beads for eyes.

"Oh, this is so perfect." I chuckled. "Okay. Now it's your turn."

He opened the little box and laughed out loud. "We do think alike, don't we? This is spectacular! He looks just like a loggerhead."

For a moment, we smiled at each other, lost for words. And in the next second, we wrapped our arms around each other and squeezed. Colton stared, but stayed quiet.

At the same time, Peyton and Sarah ran by. He slapped Chase on his back. "It's time to go, bro."

At the Food Works, our mothers stood off to the side. What else could we say? Our time together was over. We stared at each other, and painfully walked away, promising we'd talk on the phone.

Driving home, Colton lay across my lap. Not wanting to talk about the guys, Sarah put in her ear buds. My thoughts whizzed through my head like the trees outside until Sarah tapped my arm.

I twisted around.

She blinked her intense, sad eyes. "I need to think about something else. Tell me what's happening with Morgan. Is your plan working?"

Surprised, I took a moment. *What did I want to share?* "Morgan's actually sharing little bits of her personality, as long as no one else is around. Once in a while she'll come over for lunch at my house. She stays all day at the barn with no food and never knows when she's going to be picked up."

"What does she do?"

"She calls a taxi most of the time." I squinted and shook my head. "I don't know, Sarah. Something is off with Morgan. The other day I carried another box turtle out of the yard. The minute I picked him up he tucked his head into his shell. He reminded me of Morgan when she chooses not to share any more information. Every time I try to reach out to her, she shuts down. I'm hoping, if I give her enough space, she'll feel safe enough to hold her head up and share her problems."

Sarah leaned her head sideways and smiled. "You're doing a good job helping her. I just hope she doesn't hurt you in the end."

We grew quiet, again.

I looked over at her. "Okay, Sarah. We're both sad. But we have to move on. Our free time is almost gone. And since you've started soccer training and working on your campaign for Class President, I'm already missing our time together. Don't forget, I'd love to help make posters."

She patted Colton's head. "Next week, I'll tell you when we're getting together at my house. You can bring Colton."

I straightened my shoulders. "Super! Can you believe in one more week, we're going to be stuck with homework and schedules? I'll have less time at the barn."

Sarah shook her head, "I know. Is it getting harder for you to find time to ride?"

I puckered my mouth. "Yep, I had always dreamed about trying out for the Clemson College riding team, using one of their horses, and competing. If I ever learned enough. But—" I shook my head and looked down. "—That's not happening. Sometimes I get jealous watching Morgan training." I glanced out the window. "Oh, wow! We're home. I hate that this day is over."

Sarah nodded and made a deep groan.

Mrs. Neal dropped us off at home, and I couldn't wait to see Chancy. I took Colton's cape off and let him run free outside while I changed.

Mom sipped on a cup of tea as she handed me her phone. "Ms. Sue left you a text on my phone. Here, you need to read it."

"Trina. Reminding you about our lesson tomorrow. Be there at 10:00."

Mom smiled. "I wish I could watch, but I'll be at work."

My shoulders squared and my chin lifted. "I'm pretty proud of his progress. I bet Ms. Sue will be surprised."

"You'll have to tell me all about your lesson when I get home."

Chapter 20

At ten o'clock, the doorbell rang, and Colton raced to the front door. He pounced on the side window ledge and barked. When I caught him by his harness, he pulled me across the hardwood floors.

Ms. Sue watched from outside. The minute I opened the door, he quieted and wiggled.

I shrugged my shoulders and sighed. "He's getting worse instead of better."

Ms. Sue glanced down. "Hey, Mr. Colton." He stared back at her. "I know what we're working on today. If you're going to be a working dog, you must have better door manners."

He panted, swishing his tail across the floor.

"Get your clicker, Trina. Fill your pouch, and if you have a bath mat that will not slide, we can use it as his Place in the entry way. While I found supplies, Ms. Sue put Colton through his normal commands. My heart swelled as I listened to her tell Mr. Colt how wonderful he performed.

On the floor, a distance away from the front door, I laid a yellow bath mat. "Okay. I'm ready." I patted my pouch. "He'll like these."

Ms. Sue held her clicker and walked up to the mat. Without saying a word, her eyes fell on the mat, and waited for Colton's eyes to follow. The moment he looked at the mat, she clicked, and gave him a treat. When she gazed at the mat again, she added the word, "Place." He followed her eyes and looked at the spot. Sue clicked, and he gobbled another treat. Step by step, she continued this procedure until he settled all four paws on the mat and lay down.

I froze, watching. As Colton lay quietly on his Place. "That was amazing."

Ms. Sue spent an hour training one step at a time. I was to say, "Just a minute," to alert anyone waiting outside. And those words would signal Colton to go to his Place.

Smiling, she stroked Colt's head. "Have your friends help. Explain the need for them to wait outside until you're ready to open the door."

I couldn't contain my laugh. "He'll be quite the challenge. I'll try. Thanks for coming."

Later that night I called Sarah. She described all the things she had to do from now until school started. I listened to each subject and waited for her to finish rambling. Then she paused. "Umm. How about tomorrow night? That'll work for me."

"Perfect. I'm asking Morgan tomorrow at the barn."

"Ugh. You sure are getting friendly with her. I guess you're sticking to your plan. Hope it works out for you."

The next day at the barn, I approached Morgan while she readied Knight. I explained why I needed her help. She hesitated, and then shared another secret. "I didn't do well at the last competition. My parents think I'm not working hard enough. They don't know I've made a friend, and I can't tell them I'm going to your house, or they'll think I'm wasting my time. I'll be here all day. Let me see how it goes. Dad's out of town, and Mom never knows if she's going to be at the hospital all day or night, and my brother's gone back to school."

"Well. You have to come for dinner. And then we'll practice with Colton. Do you have food for the day?"

Morgan waved over her shoulder on her way to the tack room. "I'll be fine."

Which meant she was on her own again. I'd work with Colton, then bring a picnic lunch back to the barn, and afterwards, let Colt hang out by the pond.

Inside the tack room, Morgan and I chatted while we devoured sandwiches, chips, and sweet tea. I brought brownies and apples for later. Morgan even asked about Chase. I shrugged and told her I hadn't spoken to him in a week.

Morgan changed the subject and bragged in between bites about how she could do whatever she wanted, but she contradicted herself by revealing she wasn't telling her parents about Colton or me. Finally, she stopped blathering and moaned, "Oh, why not. I'll come after I feed Knight and help Ms. B. She's already invited me to dinner with her."

I frowned, worrying. "Doesn't your mom wonder what you're doing?"

"Not usually. We have a housekeeper who does most of the cooking. She always leaves food in the frig." She mumbled to the floor. "Dad cooks sometimes." Then she lifted her face and smiled. "And when he's not traveling, he's good company."

"That's good. Come over, whenever. Sarah's going to help, too."

At eight o'clock in the evening, the hot sun slipped lower in the sky and the temperature faded a few degrees. Once Sarah and Morgan arrived, I explained what I needed them to do. Colton cocked his head sideways, and his innocent, chocolate-brown eyes melted my heart, but I knew he wouldn't be an easy fix.

The girls strolled outside, out of sight. I sat on the couch with Colton at my feet, but I held his leash, waiting for them to stand at the door. Colton's ears pricked at their voices and he tried to dash to the door. I made him walk, saying, "Easy." Instead he pulled me to the door, barking.

I glanced at the door. "Just a minute."

His attention zoomed to the figures at the door. "Colton, Look!" He glanced at me. I clicked, and gave him a piece of cheese. I signaled with my hands, saying, "Back." As he scooted backwards, I pointed to the mat, "Place." He wiggled his bottom on the mat and stayed. But with people outside, the doorbell became another distraction. He fought to stay in 'Place' for a whole three seconds before he rushed at the door.

I spoke through the cracked opening. "Please, disappear again. I need him to stay on his mat when I open the door."

They giggled and ran around the side of the house.

I walked Colton to his mat and gave him instructions. I remembered Ms. Sue saying, "Let each command sink in. He needs time to process each word."

He knew what I had said, but hadn't mastered the skill.

After four more tries with the girls standing outside, Colton stayed and didn't bark at the bell. This time as Sarah and Morgan stepped inside, he waited.

"YES! Good boy!" I clicked, stroked his head, and fed him pieces of cheese. And then I bent down to be face to face. "Good boy!"

His mind and his body struggled with each other, and in seconds he popped up, barking and curving his body in a u-shape around the girls. Not the right response, but he'd made progress.

"See, Morgan? He's learning to stay back. Will you do it one more time?"

She shook her head. "Nah, I'm tired of hearing him bark, and I'm bored."

"All right. Enough. Let's go to my room."

Colton beat us, and stood at the top step. He panted while he waited. I removed his cape, and he rolled on the carpet to scratch his back. When he finished, I sat next to him, and Sarah sat on the other side.

Morgan flopped in my desk chair and leaned back. Colton darted over and pawed her leg. She cringed.

I pressed my lips together, containing my smile. "He only wants you to pet him and will probably pester you until you do. I can put him downstairs. I don't want you to get sick."

"Nah. Let me see what happens. Maybe if I touch him just a little, I'll be okay." She slowly lifted her hand and hesitated.

Colton put his nose on her knee. She raised her hand higher but made eye contact with Colton.

She snickered. "He likes a lot of attention, doesn't he?"

"Yep. And as you can see, he's a little pushy."

Morgan patted Colton's head with her fingertips. With each pat, his eyes blinked like he was being hit on the head. Gradually, her entire hand flattened on his head and she stroked his soft ears, mumbling under her breath, "When I try to get any attention, I usually get arguments. Maybe Colton can teach me new ways to talk to my parents."

Sarah snorted. "I wouldn't try barking."

We cracked up, but I saw right through Morgan's happy mask. I'd worn one of my own at the beach. She had bottled up her frustrations and carefully kept them from fizzing so she wouldn't explode.

As we quieted, I wondered if I should mention my birthday in September. Morgan had begun helping me with barn chores, and I set up fence rails for her. Fall season had creeped in and cooled our evenings, but the days were still warm. Mrs. B had offered to let me have a pool party. Even Sarah was excited since she knew how to swim. What the heck! All she could do is say "No."

"Morgan, I'm having a pool party on September twenty-first. If you're not going to a horse show, maybe your parents could come and meet mine and Sarah's."

Her face drooped. Her brown eyes grew darker, and she tried to smile. "I'll check my schedule. I can probably come, but my parents, never. Sorry. That's just the way it is at my house."

A phone buzzed, breaking the awkward silence

Morgan reached into her pocket and clenched her jaw. "Oh no!" She stared straight ahead and her arm twitched like she had been electrocuted. "Dad just called. He's not supposed to be back. He went to the house and saw I wasn't there. He's coming to get me. I have to get to the barn."

She shot to her feet and headed down the stairs. Sarah and I gaped at each other and followed. "I'll go with you, Morgan. Sarah, do you want to feed the horses?"

Morgan grabbed the door knob and shook her head. "Please, please, don't come right now. I need to leave as soon as he drives up. If he knows I have a friend and mentions it to Mother, I'll be in big trouble."

Swallowing my alarm, I sucked in my breath, aimed my eyes at hers, but she avoided mine.

I touched her arm. "Okay. If you're sure you don't want company? I have things to do."

Sarah nodded a blank face. "Me, too."

Morgan flew out the door.

Chapter 21

Mom drove Sarah and me to school on our first day back. As we sashayed through the front double doors, Sarah shouted, "Yay! We are eighth graders!"

I hooted and added, "And Sarah Neal is running for Class President. Come and join her campaign."

For two weeks, we passed out flyers with a picture of Sarah in her soccer outfit, her leg aimed at kicking the ball. Written in big bold letters under the picture, MAKE A NEW GOAL! VOTE FOR SARAH NEAL.

Finally, Friday arrived and the voting was over.

At the end of our last class, the only one Sarah and I had together, the intercom static crackled. Everyone looked towards the speaker in the ceiling and held their breath with anticipation as the principal announced, "And this year's eighth grade Class President is Sarah Neal!"

Heading into the hallway, many friends cheered and surrounded my best friend. She didn't notice I had moved out of the way and watched from the doorway. I trembled with excitement for her but knew our time together would change. A gust of sadness started at my chest and rumbled down to my feet. I banged the toes of my sandals together, knocking away the sensation. I hoped we'd still have our time at night doing horse treats.

I had always excelled at school, but after two weeks I already lagged behind. Colton had improved his skills during each of his training classes, setting an example as being the star pupil. I wished I could do the same. I spent more time at the barn and training Colton than on my assignments.

I sat at my desk and stared out the window, avoiding the stack of books and my list of homework assignments. I had Spanish and algebra to learn and an essay to write. But tomorrow was our last puppy class, and I wanted Colton to show off.

During dog classes, Wesley's obnoxious behavior sort of disappeared into an awkward kind of flirting. Being noticed was a novelty. He always paid special attention to how I looked. Only a few months ago, I had no interest in boys or clothes. Even though Wesley charmed me, guilt crept in. I wished the attention came from Chase.

My eyes drifted to the window. Chase's calls came less frequent. With the distance between us, I couldn't help wonder if he'd met another girl at school. I shook my head. Maybe the silly worries would sprinkle out like salt.

But Sarah and Peyton had totally stopped calling each other. She changed boyfriends so fast I couldn't keep up. No one seemed to keep her attention for long. For me, the idea of a boyfriend made me feel good, but they took too much effort and distracted me from the things I needed to do. The relationship with Chase on Edisto Beach had been different.

Colton crawled under the desk and waited for me to wrap my legs around the middle of his chest. As I repeated my Spanish sentences, he tilted his head and stared at me, trying to understand what I was saying. "Hola. ¿Cómo está? Muy bien. ¿Habla inglés? ¿Dónde está el baño?" I wrote my ten new vocabulary words in sentences: mesa, amigo, libro, libre, joven, leche, gracias, fútbol, escuela, and casa, and then I closed my notebook. I slapped the pile of books and moaned.

Since I couldn't concentrate, I decided to get up early the next morning and write my essay. I'd do my algebra during lunch. The moment I lifted my legs from Colt's warm body, he shot out from my desk. "Come on, fella. Let's practice one more time."

We rehearsed and ran out to the woods. A full moon glowed over head as we chased fireflies and listened to crickets. The horses neighed from their paddocks. An owl hooted somewhere in the woods and a wood pecker whittled on a tree. Twenty minutes later, Colton flopped on his stomach, panting, his tongue drooping. That was my cue. "Good boy. Time for bed."

Squeezing my eyes closed, I struggled to fall asleep, but I couldn't turn off the talking in my head. Maybe I should help at the barn only on weekends. I didn't have time for lessons now, so I didn't need the money. I curled into a ball. I probably should do my homework first, and then train Colton. I uncurled and lay on my back. No, that wouldn't work. He needed my attention and had so much to learn. I sighed. At least tomorrow, he'd be best in class, and I could figure out what to do later.

In the morning, my radio alarm blared rock and roll music. I hit snooze, twice. Then I remembered. *Oh no. My essay.*

My gut twisted inside and I swallowed to keep the acid down. Rushing to the top of the stairs, I hollered to Mom in the kitchen, using an agonizing voice. "I don't feel good. I don't think I can go to school today."

I hurried back to bed, pulled the blankets up to my chin, and pretended to be sleepy. Mom's footsteps thump-thump-thumped up the steps. She plopped beside me on the bed. Colton jumped on the other side and buried his nose in my hair.

Mom stroked my forehead. "You're not running a fever." She looked at Colt. "What do you think? Did she do too much yesterday?"

Colton whined and licked my face.

"Trina, you need to go to school, even if Colton would like you stay home. Tonight is your last puppy class, and if you don't go to school, it means you miss class tonight."

"Ah, Mom. I'm tired and my stomach hurts."

"Rules are rules. If you feel bad later, you can call me at work."

Of course, English was my first period class. There was no way getting around not having my homework. As I walked in, I bypassed Mrs. Stevens's desk. After everyone was seated, she scanned each paper. "Trina, where's your essay?"

Thinking fast, and knowing she knew about Colton's puppy mischief, I took a quick breath and rushed out the lie. "Colton ate it."

The class snickered.

I hung my head and bit my cheek. *Why did I say that?*

Mrs. Stevens didn't have the same sense of humor. She told the class about the day's assignment, and then made eye contact with me. "Trina, please step outside."

My stomach made a thousand slip-knots. And of course, wearing my hair in a ponytail made my ears stick out and burn rosy red. I walked, looking at the black and white speckled linoleum to hide my freckles from curious eyes.

Mrs. Stevens closed the door, and I moved away from the rectangle window. She put her hand on my shoulder and said, "Now, tell me the truth. Your grades last year were impressive or you wouldn't be in this class. And—" Her head titled as she studied me, "—You don't seem to be the kind of person to make up stories."

I lifted my blotched face, and blinked away a tear. "I'm sorry, Mrs. Stevens. I've had so much to do, and I ran out of time last night. I didn't want to mess up my grade, and that was the first thing that came to me. Colton does chew on everything."

She stared at me. "So you didn't finish your essay?"

Shaking my head, my finger wiped the tear dripping on my warm cheek. "I didn't even begin."

"Thank you for being honest, Trina. I've heard about what you're doing with the puppy. You've taken on a big job. I'll give you one more day. If you don't turn in your essay tomorrow, I will call your parents. They need to know if you're having trouble with so much responsibility."

I lifted my head higher. "I promise. It will be on your desk tomorrow."

As soon as I arrived home, I hurried Colton outside, and then we raced upstairs. Colton didn't like waiting for me to do my homework first, but I surprised him with a chewy filled with cheese.

Ideas poured out onto the page and my fingers typed fast. Before long I finished the first draft. I wrote and used examples of how everyone should push themselves out of their comfort zone to learn new things. Even if you are afraid, once you've found your heart's desire, you should never give up. Failure is a lack of trying. Then I revised three times and printed.

One assignment completed and now a quick romp outside. This would be my recess and then back to work.

Maybe if I get up thirty minutes earlier in the morning, Colton would have extra training time. I need another me.

With two out of three assignments completed, I started thinking about what I'd wear to dog class. During each training session, Wesley set Kaiser's mat next to where I stood. If someone walked over to visit, he made sure they couldn't get close, and he'd interrupt our conversation to add his bits of uninteresting subjects.

I watched Patrick and Annie raise their eyebrows and snicker, but I couldn't help feel little butterfly wings flapping and tickling inside my stomach. He really *was* interested in me. And he was kind of cute.

I guess Sarah had rubbed off on me after all.

Since the evenings had cooled, I decided to wear long jeans and my green PAALS tee shirt to match my eyes. Colton sat next to me, watching me blow-dry my hair. I pulled the sides of my hair up into a small pony tail, keeping the hair out of my face. I even added round, green studs the size of a pencil eraser in my ears and some lip gloss. Ready, we bounced down the stairs.

During puppy class, I spoke to Colton like he was a small toddler. He understood what I said, and I hoped he wouldn't be overly social. "Tonight,

Colton." Hearing his name, the top of his ears pitched forward, his head tilted, and his warm brown eyes looked straight into mine. I pointed my finger to my nose. "Colton, listen. You must Come when I call you."

He blinked, and wiggled his nose.

Each dog was attached to a long rope. When it was my turn to demonstrate, I gave the command Stay and ran as far as I could the other direction. I dropped the line and called, "Colton. Come."

He ran straight to me, his tongue lolling to the side, showing all of his teeth, forming a giant smile.

"Yes! Good boy!"

Everyone did this command in their section. Every few minutes a dog or two ran loose, dragging their rope to the other side of the room for a quick visit with another buddy. I kept Colton's attention. The frustrated students called their dogs, and before long it was quite noisy and confusing. Ms. Sue caught the rowdy dogs and returned them.

For the last performance of our six-week training class, our dogs were put in their place. We had a list of new commands to perform: Wait, No, Drop, Leave it, Kennel, Hurry, Place, and Stay.

Most of the puppies did well. Now, we had one final command. Every dog sat on their Place and was told to Stay. We backed away, and had only one chance to silently hold our palm flat, signing Stay

Standing by the wall for three minutes, seemed an eternity. The puppies sat or lay, panting, casually glancing at each other. I held my breath and tried to ignore Wesley nudging me. I needed to concentrate on Colt.

Colton squirmed and grew antsy. It was against the rules to give any coaching signs or encouragement. Uh, oh. My heart played Dad's favorite tune: *Help! I need somebody! Help!*

First, his tail switched back and forth, and then he looked both directions. He licked his lips, and shook from his head to his tail, trying to calm himself. Maybe to find his self-control, but it didn't happen. His expression told me trouble brewed, and he meant to cause a ruckus.

I swallowed, but I couldn't respond to him. His true personality craved to surface.

He took one step and he was off. He ran to Tanner and nosed him. Lucy watched and followed. Then he corrupted Sasha and Kaiser. One at a time, Colton told each puppy to misbehave without any sound. In seconds, all five dogs were having a free-for-all.

Ms. Sue attempted to look stern and quietly said, "Trina, get Colton and put him back in his Place."

All my friends and their parents chuckled. Each student retrieved their pup. We tried one more time with success. My little rascal was a handful for sure.

He wasn't the star pupil I had expected. Tonight, he was the class clown like me. I had to do something. How could I deal with our futures if I couldn't pull it altogether?

Chapter 22
September

Sitting at my desk after school, I changed the calendar page. A warm rush spread through me as I spotted the purple circle wrapped around my birthday. I planned to cross out each day until the twenty-first. Fourteen years old! My heart danced as I daydreamed about my surprises to come.

Since Colton's scare with the horses, Morgan had opened up a tiny bit about herself. Depending on her mood, she jabbered without thinking, and on other days she never said a word.

Saturday afternoon, Morgan helped me with barn chores. As I swept the barn floor, she casually mentioned her grandparents. I almost stopped breathing. Hiding my surprise and excitement at hearing her intimate secrets, I never glanced at her.

Morgan continued to speak from Rapp's empty stall. "My grandparents on my father's side—" Her voice grew softer. "I wish they lived closer."

I shied away from being nosey and hoped she'd tell me more. As I walked up to the hayloft and threw bales down to the feed room below, I kept the conversation moving. "My grandparents live in Virginia. I know what you mean. They always make me feel special, but I see them maybe twice a year." I carried a flake of hay to Sonny's stall, and Morgan's loud voice filtered from the other end of the barn.

"I'm thinking about going to see them so I'm not sure if I can make it to your birthday party."

"Oh, no! I'll be so disappointed."

Then her eagerness to talk hit me in the head. Morgan couldn't talk face to face. We went about our chores, having a distant conversation until we met in the tack room. I opened the cooler and offered her an apple and some chips.

As she chomped into her apple, I asked, "Do your grandparents ever come to your house?"

With her apple between her teeth, she grabbed items from her trunk, stashed them under her arms, and walked out. I stared at the empty doorway as my stomach churned. *Did I say the wrong thing?* She avoided me the next hour, and I walked home. She had made it clear not to ask questions about her grands.

Early the next morning, I woke, worrying about Morgan's distress. But when she arrived at the barn, she rambled on as if nothing had happened.

I pressed my lips together and just listened.

She cleaned Knight's stall, and blabbered. "You know, Trina, if I save some money, I could go see my grands. They'd never come here. It's something I've thought about since we moved out of their house, and that was three houses ago. I found out there's a train that goes to Florida, and I could be there in one day."

I stopped picking Chancy's stall and stuck my head out the door. "You used to live with your grandparents?"

She walked up to my door, and made eye contact. "Trina, now that I can do most of the barn stuff by myself, is there any chance I can cover for you when you need extra time?"

I choked. "You want to earn money? Doing menial work?"

Morgan leaned her head. "My parents never give me any money. They pay for everything or set up accounts at the stores for me to purchase what I need. That way they know everything I buy. Even the taxi driver is covered when I need a ride. It must be nice to have your own spending money."

"Why wouldn't your parents pay for everything on your trip?"

"Well, I may go with a friend from school who has grandparents in the same town. And I'd need to have my own cash."

"Yeah?" My jaw dropped, and at the same time, I wanted to say, "Your story is getting stranger." But I grabbed a wild strand of hair, twirled it around, and told myself not to react. I breathed through my nose and whispered it out my lips. "I'm glad to hear you've made a new friend at your school. Why don't you invite her to hang out at the barn?"

"Well, she doesn't live in my neighborhood, so we don't ride the same bus."

"Morgan, just the other night, I tried to figure out how to make more time for all of my homework and training Colton. I'm kind of struggling. And my parents don't know yet. I still have time to get my grades up. But if you really want to earn some money and do some of the chores, you'd be a huge help. Which days can you work?"

Morgan chuckled. "I'm here every day. Just tell me what you want me to do."

"Wow! This is perfect timing. Now that I'm not riding much, I don't need money for lessons. Let's go tell Mrs. Brown."

Morgan sucked in a panicked breath and wrinkled her eyebrows. "Can't we do this between us? If Mrs. Brown knows, she might say something to my parents, and then they'd get upset with me and probably with her."

"I guess?" I bit my bottom lip and frowned. *Should I believe her?* "Okay. I'll keep my name on the chalkboard. When you help me, we'll share the money. And if you work without me, you'll get it all. I'll keep track of what I owe you. I get paid every two weeks."

Morgan smiled at the floor. "Thanks, Trina. That'd be great."

"Where in Florida do your grandparents live? When are you planning to go?"

She shrugged. "In Bristol, a little town close to Tallahassee, Florida. I don't know when. We're still in the talking stage. But we're working on it. The time has to be just right."

I walked away and processed what she had said. I worried about not getting Mrs. Brown's permission, but I sure needed an extra hand. After sweeping the barn, I found Morgan cleaning her leathers in the tack room.

She glanced up at me. "Look. I've learned how to do another thing. You've taught me well."

I sat next to her and examined her bridle "Good job. I..."

Morgan stared at me. "What?"

"Umm. Since you've asked, would you mind helping me, today? I have to work Colton at the grocery store, and mom's waiting for me."

Morgan straightened and for the first time beamed. "Yes, that'd be awesome. I'm here until who knows when. And it will give me something else to do. And—" Morgan glanced each direction, "Mrs. B isn't around."

"That's true. But at some point, she'll find out. I'll need to explain before she gets upset about me keeping it a secret. I know she'll be fine with it."

Morgan looked at her boots. "Well, if we can wait just a little longer, maybe I'll have saved enough money, and she won't need to know."

Her comment caught me off guard. As she headed to her stall, I stared at her back and concern welled up inside of me. Morgan had everything she ever needed, except for parents who cared. What did she mean, "The time had to be right?"

Chapter 23

As I walked in the house, Mom popped up in her recliner. "Oh, good. I was getting ready to call you. Everything okay at the barn?"

Another rock hit the bottom of my stomach. I didn't look into her face. "Yep." I swallowed. "Come here, Colton." I pulled out his newest cape from his supply bag. His little bottom jiggled, and his tail waved. "Want to go to the store?"

He wiggled faster, making his long body into a U-shape. I fastened his cape around his chest and read the writing: "Please don't pet me. I'm working." My heart sputtered, feeling the pride in what I was accomplishing.

Mom parked the car. Colton leaped out, and heeled next to my side. As we approached the store, the automatic doors slid open. He took two steps back and stared. The doors closed, and he froze. He walked forward again. The doors split apart, and he looked both directions as we walked through. Once through, he turned sideways to watch the doors close behind him.

While we waited for Mom to speak with the manager, Colton analyzed the doors. He put his front paw on the black rubber mat, and the door slid open. His head tilted, and I could see his brain ticking. Curious customers let him experiment. His eyes glowed at the magic.

Mom returned. "The manager is excited you're here. I need to pick up a few things. You go ahead without me."

I stood taller and made Colt pay attention. "Ready? Walk." Before we entered an aisle, I said, "Sit." He listened and followed like a pro, showing off.

A couple of children dashed up and down the aisle, passing an inch from his body, laughing. He showed great restraint, watching their excited behavior. His ears moved, and his mouth stretched across his teeth in a grin. I knew if he had the opportunity, he'd enjoy chasing them. I called, "Colt, Heel." He kept his eyes on me and walked at my side.

The next challenge was to walk down the meat aisle. Colton's nose lifted toward the refrigerated shelves. His nostrils opened and closed.

I looked at him. "How can you smell anything? All the meat is sealed."

He blinked at me.

I sniffed, trying to detect any odors, but I didn't have a dog's nose.

He had been fed people food as treats, but he learned to sit under a restaurant table without begging. We stayed in the meat section until he no longer showed any attention to the aroma.

We strolled up another aisle where a woman pushed a grocery cart with a pretend blue plastic truck cab on the front. Her toddler sat inside the cab, twisting the steering wheel back and forth and roaring loud motor sounds.

The lady stopped and stepped toward us. "Can my son pet your puppy?"

"Thank you for asking, but right now he's in training. I'm teaching him to ignore his surroundings and to listen only to my commands."

The woman smiled. "I understand. You're doing something wonderful. He's a beautiful dog. My brother has diabetes, and he's had an Alert Dog for three years. Whenever his insulin goes haywire, his dog smells it through his skin and will lick his arm or leg to warn him. Having a service dog has improved his health."

"That's great. This is my second dog to train. He has a lot to learn before he qualifies."

Colton stayed in a Sit while I spoke. He did the best he could, waiting for me without squirming. He could only restrain himself for a short amount of time. Talking was my first mistake and my fault for what happened next.

When the child rumbled like a truck, Colt bounced up at the noise, and poked his nose inside the truck window. The child screamed like he had been stung by a bee.

Colton backed away and hunched down to all fours.

The mother apologized about her child scaring Colt. She looked inside the cab and calmed her crying son, "The doggy wanted to say hello, Thomas."

As her son quieted, I squatted eye-to-eye with Colton and soothed him. Then I glanced up at the mother. "This is my dog's first visit to the store, and it's not good that he became frightened. He has to be numb to noises and quick movements. Do you think Thomas would mind letting Colton greet him again?"

The lady smiled. "I'd be glad to help." She leaned into the truck cab. "Thomas, the puppy wants to give you a kiss. Is that okay?"

He poked his head out the window and stared at Colton. "Okay. Kiss."

"Thanks, Thomas. Hold your hand out the window." Then I gave the command, "Heel."

Colt walked next to me and up to the cart.

"Greet."

Colt bumped his nose on the boy's hand.

"Yes!"

The boy giggled like someone had tickled him and squeaked "Do again!"

We walked away and I repeated, "Greet."

Colt moved forward and nosed Thomas's hand. Then he sat in front of the boy.

I bent down and smiled at Thomas. "Thank you for helping train my puppy."

He laughed and pretended to beep his truck horn, sounding like a goose honking.

Before the mother pushed the grocery cart down the aisle, she beamed and said, "Thanks for doing what you are doing. Service dogs make miracles."

Colton sat and watched them leave.

Mom had observed from a distance, walked over to us, and put her hand on my shoulder. "He's doing fine. It'll take a few outings for him to get accustomed to new people and new sounds. Take him up a few more aisles, and I'll be waiting at the door."

We headed to the produce aisle, and then to the restroom. Inside, he needed to see the stalls and hear the hand dryer. I had him follow me inside.

"Sit." I pointed to the door. "Wait."

After washing my hands, I put them under the automatic air dryer. Colt's head flew up. He backed away and stared at the noisy machine. As soon as it stopped, I repeated drying my hands. This time he moved closer with a questioning look. I knew each time we used the restroom, he'd get more relaxed with the sound.

At the front of the store, he wiggled up to the doormat and waited for me to say, "Open."

He pressed on the mat and swaggered through the open door. Colton walked at my side all the way to the car. I opened the door, and he waited for the command.

"Okay. Up!"

Mom twisted around and beamed. "Trina, Colton did a super job for his first visit. We can do another outing Tuesday after school. I'll have the afternoon free."

I grinned and climbed in next to Colton. "Let's go to the Mall."

"Really?" Mom's eyes widened. "I've waited a long time for you to ask to go to the Mall. Why don't you invite Sarah?"

During my evening with Sarah, treating the horses, I talked about Colton's grocery store experience and invited her to go to the mall.

Her expression was priceless. She studied me. "Really? Why are you going to the mall?"

"Besides having a people watching session for Colton, I need some new clothes. Will you help me choose?"

"Wow!" She clapped her hands together. "Trina, I never thought you'd be interested in shopping for clothes. Is it okay with your mom?"

I beamed. "She's excited. Before the beach trip, she tried to get me to look at new clothes."

"So what's with the new interest? Chase is a long way away."

"Yep, he is. I've outgrown everything. Look, I'm almost as tall as you. I need some new stuff that fits. Nothing fussy. Okay?"

With no conversation about Morgan, we finally said goodbye and headed home. I stretched out on my bed and tried to read but the words all blended together.

This day had been full of surprises. Not the fun kind I had thought of. After riding and then working with Colton, something new tickled inside. And it was a scary.

Chapter 24

Every time I rode Chancy, I told myself I might be a better rider if I practiced more, but being honest with myself, I realized my riding skills might never improve. When Colton and I worked together, we clicked. We were a special team, doing something important for others.

So many new feelings to explore. I was unsure of what I actually wanted to do. I doubted my thoughts and seemed to be confused most of the time.

With two more weeks until my birthday party, maybe I'd figure out what was going on inside of me. I tried to erase my worries and let the thrill of my party seep in. My dog friends, Annie and Jessica and, of course, Wesley were coming. I hadn't heard from Chase and still hoped he'd come. That would make things interesting with Wesley.

Is it silly for me to be so eager to turn fourteen, have cake and ice cream, and open presents?

I didn't even know what I wanted for my birthday, but I knew I'd be surprised. And I loved surprises.

Hoping to get sleepy, I read until my eyeballs hurt, but the moment I closed them my thoughts shot from horses to dogs to boys and my birthday. I tried harder to leave out the guy stuff. As I lay on my side, staring out the window, my phone chirped.

My heart fluttered before I answered. Chase had promised to call before my birthday, and we hadn't spoken in twenty-six days. His voice always brought me back to our week on Edisto. Tingles crept up my arms. I closed my eyes, and concentrated on slowing my pulse. Who else would be calling at this hour? Before the phone stopped chirping, I checked caller ID with shaking hands and answered in a gasp, "Hey!"

His deep voice said, "Hey, Trina, It's me."

I swallowed and took time to calm my voice. "Wow! How are you?"

He chuckled. "I'm extra good."

I sat up, rocking back and forth, waiting for him to explain why all of a sudden he was calling.

His voice grew higher in pitch. "I have some news. Is it too late to talk?"

"Nope, I'm just reading. It's been a busy day."

"Trina, I'm sorry I haven't kept up with calling, but you know how it is. I get busy and forget. That didn't come out right. I think of you every day, but it's too hard not seeing you."

"I know. Maybe when you get involved with PAALS, we'll be able to see each other."

Chase snickered. "That's why I called. Ms. Jen decided to have an early session with graduating some of the dogs. She couldn't do all of the people at once. Logan's name came up on the list three weeks ago with the dogs that were ready." Chase's voice grew louder. "Logan's getting a dog!"

I stopped breathing. Two seconds later, I screamed, "Yay!"

Colton stared at me wide-eyed as I choked and pumped my left arm up and down.

Chase spoke slower. "I know you're excited. I am, too. Breathe for a minute."

I turned my mouth away from the phone, I didn't want him to hear my rapid gasping. "I'm okay now. Tell me. Tell me everything."

"Mom and I went with Logan for our first Meet-and-Greet session three weeks ago. Mom and I will be the caretakers, and they told me what you said earlier. I can't interfere with Logan's connection.'"

"Okay. So where are you in this process?"

It was Chase's turn to pause. "Logan had to stay with Dad while Mom and I tested. We had to prove we knew what to do with the dogs. That took weeks of us practicing and testing, which is why I haven't called. And I'm sorry for that."

"That's okay. I understand. Tell. Tell me!"

"Last weekend Mom and I took one dog, Cassidy, a Golden doodle, to a hotel on Friday night. Whew! That was scary! We had to walk her, take her to a restaurant, settle her into a new room, and sleep. Then on Saturday, we had Sydney."

I couldn't help but giggle. "You're going to make me wait until you've told me the whole long story, aren't you?"

"Uh-huh! Listen. You need to know *all* of this. By the way, there were six of us training. The next week, I missed school. Each day, Mom and I had outings with Logan and both dogs. We used our training cues in Walmart with lots of people and noise and switched dogs.

"At the Columbia Airport, we practiced getting in and out of an airplane and teaching each dog to sit by our feet. On Wednesday, we were tested at the

Mall. Mom and I were totally exhausted, and I know the dogs were, too. We passed, by the way."

"Yay!" I switched the phone to my other ear. "Go on!"

"Well, on Thursday, Ms. Jen handed us Sydney to begin another practice session. And Logan, for the first time ever, had a seizure."

"Oh, no!" I sputtered. "Is he all right?"

Chase exhaled in the phone. "Woo! That was the most scared I've ever been. You should have seen Sydney, Trina. He lay next to Logan, his paws over Logan's chest, sniffing his body and checking his breathing. The other dog, Cassidy, saw Logan on the ground and lay on Logan's other side.

"At the hospital, Logan had tons of tests. The doctors believe it was an event that may never happen again. Maybe too much excitement and being too tired. Anyway, the next day, Logan felt okay. Maybe a bit tired. But then we returned for the final testing, and Ms. Jen didn't have him do any training. Are you ready for the outcome?"

"No, not yet." I chuckled, but my pulse speeded and tears welled up and leaked down my cheek. I sniffed. "You're enjoying yourself too much. Are you really going to tell me?"

His voice grew louder. "You have to know the answer." He paused, exhaled into the phone, and thumped his hands on the table. "Drum roll, please! It's Sydney!"

"Yay!" I screamed, "Yes!"

He interrupted my yelling. "I need to tell you this. Ms. Jen shared later, she had planned on giving Cassidy to Logan. But after Logan's seizure and Sydney's reaction, she knew he was meant for Logan."

"Oh. My. Gawd! I can't wait to tell mom. But Chase, now *I* need to tell you something." I took a long breath, making him wait and wonder.

He hooted. "I know what you're doing. I guess it's payback time. How long can you hold out?"

"Not long," I cackled. "It's not something I want to say. You need to know that I can't see Sydney for maybe six months. He needs time to bond with Logan and then when he's off duty, I can play with him. So, if we see each other again, Sydney can't be with you."

He blew out a sigh. "I thought you were going to say we could never see each other again. That's an easy problem. I love the idea of being with you *and* getting a break from Logan. Let me work on our next get-together. Transportation seems to be the biggest problem."

"Yeah, I guess so. Any ideas?"

"One day Peyton will be driving, and then I will. Will you forgive me for not calling?"

My body seemed to float above the floor. "You are too much, Chase," I moaned. "You are forgiven. For a while."

"Good. I promise I'll call tomorrow."

Chapter 25

Days passed and the only thing for certain was I'd talk with Chase at night. On Friday, the day before my birthday party, Sarah chatted with me in the barn after school. I told her about Chase's phone call. She followed me from place to place holding Colton's leash as I readied my horse for a short ride.

"Wow! That's great about Logan!" She gave me a half smile but didn't look straight at me. "It's nice you're still hearing from Chase, even if it's not often."

She stroked Chancy's sleek neck as I put on her saddle.

I wanted to ask about Peyton, but the familiar diesel noise rumbled up the drive, and we knew Morgan had arrived. Sarah waited for the truck to leave, and jogged outside with my wagging puppy. I looked into Chancy's brown eyes, "Well, isn't Sarah getting friendly with Morgan."

Chancy snorted and shook her head. She had no idea what I had said, unlike Colton, but loved the attention. The two girls wandered into the barn, giggling.

I glanced over. "All right you two. What's the joke?"

Morgan grinned. "No joke. Just excited about your party tomorrow. It's worked out. I can come."

"Yay! I'm glad you'll make it." I leaned my head. "Do you want to bring one of your new friends? The more the merrier. I've invited my class of puppy trainers."

Sarah poked her elbow in Morgan's ribs. "She has a new friend in class. And she's invited Chase, too. That should make the party interesting."

I jolted upright and gave her The Look. "Wesley is just another puppy raiser, and we have something in common to talk about. And I don't think Chase is coming."

"Wow! Good for you, Trina." Morgan snickered. "Two guys at one time! I have enough trouble with girls, let alone guys. So as for *my* friends, forget it. They're busy with their own activities. Anyway, tomorrow is supposed to be hot, with only a small chance of that big storm hitting us, and we'll have fun at the pool."

"Storm?" I asked.

Sarah rolled her eyes. "On the news for the last week and a half. Tropical storm in the Atlantic headed this way."

"Guess I was too busy with Colton. So when's it supposed to hit?"

"After your party, and then only if it turns this way." Morgan shrugged.

"That's good. I'd hate to have to cancel my party." I reached up for the bridle. "Any chance *your* parents are coming, Morgan?"

"Nope. None at all."

"That's okay. We'll have fun. Mom and Dad have planned all the food, and of course Mrs. B will be there, and Sarah's parents will keep mine occupied."

I swung myself up onto Chancy, sat up straight, and then took a deep lungful of air. I closed my eyes. There's nothing like swaying back and forth and hearing the clump, clump of her hooves on the ground. Every sensation reawakened my desire to be a good rider.

I had accepted not having my own horse since I had the opportunity right here. My out-of-shape legs brought me back to reality. A shiver went through my body. I squeezed Chancy's sides with my legs and directed her to trot. My helmet shaded my eyes from the sun, and today I was thankful to be alone with my thoughts. My heart hurt being stretched in two directions.

In a few minutes, Chancy warmed-up her muscles, and I practiced old skills. Sarah stood at the fence with Colton. His chin lay on a rail and watched all of the action. Morgan appeared in the ring. She set up a low rail for me to jump, coached me over it, and added one more jump on the other side of the stadium.

My grin grew larger and larger. "One more time!" I pretended for those few minutes, I was flying over four foot jumps at a cross country event. Soon my legs lost all control, and Chancy panted. We headed to the barn.

"Thanks, Morgan. That's the most jumping I've ever done. Do you guys want to come over for a snack?"

"Nah. I have things to do with Knight, and I'll help Mrs. Brown. I'll see you tomorrow afternoon. Around 2:00?"

"Yep. See you then. Thanks for helping me today."

Sarah chimed in. "I've got stuff to do, too." She waved me away.

I shuffled over to Sarah. "Aren't you walking home with me?"

She made a crooked smile. "I'm going to stay here for a few minutes and visit with Morgan."

My chin landed on my chest and I couldn't help giving her a questioning look. Even my voice came out puzzled. "Okay! See ya."

I walked a couple steps and turned around. "Do you want to do horse treats tonight?"

"Yep. Let's plan for eight o'clock."

"Perfect." But I walked home confused.

What's the deal with Sarah and Morgan?

Chapter 26

During the month of September, the evening air cooled, and days warmed with less humidity. I never knew how to dress during the changing seasons. Some mornings, the fog rolled in and covered all the low places in the woods. I'd wear a sweater, but by late morning the misty cloud burned off, only to grow as warm as a summer day.

A sprinkling of green leaves sprouted yellow spots like they had grown freckles. In the months to come, they would magically turn all shades of reds, oranges and yellows. In time, they'd turn brown, fall to the ground, crumble and disappear. Maybe my freckles would do the same as I grew older.

The sun rose later in the morning, letting Colton sleep longer. Now that he slept in my room, if I woke too early, he reacted like Sydney had done. Any movement from me alerted him. This morning my body tingled as if ants marched up and down inside my pajamas.

"Okay, Colt." I patted the bed. "Up!"

With invisible springs in his legs, he bounced on the mattress, and plopped his front legs across my stomach, knocking the wind out.

"Humph!"

He leaned over and licked my cheek.

I held his face. "Good morning to you! Today's my birthday party. We have to stay busy, for hours, to make the time go fast."

He panted, listening.

Colton lay on the carpet, watching me dress, but the minute I grabbed my tennis shoes, he spun in circles, his tail swinging in full motion. His idea of hurrying me actually slowed me. His head lunged under my arm, preventing me from pulling on the shoe. Or as I pulled the laces tight, he'd slide his nose under my fingers.

I looked at him. "Wait."

His bottom plopped right where he stood, and he quivered.

Laces tied, I stood and walked to the door. Colton stayed.

"Good boy! Come."

Every morning new scents caught his attention in the backyard. Deer wandered outside our fence during the daytime but left round, black pellets in our woods while we slept. To a dog, they must be as delicious as our chocolate chips. Colton's nose tunneled into a pile, eating one at a time.

I wrinkled my nose. "Yuck, Colt. Leave it!"

After a couple more hurried nibbles, he backed away and gave me a look as if saying, "Why did you make me stop? These are so yummy!" His tongue swiped his lips, and he sprinted to the house.

"I know what you want."

He stared at me.

"Breakfast?" I picked up his food bowl.

He blinked, and nodded with each pant.

I patted his head. "Me, too. Let's eat."

I ate my cereal one piece at a time, chewed it three times, and took one sip of my orange juice. This only made breakfast last ten minutes. I had hours to go before my party. I stayed at the table and watched Mom eat, and chatted with her as she sipped coffee. Everything happened in slow motion.

Dad hid behind the newspaper for a few minutes and then announced. "Uh-oh. That second tropical storm could turn out to be a hurricane and may come in earlier than expected. It could hit the coast sometime tonight. This one they've named Billy." He smiled and pulled the paper away from his face. "At least the rain and wind we'd get should hold off until later tonight or tomorrow. You should have perfect weather for your party."

Mom looked at me. "So what are you going to do to stay busy?"

"I guess I'll do some homework, have a Colton practice session, and maybe clean my room." I sighed. "But that still leaves hours before the party."

The minutes got stuck somewhere around twelve o'clock. I dressed in my bathing suit and filled my beach bag with necessities. Colton took a nap. If I at least picked up my clothes, that would kill some time. Then I could start reading a new book or sketch a picture of Colton.

Dirty clothes went to one corner. Towels lay in another pile next to the door. My phone chirped.

I lost my breath seeing the caller ID. "Hey!"

Chase sang, "Happy Birthday." I giggled at his voice. After our basic chatter, he paused and gave me an order. "Don't ask any questions. Turn on your computer."

Rushing to my desk, I clicked it on." Okay. It's coming up."

"Go to your emails. When you find the one from me, open the attachment."

A surge of excitement exploded through me. "I'm sorry you couldn't be here. We're having a pool party."

"I'm disappointed, but it's just too far for me to make it with Logan needing my help. So I sent you my present. Are you watching?"

I sat in front of the computer wide eyed. "Yes, it's opening. Oh, Chase! I see the sand dunes. You're at Edisto."

"Yep. The weekend after Labor Day."

As I stared at the screen, my fingers to my toes throbbed, waiting for the video. "Oh my! They're precious. So tiny! Baby turtles! Is it from our turtle? When did they hatch?"

"Dad received an email telling us a nest would hatch sometime around those days. Don't know if it is the same nest you and Sarah checked on each day. I took my camera and planned to send you their pictures. Happy Birthday!"

"I leaned in closer to the screen. "What a cool present. Thank you! Look at how many! Over a hundred I bet. Oh, this is so exciting. I'll share this with Sarah."

"Peyton is sending this to Sarah now. I wanted it to be a surprise, so he waited until you saw it first."

My eyes stayed glued on the babies. "Did you see them swim away?"

"Yep. Keep watching."

"Oh, you helped that little guy. Those birds were hoping to have dinner. Did they all make it?"

"With the crowd protecting them, they all made it to the water, and then they were on their own."

"Oh!" I sighed into the phone. "I hope next summer we get to watch another turtle lay her eggs. We were really lucky on our first night."

We talked for a while, dodging the subject of my party. After a long moment of silence, Chase asked, "So who's coming to your party?"

"Sarah, Morgan, Jessica, Annie, and Wesley."

"Wesley?"

His questioning tone stabbed my heart. "He's just another dog trainer in our class."

"Hmm. Maybe *I* need to become a Puppy Raiser?"

"You could do that."

Chase paused for too long.

I cleared my throat. "Are you still there?"

He quietly breathed into the phone and changed the subject. "Logan's been saying new words, and he's so happy. Sydney opens Logan's drawer, gets his socks and underwear out, and nudges him awake. Logan gets up happy each morning and ready for school. The teacher is a dog lover and invited Sydney to attend class with Logan. She's worked with PAALS and knows how to work with service dogs."

"Wow, Chase! That's awesome! Hearing how good he's doing, makes me happy I'm training another dog. There are so many people needing help. You know, we could use your experience on weekends when we train new puppy raisers. It would be one way of seeing each other."

He inhaled. "Really?"

"Yes, I'll say something to Ms. Jen. Thanks for my fun present. I'll think about you today."

In a low voice, he groaned. "I hope so. Miss you."

After hanging up the phone, my heart sputtered. All I could do was think about our times together. I clicked on the video two more times.

Once I finished folding my clothes, I sat cross-legged and put Colton's toys in his basket. Chase's video replayed in my head.

Footsteps approached the door. Mom called. "Are you ready, Trina?"

Colton and I flinched. I bounced to my feet and yanked the door open. "Are you kidding? This has been the longest day. Until, I got the best present, ever!"

Chapter 27

Mom, Dad, Colton, and I strolled up the path as I chatted about Chase's surprise video. I wanted to run, but I contained my excitement and tried to act fourteen. Mom and Dad's voices grew more excited and couldn't ask enough questions. I had no more answers, but I enjoyed sharing my wonderful surprise.

We talked so fast, I wasn't paying attention to Colton. Off leash, he bounded in and out of the woods but came back when I called him. At the gate to the pool area, Mrs. Brown's purple banner, HAPPY BIRTHDAY, swayed in the breeze.

Wandering in, we set our towels and beach bags on patio chairs, and I waited for someone to scream, "Happy Birthday!"

I glanced around and my heart sunk. "Where is everyone? They did say they were coming."

"I don't know." Mom looked over the fence for my friends. "Let's walk over to the barn. Maybe they're with the horses."

I attached Colton's leash and we went to the barn. Three horses stood in the middle of the barn, saddled, and wearing bridles.

"SURPRISE!" Shouted Morgan and Sarah.

Mrs. Brown's grin made me laugh. Morgan wore her riding clothes, and Sarah wore jeans and a pair of brown half-boots with a small heel.

I blinked and did a double-take. "Are we all riding?" Before anyone could answer, I gazed at Sarah. "Sarah, are you going to ride?"

She lifted her head. "Morgan and Mrs. Brown promised me it'd be easy, and she wouldn't let go of the leash."

Morgan poked Sarah's arm with her elbow, laughing. "Not leash, silly. Reins."

"What-ever! I'll give it a try. Just for your birthday."

"Wow. This is really special." I beamed at my parents. "You knew all along, didn't you? What about the others coming?"

Mom laughed. "I told them to be here at three-thirty."

Seconds later, Mr. and Mrs. Neal walked in clicking their cameras.

Mom pulled the bag off her shoulder. "Here. Go change. We'll meet you at the pool after we see Sarah get on Sonny and ride."

Giggling all the way to the tack room, I changed and rushed Chancy to the ring in time to watch Mrs. Brown lead Sonny to the stool for Sarah.

"Okay. Sarah. First rule. You must always get on the horse from the left."

Sarah interrupted. "Why always on the left?"

Mrs. B quickly added, "Ask Trina later. Now, put your left foot in the stirrup. That's it. Hold onto the reins, and some of his mane. Pull yourself up and swing your right leg over his back."

After three attempts of swinging up and over, Sarah groaned. "This is harder than you said." Her nervous laughter grew louder.

Sonny threw his head over his shoulder. His stare meant, "What are you doing back there?"

Sarah tried one more time. "I'm on! I'm on! Oh Mrs. B, hold him still. I'm a long way from the ground. Oh. My. Gawd. This feels weird."

"You're doing great." Mrs. B cackled and tried to sound encouraging in between her words. "Sit up. Now hold the reins in front of you. I'm going to walk him. Let you get a feel of his movement."

"Whoa! Not so fast!" Sarah wobbled to the right and to the left as Sonny stepped with each opposite leg. Her eyes grew larger and larger. Her voice shrieked. "I'm going to fall off."

Morgan bent over, laughing.

I snorted with giggles. "You're riding!" I choked out. "I'm so excited to see you on a horse. After all this time, you finally decided to try. Thank you!" I walked Chancy along Sonny's side. "So. What do you think?"

"It's—it's okay." Then Sarah grew quiet. Her head never moved. Her face showed no expression and paled blonder than her hair.

Mrs. Brown, patted Sarah's leg, "Honey. Breathe. That a girl. Now blow it out. Breathe again, hon. Okay. Now I want you to know how to steer him. Take the left rein and pull slowly to the left. See how he goes left. Now pull the right rein. That's it. Okay. Pull both reins toward your stomach. Pull hard. That makes him stop."

Sarah pulled, and Sonny stopped. Her smile spread from ear to ear. Some color returned to her cheeks. "I'm getting the hang of this. I'll try again."

Mrs. B stretched taller and smiled. "That's the spirit. Now wrap your legs around his stomach and press with your thighs. Give him a little kick with your heels and make him move."

Morgan and I rode along each side of Sarah while Mrs. Brown held on to Sarah's reins. We walked our horses, giving Sarah compliments. When Mrs. Brown let go of Sonny's reins. Sarah swayed on Sonny's back, and managed to ride along the fence.

After two trips around the ring, Sarah moaned. "Okay, guys. My butt's numb. Let's go swimming." She pulled her reins to the left and moseyed over to the stool.

Mrs. Brown coached her on getting off. "Lean forward. Swing your right leg behind you, and step onto the stool. That's it!"

Sarah walked toward the fence like there was a small horse still under her. "I've heard about sea legs, but I've never heard about horse legs."

Morgan hooted and galloped off. I followed. We needed a more aggressive ride. Mrs. B held Sonny's reins, and Sarah watched. After a hard ride, we let our horses set their own pace, and they strolled back to the barn, ready for their cool down.

I slid off Chancy's back. "After a ride, Sarah, we remove their sweat and give them a good rub."

Sarah complained as she attempted to hose Sonny and scrape off the excess water. "You guys are crazy to want to do this much work every day."

Morgan grinned. "It took me a while to understand all of Knight's needs, but because of Trina, now it's routine. She was right about him becoming a friend."

Mrs. Brown finally shooed us out of the barn. "Go. Get out of here. I'll finish. Heather's on her way."

Hot and sweaty, we changed into our bathing suits and talked about the turtle video. Morgan asked about the turtles and who sent the video. I made Sarah promise not to mention Chase in front of Wesley. She smirked. "For someone that didn't want to like boys, you're learning quick."

My face heated up. "They're both just friends. I can have boys and girls as friends."

"Uh-huh." Sarah nodded and smiled. "I say, good for you."

When we arrived at the pool, Annie, Jessica, and Wesley were screaming "Marco! — Polo!" Our parents lounged with drinks in hand, having some kind of discussion. Sarah went to the pool steps, Morgan did a cannonball, and I jumped in. Colton ran around the edge of the pool, barking.

Mrs. B told Colton to swim. Playing tag while Colton dogpaddled was a challenge. When he panted heavily, I rushed over and put my hand under his body so I could lead him to the steps. That day, he learned how to get in and out of the pool.

During our water games, Wesley decided he was the captain and shouted orders. As everyone tired of his commands, we took a break and laid our towels on the grass to rest. Of course, Wesley put his next to mine before anyone else had a chance to open theirs. I smiled, but felt a rush of warmth go up my neck. I grabbed my sun lotion and rubbed my arms and legs. Wesley offered to rub my back. Crashing waves banged the insides of my stomach.

I shook my head. "No, thanks. I'm fine."

He stared at me, and neither of us spoke. The awkward silence lasted for an eternity until Annie started telling funny stories about Sasha. Then Jessica shared stories about Tanner, and Wesley talked about Kaiser's antics. I told them the story about the little boy at the grocery store. I glanced up and noticed Morgan and Sarah had moved to the table under the umbrella, having their own discussion. I leaned in and watched them laugh and smile. After a couple minutes, I stretched my neck like a satisfied cat and turned my gaze back to my other guests.

The wind picked up and dark clouds floated in, hiding the sun, so Mom summoned the group. "We better hurry and do presents and cake. We're running out of good weather."

The cake, decorated with a chestnut horse that looked like Chancy, made me smile. I'd fallen in love with Colton, so I thought Mom would've put Colton on this cake. But she still believed I wanted to be a great rider.

I received a pretty bottle of leather cleaner from Mrs. Brown, and a new grooming brush and shedding blade that also worked as a water scrapper from Morgan. Wesley wiggled and beamed as he plopped a cardboard box in front of me. "This is from the three of us!" The group grinned and slid forward to get a closer look. Inside lay a lavender stuffed dog with a squeaker in each leg, both ears, and tail.

After hugging the dog and thanking everyone, Sarah handed me her package. I unwrapped a tee shirt with a black Lab on the front. It looked just like Colton. I nodded, leaned my head sideways, and we smiled at each other. She still knew me best.

Mom and Dad surprised me with a new pair of gloves and a homemade coupon for one free riding lesson anytime.

When I started to put the gloves in their box, Mom tapped my hand and grinned. "Please try on the gloves and see if they fit. I wasn't sure about your size."

I caught a sparkle in her eyes. Dad had the same electrified expression. I slid my hand into the left-handed glove. Something hard blocked my hand from going inside. I opened the glove and peeked in. I screamed. "Oh, yay! Yes. Yes!"

I pulled out my new cell phone with a purple case. "Now, I'll have reception anywhere I go, and I can listen to music."

Sarah laughed. "And GPS. Don't forget that."

"That's okay with me. I don't ever go anywhere that's a secret." I hugged Mom and Dad. "Does it work now?"

Mom smiled. "Yep. Same phone number, too. You're old phone is retired."

Mrs. Brown excused herself. "I don't like what I'm seeing up there. I'm going to check on the horses. The weatherman reported a while ago the storm may be changing to a Category Two hurricane. I wish they'd make up their minds. If that happens we could have tornadoes blowing in our area. Let's hope it doesn't get too bad."

Minutes later, the wind propelled my Happy Birthday banner up and down until the strings popped on one side. It twisted around and around, and with the next gust, it freed itself, and took to the sky.

Everyone filled their arms with as many items as they could carry and rushed to the barn. Mom shielded the cake, Dad and Mr. Neal hefted the cooler and card table, Mrs. Neal grabbed presents and totes.

Once inside the barn, Dad set up the card table in the tack room, and Mom cut the cake.

Just like dogs, horses catch a scent in the air when there's thunder and lightning before we ever know a storm's brewing. Sydney had shivered as a young pup, and I was relieved when he conquered his fear at Edisto. Colton sat and panted without even a hint of uneasiness. That was a great sign for becoming a secure service dog. I rushed to the stalls to check on the frightened horses.

Chapter 28

Pine trees swayed and tall hardwoods leaned sideways. The wind wheezed through the woods, plucking off freckled leaves from each limb. They swirled in the sticky air until the wind stilled and coasted to the ground. In a few short minutes, the beautiful day became creepy and cool. The bright, blue sky disappeared under billows of angry, gray clouds.

Annie's parents had driven Jessica to the party and returned earlier than planned from shopping. Soon after their arrival, Wesley's parents joined the group. Worried about driving south to Columbia, everyone scurried into their cars, ready for a wet and windy drive home.

Mrs. B flew into the barn, her face creased with worry lines. "The weatherman says it is definitely a hurricane and is coming ashore somewhere around Charleston."

I pictured Edisto and the older houses along the shore. "Oh, no! I hope Edisto's okay."

She stopped for a second and made eye contact. "It's been years since Edisto's been hit by a storm. It's tucked in more than Charleston. I do remember when Hugo hit Charleston and traveled all the way inland. I don't want to take any chances. The horses are getting nervous. Let's get everything put away and meet back in the barn as soon as y'all can."

Grabbing Morgan's hand, Mrs. B pulled Morgan closer. "See if you can stay with me tonight. I may need your help."

Morgan nodded and headed into the tack room.

Mom and Dad hauled supplies home and offered to come back if they were needed. I leashed Colton, carried what I could, and yelled. "Be back in a few!"

Colton followed me to my room as I changed into jeans and a sweatshirt, and rushed downstairs. After he settled in with a full stomach, I hurried to the barn.

I checked water buckets while Morgan prepared the horses' dinners. Each horse snorted and whinnied as they pawed the stall floor, whipping their tails side to side. The strange scent lingering in the air made them short-tempered

and restless. If the storm came any closer, we'd let them loose in the back paddock, but right now they were safe in their stalls.

Morgan and I sat on a bench outside Knight's stall. Her worried eyes
flicked from corner to corner of the barn. Attempting to distract her, I patted
her arm. "What'd your parents say?"

She shrugged. "I left a message. No one's home."

My heart ached for her. "I'll stay with you tonight, and it'll all be over in
the morning."

Her eyelids fluttered. "And you'll go home to your cozy house and parents
who care what you're doing." Tears trickled down her cheeks. "I had my trip all
planned. I didn't know about the storm, and obviously my parents didn't either."

My shoulders flew back. "What are you talking about?"

Morgan's eyes narrowed, deciding if she was going to explain. "Trina, this
has to be between us. It's taken a long time for me to feel I can trust anyone."
Her cinnamon eyes darkened and zoomed into a daring glare. "This is the first
chance—" She clasped her hands together. "—the first chance I've had to talk
to you alone, today."

She paused, watching my reaction. My heart hammered in my chest. I held
it in place with both hands, took in a lungful of air, and exhaled. My instincts
had been correct. She hurt underneath all that anger and desperately needed
someone to care. I held Morgan's glare.

She scanned the barn. "My parents left yesterday. Dad had some work to
do at one of the beach cities and Mother decided to join him since it was a
three-day weekend at school. Of course, I wasn't invited. I had a horse to ride
and needed more study time. They used to leave me often, but I always had a
brother around. Now both of them are gone." She started to say something
else, closed her eyes, and pressed her lips together.

In a second she recovered. "I'm old enough to stay by myself. It's usually
only overnight." She made a scary sneer. "Maybe my parents will get caught in
the storm and think twice about me being alone. They hired a woman from
an agency to babysit me for the long weekend. Our maid had the weekend
off." Morgan stomped her foot. "I called the agency, pretended to be my mom,
and canceled the lady."

My eyebrows lifted as I imagined faking my mom's voice. "And she believed
you?"

"Yeah." Morgan lifted her chin. "I learned a long time ago how to sound
like her, and I've had lots of practice."

"Okay. Morgan." I gave her a questioning glance. "What's going on?"

She dipped her head and sucked in a breath. "My brothers have always protected me and acted like my parents. They are six and eight years older."

"Where are your brothers now?" I examined her expression. "You never talk about them."

Morgan shook her head, and wiped each eye with her pointy finger. "I've been told many times that I was a surprise. That's when they moved in with my grandparents." She stared at me and paused. "Do you remember when you found me crying in the woods?" I nodded. "My oldest brother, Quintin." Her eyes softened at the thought of him. "He's the one who spent the most time with me. He's in the National Guard. He flies." She paused and looked away. "Flew helicopters and, and, I—I can't talk about it." She sipped a breath and let it out slowly. "I'll explain another time. Phillip, my other brother, is almost finished with college and comes home sometimes."

I let her ramble, hoping she'd come back to Quintin. I could wait.

"Dad worked in Florida redesigning cities there, and mom worked as a nurse. Mom has been going to school forever trying to become a surgical nurse. As soon as she received her credentials, she became a traveling nurse. She stayed in places for months at a time. Grammy and Gramps helped raise me with Dad, spending more time with me than my mom. And now she's decided to stay in one town. This is her third permanent hospital job. Maybe we'll stay in this city. Since Dad travels so often, he has no idea how often Mom is doing her thing."

I tried not to show my shock, but I'm sure my shoulders tensing gave me away.

An ear-splitting banging, brought us to our feet. Morgan and I ran to the open area of the barn and stuck our heads out. A huge branch from an over-hanging tree clung to its trunk, not wanting to let go, but with the next gust of wind, broke loose, and crashed on the roof.

Looping my arm through Morgan's, I lifted hers. "Let's go in the tack room. Mrs. Brown should be back soon." I pulled her in and didn't let go of her arm. "So, what were you planning?"

"I was going to hang out here and then call the taxi. I saved enough money for a one-way ticket, and he'd drive me to the train station. The problem was he'd tell my parents where I went, and I didn't want them to know. So instead, I had the driver put my bike in the trunk, and I told him we were going for a long ride, and I wouldn't need him again. I hid it in the storage barn."

Morgan's face streaked with tears.

"Mrs. Brown has been a better mother to me since I've moved here. So have your parents. I even told Mom that before she left with Dad. She hit the roof, screaming about all the things I do wrong and said that she'd had enough. She's going to sell Knight."

"Oh, Morgan!"

"Well, she thinks I don't appreciate what she does for me. I really think she's jealous of Mrs. Brown and your parents. You all spend more time with me than she does. Her life is more important than mine."

Morgan caught her breath. She had opened the genie bottle of emotions and they came whooshing out. "And—and, I'm tired of being dropped here and there. I know I act like a brat sometimes, maybe all the time, but that's what they expect. It used to work with Dad, but now he's getting concerned and frustrated. That bothers me 'cause he really does care, but I'm hoping he'll figure out what Mom's been doing."

Mrs. Brown's boots thumped from the other end of the barn. Morgan took her sleeve and wiped her cheeks and blew her nose into a crumbled paper towel.

"You girls okay?"

"Yep." I smiled. "We're just relaxing and keeping an eye on things. It seems to have quieted a little. What'd you find out about the weather?"

"The weatherman is watching and waiting. It's still building and heading toward Charleston or below. He's concerned about tornados spurring off from the storm. Right now, everyone is preparing for some kind of blast of air and water. Just don't know the category they're dealing with. They're boarding up windows and people are stocking up on necessities. The best news is many people are evacuating."

"I'm glad we're inland. The horses have quieted and are resting. I'm going to take Morgan to my house for a few minutes, but if you need us we'll rush right back over."

"That's fine. See you girls in a bit."

As soon as we escaped Mrs. Brown's, I stopped under the trees and put my hands on my hips. "So, were you planning on riding your bike to the train station?"

"I hadn't decided."

"Are you crazy?" The more upset I got, the faster I spoke. "You know how dangerous it would be to be on the road, all by yourself for miles." I gasped for air. "You could be kidnapped, molested, and never see Knight again. And with this weather? What were you thinking?"

"I expected the storm to hit after I left for Florida. I only wanted to get away and make my parents worry."

I groaned. "Just come spend the night with me."

She cradled her head in her hands and stared at the ground. "Your parents can't know. If my parents call yours, they'll want to tell them I'm at your house." She raised her eyes. "That won't work. When my parents come home on Sunday, I won't be there. Mom will be too embarrassed to ask for help."

"What if they call the agency?"

"Then my mom will know I did something critical. And if Mrs. Brown needs help here, I'll stay in the barn and help with the horses. She won't know that I haven't gone home."

"Well, that's not any different than if you stayed at my house. Mrs. Brown will tell them you're here."

Morgan froze and stared off into space.

"Come on, Morgan. Let's go!"

At the house, we rushed upstairs with Colton. Nothing more was mentioned about her plans, and we avoided the subject.

As the evening continued, the winds died. The weather man showed why the storm had lost its velocity and would be no more than a category one. That would still bring danger, but the towns around Charleston were prepared. Edisto being farther south would be safe.

Mom invited Morgan for dinner. Sarah wasn't interested in feeding the horses during a rainstorm and complained she could hardly walk from her ride. Morgan and I treated the horses. Knight enjoyed Morgan's extra attention, and she learned about his playful side.

"Are you sure you don't want to hang out with me for one night?"

She stared at the barn floor, and shook her head. "I'm exhausted. I'll go home. I'm not going to ride my bike in this weather."

Not trusting her, I watched her call the taxi, and stayed with her inside the barn. As soon as he drove up, she hopped in the backseat, and waved to me through the side window.

Around eleven o'clock, the weather changed again. Dad's weather siren blared through the house. "Warning. Tornado spotted in Simpsonville." Colton howled at the noise. I texted Mrs. B. "Do you need help? Tornado close by."

Mom held Colton as he ducked under her arms. I paced, waiting to hear from Mrs. B. "Dad, let's go. I bet she's outside. And she won't be able to hear us."

We ran to the barn and hollered for Mrs. Brown.

I looked up at Dad. "The horses are riled up, and I'm worried they might kick the stalls and get hurt. We need to put them out, but first I need to know the gates are closed."

Dad stood at one of the windows. The rain poured and the wind rattled the barn structure. The sky turned a greenish gray, eerie, and still like someone had vacuumed all of the oxygen out of the air.

"This is really scary, Dad. The tornado must be close. Listen."

As the sound like a freight train rumbled and roared through the dark night, Mrs. Brown burst into the barn and screamed. "All gates are locked. Let them go!"

The horses' wild eyes told us something was going to happen in a matter of minutes. Mrs. B stood in Chancy's stall and pushed open her back door with her whole body. Each of us did the same in each stall. The horses' instincts took them galloping to the lowest place on her property where the trees crowded together, giving them some protection.

Mrs. Brown shouted. "We've done all we can do. Scoot home. Thank you!"

As I started to jog away, Mrs. B hollered, "Morgan went home, right?"

I screamed back, "I saw her get into the cab."

Waving, Mrs. B hurried into her house.

Chapter 29

Mom threw towels to Dad and me as we hurried into the house, dripping wet. We stripped off the outer layer of clothes in the laundry room. Dad dashed to their bathroom, and I shivered to the downstairs guest bathroom. Mom watched for a tornado.

Colton sat by the shower while I defrosted under the hot water, fogging the mirrors and window. After towel-drying my hair, I decided I'd let the humidity create my very own red afro. And that made me think of Morgan. My stomach dropped without a parachute, and I ached for her. Was she afraid all by herself?

I jogged upstairs for new clothes with Colton leading.

Dad called up to me, "All clear. Come have some ice cream before you head to bed."

"On our way. And I bet Colt would love a goodie, too. I don't think he wants to go outside right now. He's kind of clingy."

The second we sat at the table, the lights blinked, and a terrible boom rattled the house. "Dad, I thought you said all clear?"

Colton sensed my nervousness and laid across my leg, doing a hug. I groaned, picking up my almost grown dog. He hung over my lap and looked straight into my eyes. The wind wailed, shaking our walls.

"I think it's just a blast of wind. Our alarm will warn us."

I almost mentioned Morgan being home alone, and caught the words before they shot out of my mouth. Instead I said, "It doesn't seem to be going away. I can't even begin to think what it must be like on the coast."

Before I finished my sentence, lightning spiked, and I started counting. I made it to one-thousand-one. I squeezed Colton close and whispered in his ear. He stayed distracted for a moment, and then another noisy gust hit. He crawled closer, but didn't shiver or pant. I leaned over the bowl and ate my last bite of ice cream. "I'm taking us to bed. I want to snuggle with Colton under the covers. He'll help calm me."

Dad suggested. "Take a flashlight before you go up. We could lose power, and I don't want you lighting candles."

I grabbed the flashlight, and pointed it on the steps. Colton pounced at the round light like a cat and chased it up the stairs.

Ready for bed, I silenced my new phone, patted the mattress, and called, "Colton, come." I lifted the sheet and we burrowed. He poked the tip of his nose out while I read my book using the flashlight. Time evaporated, but I couldn't close the book. I kept telling myself, *One more chapter.*

When I couldn't keep my eyes open, I scooted up to my pillow. "Okay, Colton. Time to sleep." He curled up close to me, breathing in my face, and just as I whispered, "Night-night, little—" my phone vibrated on the night stand. Who would be calling at this hour?

Reaching for the phone, it vibrated again. "Hello?"

A voice shrieked. "Trina, it's me!"

"Who? Sarah? I can hardly hear you."

Silence.

"NO! This is Morgan. I'm in the barn."

"Morgan? You're where?" My heart beat in double time. I caught a breath and tried to keep my voice low. "You're in the barn?"

She screamed. "Yes!"

I couldn't understand through her sobbing, and I made her repeat herself.

She stopped blubbering. "Oh, Trina. I'm so frightened. I think part of the roof has blown off. Please, can you help me?"

"Yes! Yes! Of course. Let me get my dad, and we'll come over."

"NOOO!" She shouted. "They can't know. I'm hiding here to frighten my parents, and they don't even know I'm missing. I could be killed, and they'd never know, and they'd be free of me. But I don't want to die!"

"Why can't I get my dad to come with me? I'm scared, too. If I leave Colton, he'll whine and bark, and they'll hear him."

"If you tell your parents, they won't be able to keep it a secret. My parents will be back on Monday, and I'll be gone. Maybe then they'll think about if they want me or not!"

"Oh. Hold on while I think." *What can I do? What can I do?* Another bolt of lightning made me sit straight up in bed. "We need to talk this through. I'm taking a chance by putting Colton in the garage. When you come over he'll bark. I'll have to keep him quiet. Do you have a flashlight?"

"Yeah. Found one in the tack room. I'm afraid to walk over. I stayed with the horses for a while and actually felt safer with them down by the creek than being in the barn. But I got so wet and cold, I came back. I just want to get out of here. What if I get hit by lightning? Would you take care of Knight? He likes you."

"Morgan. Stop talking like that. You're going to come in my house, and you'll be safe. Grab a hooded jacket from the tack room. Don't use an umbrella. Let's wait until the next flash of lightning, and then you make a run for it. As soon as we hang up, I'll head your way. I have a flashlight, too. Look for my light."

We stayed silent for a moment. A bolt of lightning flared in the sky.

"Okay. Let's go."

I slid my feet into my flip flops, crept down the stairs, and grabbed my raincoat. Colton plopped down the stairs like a heavy-footed elephant. If my parents heard us, I'd say, "I need a glass of milk."

As if we were talented burglars in the middle of the night, no one caught us. I threw pieces of biscuits around the garage floor and snuck out the door. Without a star in the sky, or a moon for light, it was spooky dark. I couldn't even make out a tree or the path. Lucky, I had the way memorized and headed toward the barn. I saw another flash, but it seemed farther away. That made me charge forward.

Morgan's flashlight glowed ahead. I called to her, telling her she was safe and making me believe it, too. I followed my flashlight straight ahead, not thinking about holes or tree roots crossing the path. My focus was to reach Morgan and bring her to my house.

I shouted over the rush of wind in the trees. "I'm right in front of you. Do you see me?"

I tripped and tried to catch myself and swallowed a scream. My ankle twisted, and I remembered going down.

The pain made me dizzy and woozy. Morgan cried as she held me. "Are you okay? Trina. Are you okay? Answer me!"

Morgan's shape blurred, but I knew it was her. "What happened?"

"That's not a good sign. You fell. I saw your light go down. Do you hurt anywhere?"

"My elbow's sore. I feel funny. Let me stand up." Morgan put her hands under my arm pits and helped me stand. My vison blurred, and the trees seemed to be spinning. My guts turned. "Ooo. I think I'm going to throw up. My ankle."

Morgan shuddered. "Oh crud. This is great. How are we going to keep this a secret?"

I stood, inhaling short choppy breaths. "All right. Give me another second." I blew out my frustration. "If I don't get back before Colton wakes my parents,

I won't be able to keep it a secret. Can you balance me? Let's see if I can walk." Pain shot through my leg and I gritted my teeth. "Oh. My. Gawd! Standing is making every nerve come alive. They're yelling at me, 'Don't move!' Oh, Morgan. It's like I'm being poked with hot knives. Wait. Wait a minute. I-I can't handle the pain."

The wind quieted off and on, letting us maneuver. Since I couldn't put any weight on my right foot, I had to hop on my left foot. Morgan balanced me on the right. I swallowed my screams with deep moans and cries.

Maybe the worst of the weather is over, but what about me?

I opened the door to the garage, and Colton met us. He sniffed me and circled Morgan. "Good boy, Colt. Good quiet."

"Okay, Morgan. We have to go upstairs without waking mom and dad. "I'm not going to be able to walk up. You're going to have to go ahead with Colton. I'll sit on the steps and pull myself up on my bottom."

She puffed out her cheeks and stared.

"Morgan don't give me that look. Colton's fur won't bother you if it hasn't already. I need your help. Or you need mine. Either way, we need to get up the stairs."

Colton didn't want to follow Morgan. I sat with my back to the stairs, and lifted myself up one step at a time with my leg straight. He slapped his front two feet on each step and waited for me to move to the next step. And then his hind legs bounced forward ready to do it again. Morgan stood at the top of the stairs, holding her breath and wringing her hands.

As I lay across the bed, she rushed back and forth to the bathroom, cleaning my elbow. Then she found dry PJ's for me and a night gown for herself. I snickered. "It may be a shortie nightie for you, but that's all I have. Did you pack anything before you decided to run away?"

Her glare scared me.

"How did you get here?" I gave her my evil stare. "I saw you get in the cab."

She put her hand under her long hair and flung her curls, and then shook her head. "I pretended I was going home. I told Mr. Cabbie, to drop me off at the corner store."

"What?" I covered my mouth, hoping I hadn't woken my parents. I listened for a second. All was quiet. "Why would he leave you there?"

"I pretended to get a phone call from Dad, saying he was on his way to get me at the barn." Morgan paced in the room. "So I told Mr. Cabbie Dad would pick me up there."

I hit the mattress with my hands. "So you walked all by yourself down that busy street to Mrs. Brown's?" I shook my head and shot her a nasty look. "Do you have any idea how dangerous that was?"

"Yeah. At that moment, I didn't care." Morgan sat on the edge of the bed, her eyes flooding. "And with the bad weather there weren't many cars. But by the time I got to Mrs. Brown's, the weather had gotten worse, and I was wet and hungry. I raided the tack room frig and dried off, and found Mrs. Brown's raincoat. All the horses were way down by the stream, bunched in a group, and I thought I'd be safe with them. I patted and talked to them. But I got so tired. I was afraid I'd fall asleep, collapse on the ground, and get stepped on. I decided to settle into the hay loft, but the wind picked up, and then Mrs. Brown's tornado alarm went off. I rushed down to the tack room, hid in a corner, and it sounded like the barn was going to blow away." Morgan stopped talking and panted. "That was the most frightened I've ever been."

"Oh, Morgan, I'm so tired, and my leg hurts so bad!" I cringed and cried out in pain as I tried to scoot to my side of the bed.

"I don't know what to do." Morgan ran her fingers through her bangs. "Let me sneak down and get some ice. Maybe it will help by morning."

"I'm supposed to help with the horses in the morning." I sobbed. Tears streamed down my cheeks. "What if I can't walk?"

She caught my quivering chin and flinched. "I'll be right back. Do you have any Tylenol close by?"

I nodded. "Downstairs in the guest bathroom medicine cabinet." I patted the bed. "Colton, up!"

Without any effort, he bounced up as Morgan slipped out of the room.

Chapter 30

On my back and Morgan on her stomach, we buried ourselves under the covers with our flashlights, whispering. "Morgan, what are you going to do tomorrow?"

She lifted the sheet higher, letting air slip in. "Well, I know I'm not going home. After all I've gone through to stay away. I'm not going back."

Colton pushed his nose under the sheet as he laid on my pillow.

As I rolled onto my left side, I shrieked and jammed a knuckle into my mouth.

When the pain eased, I shined the flashlight under my chin, and made a scary face at Morgan. "You're going to be in so much trouble."

She exhaled. "I don't care! My house is like tomb. The quiet kills me." She opened her mouth to tell me more, but a look came across her face. She stopped.

"Morgan, tell me. I took a chance for you tonight. You have to trust me." I accidently moved and caught my scream with my hand.

Eying me, she ducked her chin, and twisted her head the other direction. I didn't speak. Her breathing rushed in and out.

Morgan finally muttered, "All right. I want to tell you. When I was six, my parents bought me a horse so I'd have something to keep me occupied, and Mother wouldn't have to take care of it." Morgan snickered and made eye contact. "But, I've discovered through the years, Dad would love to have a dog, but he's never home, and there's no way Mother would ever allow one in the house."

My eyes grew larger. She had told me that *she* was allergic. But not wanting to distract her, I pressed my lips together.

"They got me the cutest chestnut pony they could find. She was so pretty and sweet. Then they started planning my future. When I outgrew Melody, that was her name, and I had to get another horse. I guess, I was around ten. No questions asked. No discussion.

"One day she was there, and the next she was gone. I never wanted to ride another horse. But one day, they took me to a horse show and showed me

Sally, a small thoroughbred, and said she was mine. I almost died inside. I didn't want to get attached again. She had been trained already, and all I had to do was learn to ride her. I got bucked off three times at a riding event, and I refused to ride her. But when another really good rider eyed Sally and offered to buy her, I quickly had to rethink what I wanted to do."

"You sound like me. I can be stubborn, too." I laughed.

"I decided to learn how to ride her, and we won most of our shows. Mr. Grumbly took care of her, but I'd hide in her stall and keep her company. I didn't want to go home. Of course, I grew, and my parents switched horses again. I'm always starting over."

Surprised, I huffed. "Really! Me too. So you know what it feels like to lose your best friend. And now you have another horse. It's weird isn't it?"

She put her face closer to mine. "What's weird?"

I groaned, and chose not to move any part of me but my mouth. "We have so many things in common. We've both lost our best friends. The first dog I grew up with died, and then my first service dog had to be returned to be matched to his forever companion."

"Wow, I hadn't thought about Sydney leaving." She looked over at me.

Colton shoved himself forward and lifted the sheet with his nose.

I got another whiff of cool air. "It's awful, though."

Her dark eyes studied me. "What's awful?"

"How you had to give up your pony and your first horse. That your parents didn't ever ask you about what you wanted." A sharp jab in my chest took my breath away as I thought about losing Sydney. "Do you love riding?"

"I did at first with Melody." She closed her eyes for a second. "Then my parents took control. A horse was their perfect pet, knowing someone else would care for it, and they'd never have to do anything but pay for it. They chose Knight the same way. I've never had a say in anything."

My frizzy hair scratched the sheet as we wiggled underneath. "You're such a good rider. Are you saying you don't want Knight? You're not enjoying competing?"

"My Mother uses Knight as her weapon, and it takes a lot of the enjoyment away," Morgan whined. "But if I take her out of the equation, I'm beginning to like him. You showed me how he can be my friend. I've begun to think about being a trainer. Have a barn like Mrs. Brown. I can't lose Knight. Not yet. I will one day."

"Why would you lose him?"

"I'll outgrow him, or need another horse that can jump higher, or do more difficult dressage."

I pushed back the sheet and tried to sit up. The pain stole my breath for a moment, and then I used a forceful whisper. "Morgan, do you see how much we're a like? You're already training horses, and I'm training dogs. And we're both going to have to give up another."

"You are so right!" Morgan's voice grew louder. "I never ever thought about how much we were the same." And then she cackled. "But, we sure do come from different families!"

Her laughter was contagious.

I straightened as much as I could without hurting. In between snickers, I added more advice. "When your parents get home, tell them what you just told me. My mom is always asking me to tell her what is going on in my head." I held the flashlight under my chin. I wanted Morgan to pay attention to what I was saying. "See? I'm serious." I made a quirky face. "Remember when we worked with Colton on door manners? He showed you that he wanted your attention. You need to tell your parents in words instead of acting angry."

"Trina. You make it sound so easy."

"Maybe they don't know how lonesome you are. Tell them you understand they're busy making money, but you don't like that they leave you alone." I glanced into her eyes. "Have you ever thanked them for Knight?"

Morgan flinched and shook her head.

I started to pop up, but caught myself. "Oh. My. Gawd! I've always dreamed of having my own horse and competing."

Morgan shifted on the bed. "But now you're training dogs!"

"Yep, I am! And I can say I've chosen to do this." I closed my eyes, grabbed a long breath, and thought about what this all meant. I cleared my throat. "Don't change the subject! Tell them how Knight is keeping you from being lonesome and how he's making you more independent." I snickered. "Your mother will like that one!"

Morgan giggled with me.

I had to say, "Shhh!" and we laughed some more.

Once we quieted, we listened for footsteps.

Nothing.

Chapter 31

Every time I drifted off, the pain in my ankle shot upward through my leg and made my breath catch. Morgan snored right along with Colton. I sobbed quietly, resting on my back with my foot propped on a pillow under the sheet, waiting for the nightmarish minutes to end.

What am I going to tell my parents? I've never kept any secrets from them, but I knew that if I told them the truth, they would probably tell Morgan's parents where she was hiding.

Not only did my ankle hurt, I'd never been in a situation like this. Common sense said, "Be honest." But my heart said, "Help, Morgan."

Daylight barely peeked through the blinds. I twisted onto my left shoulder to see the time and shuddered from the pain. I nudged Morgan.

"What? What?" She rolled over on her side. "Oh! Hi, Trina. Boy oh boy, am I tired." She rubbed her eyes, and as if remembering about last night, she bounced upright. "How are you?"

"I'm not good. You're going to have to make up a story about going to the barn early. There's no way I can help feed the horses. Hurry and get up. Grab a pop tart or anything you like from the pantry. My parents won't be up yet."

Morgan grumbled. "Oh, no! What are you going to say?"

"I've thought about it all night. I want to help you, and you are right. My parents would want to tell the truth." My stomach revolted. *Is it the lying, or the pain I'm in? I'm going against all I've ever learned. I'll be in big trouble for this. I hope it's worth it.*

Sitting on the side of the bed, Morgan stretched. "Can you believe the things I did last night, and my parents don't even know I'm missing. I hope they got caught in the storm."

Colton jumped up for his morning snuggle.

I puckered my face. "Be careful what you wish for."

Morgan bowed her head. "I know. I need to hurry. Thanks for listening. I probably made it sound worse than it really is. I know you're going to get in trouble at some point, and I'll try and help you when this is over."

"I believe you. I just want you to get to the barn. Mrs. Brown has probably brought in the horses. If she even slept. Just tell her I called you early this morning and said I hurt my ankle while walking Colton in the storm."

She jumped up. "And I'll tell Mrs. B I'm going back home. I'll take my bike and disappear when I'm finished. She won't see me again and can't tell my parents anything. They'll start looking tomorrow. They haven't even called. What are you going to tell your parents?"

"The same thing you are telling Mrs. Brown. It's partly true."

"How are you going to care for Colton this morning? You want me to walk him on his leash and put him in the stall."

"Nah. I'll scoot down the stairs on my bottom, and let him out. He can run in the woods by himself, and when my parents get up, they'll find out I'm hurt."

After putting Colton outside, the pain stabbed straight up my leg, and I fought to keep from throwing up. I left the door cracked, and sat on the chair next to a window. Colton ran and entertained himself until he realized he was alone. He dashed inside, panting, and hungry for breakfast.

I wasn't quite sure how I was going to make it to the kitchen and feed him. Biting my lip, I scooted across the carpet with my leg pointing straight in front of me, tears dripping down my cheeks. He followed behind, pouncing at me as if we were playing a new kind of game.

Mom shuffled across the kitchen floor to make coffee. She choked on her scream as she caught her balance before tripping over me. "What in the world are doing, Trina?"

"Um. Umm." My butt hit the floor. I swallowed and let the words fly. "I-I hurt my ankle last night taking Colton out in the middle of the night."

"What?" Mom's face went pale. "Are you okay? Colton doesn't usually do that."

"He never went out before bed last night. I'm not sure if he heard a noise or he just wanted to do his business. He didn't want to stay out long, but I forgot my flashlight, and I stepped in a hole or tripped on a branch. I hobbled in and pulled myself up the stairs."

Mom squatted and examined my ankle. "Oh, honey. Why didn't you wake us? This looks awful. Are you in terrible pain?"

Tears flooded my eyes and regret tore at my heart. I had made the right decision and now I had to follow it through. I bit my bottom lip and nodded. I didn't want any chance of saying something I'd regret later.

"Stay right there. Don't move. Better yet. Let me get you to the couch so you can stretch out. Then I'm waking your father." She helped me shuffle to the couch and set a blanket over my lap.

"No! Please don't wake Dad. I'll be okay in a couple days. Let's just wait and see if it gets better. I don't—"

But she disappeared into their bedroom. Dad's deep voice boomed through the door. "Let me get dressed, and we'll take her to the emergency room."

My heart throbbed, making it hard to breathe. I cradled my face in my hands, and slowly shook my head. Now I had really made a bad situation worse.

Mom fed Colton his breakfast and as soon as he finished, she told him, "We're going to the store, and we'll be right back." He had learned that meant, we'd be gone for a little while, and he walked into his crate downstairs.

Mom leaned her head with a questioning glance as Dad lifted me. "Weren't you supposed to take care of the horses this morning?"

I gulped. More lies. "Yep. I called Morgan late last night after I fell. She stays awake late. And she promised to go over early and take care of everything. She had somewhere to go this afternoon."

Mom smiled. "That's nice of her. I'm proud of you for taking the initiative to be her friend. Goodness knows she needs a friend or two. I sure hope to meet her parents one day."

"Me, too. But you might be surprised by what they're like." I held onto Dad as carried me to the car.

———

After X-rays, Dr. Mack, an orthopedic specialist, decided to check on me. "Want to tell me what happened?"

I whispered. "I tripped over a root or a hole. I don't remember."

"Well, I'm going to make you feel better soon. First, I have to put your ankle in place." He gave me a minute to relax. "Ready? This shouldn't hurt."

I sealed my lips and squeezed a pillow in my lap as he positioned my ankle at a ninety-degree angle.

"That a girl!"

I nodded.

Then he pulled a white sock up to the middle of my calf and wrapped layers of gauze around the sock for extra padding. After he smoothed the material, he applied the fiberglass.

"This is just a temporary cast," he said. "It will need to be changed in a couple days after the swelling goes down." He gave me a long, stern look. "Now, you have to promise me that you won't put any weight on the ankle and you'll keep it elevated."

I lowered my chin. I hurt too much to talk.

"The next time I see you at my office, you can choose any color you want." He patted my shoulder. "Do you have a favorite color?"

I whispered, "Purple."

The nurse scheduled our next appointment on Wednesday morning. A piece of my heart broke off and disappeared. *If I can't take care of Colton, what will happen to him?*

Three hours later, Dad carried me to the couch and Mom propped my leg on two pillows. The nurse had given me a pain pill, and I couldn't stay awake. I'd be sleeping downstairs again.

Colton rushed over, sniffed me, and worked his way down to my cast. He glanced at me, and lightly pawed my knee. He knew I hurt. For the next few days, I could only get up to go to the bathroom.

Mom hadn't mentioned what we'd do with Colton. What would Ms. Jennifer do? Would she place him with another family while I healed?

What if he never comes back?

I pictured saying goodbye to Sydney. My whole body shuddered, and I couldn't see through my flooded eyes.

Mom sat on the edge of the couch and rubbed my back in circles. "I'll take over today with Colton, but I need to call Ms. Jennifer and Mrs. Brown to explain the situation."

I buried my face in the pillow. I drew in a deep gasp and tried to pull away from her touch. I had no place to go.

She paused and silence filled the air. "Maybe Morgan will help out for a few days? And Heather?"

I shrugged.

My aching heart strummed a wild beat like a bass guitar. I stayed hunched in the corner of the couch, thinking. *Morgan's going to disappear.* Where would she go on her bike? I worried about her and what she was planning to do. I had to help her. But how? In my situation?

I'd be using crutches for weeks.

Chapter 32

The meds dissolved the pain and knocked me out cold. Waking with nightmares and the sweats, I fought dozing off, but sleep always won. I dreamt more about Morgan missing, or Colton being handed to another family.

Mom crumpled in the recliner and called Ms. Jennifer. Her side of the conversation came as murmurs to me. I held my breath so I could hear. She spoke about how I'd be down for at least a week and a half, and then I would be able to get around using crutches. Mom's head bobbed to what was being said on the other end. When I was forced to breathe, I had a coughing spell and started crying.

After Mom hung up the phone, she sat next to me with a long face. "Ms. Jennifer thinks it might be good for Colton to be with a foster family until you're mobile."

"No! No! I'm going to lose him. Like Sydney came to me after his first family deserted him. I can't let him go! I can't!" I cried so hard, I threw up.

Mom grabbed the bowl next to the couch, but it was too late.

She didn't say a word. Like a robot programed to clean things up, she walked to the laundry room and returned with the dust pan and towels to clean up my mess.

I snuffled. "I'm sorry Mom." In slow motion, I leaned back and let my head fall back on the pillow. "The medicine is making me sick."

Mom wiped my face with a cool rag. "It could be the meds, but I have a feeling you are all worked up over Colton." Mom bent down on her knees and took my face in her hands. "Honey, I don't have the time to do his training."

I shook my head until the room spun. "No! No. No. Mom, please don't let him go."

"Trina, you're going to be down for a week after the hard cast is on, and Dad is going out of town. Ms. Jennifer says, 'Two weeks. That's all.'"

"I can't be without him!" I covered my face and wept.

"I don't think you have a choice." Mom squished next to me with a twinkle in her eye. "Now listen to the good part."

Forcing myself to sit up, I glued my swollen eyes to hers.

"When Colton comes back, Ms. Jennifer would like you to do some special training with a wheelchair, and teach Colton skills that a person needs from a mobility dog. Dad has already ordered a wheelchair for when you're feeling better."

I stopped crying and sniffed. Mom handed me a folded Kleenex from her pocket, and I blew my nose. "Really?"

"Ms. Jennifer believes Colton is going to be a sturdy Lab and will make a great mobility dog." Then she fingered my tangled bangs off my wet face. "He's calm and steady. He'll be strong enough to help with a wheelchair, open doors and drawers, turn lights on and off, and pick up objects that fall to the floor. So, you see, this will be a chance to do some new kind of training. And, he will be coming back to you."

I bent my head, breathed in and out, and thought about what she said. *This happened because I lied to my parents, and this is how I'm being punished.* Only my eyes lifted. "When, when is Colton leaving?"

"One of her volunteers is on her way. I'll put a few of his favorite toys in a bag and send his dog food and treats. Can you think of anything that he'd want or need?"

I fell back on my pillow and stared at the ceiling. Suddenly, I remembered Sydney carrying my sock as his pacifier. "Mom, could you get one of my dirty socks."

She smiled and headed upstairs.

Colton sensed I was sad and pawed me to make me happy. That wasn't going to happen until he was back at my side.

I cried myself to sleep, and then Colton barked, jolting me awake. Someone was here. I thought about hiding Colton, but of course, I couldn't move. He bolted to the door, forgetting all of his door manners. *Oh no. What if this person believes I'm not training him correctly?*

Ms. Sue walked into the room, speaking softly to me. Relief filled me, but I didn't make eye contact. My favorite trainer. Her words entered my ears, but stung my heart.

"Trina. I promise, he'll be back as soon as you're ready."

Afraid to look at her, I glanced sideways.

"Honey, I will love him and work with him on just the things you've recorded. He's yours to keep until he moves on to a permanent family."

I grimaced. "You're sure?"

She smiled her big grin and kneeled by my side. "Ms. Jennifer and I wouldn't want it any other way."

Without really believing her, I muttered. "I'll have my new cast and will have a wheelchair by Thursday. He could come back then."

"Trina, I won't have time to bring him back until the following Saturday." Ms. Sue stood. "We have a number of dogs to work with and take on outings. We'll include Colton. This will give you time to rest and get well faster."

I stared up at her and blinked away my tears. "How about if Mom or Dad picked him up this Saturday?"

"Trina, no more." Mom patted my shoulder. She handed me my purple sock and spoke in a strong voice. "You need at least ten days. Stop pleading."

I wiped my tears with the sock and tied knots. "Here, this will help him remember me." I handed Ms. Sue the damp sock.

She leaned down and hugged me. "Trina, call anytime you want to know how he's doing."

Out of the corner of my eye, I watched Mom walk Colton out the door with Ms. Sue carrying his supplies. What was left of my heart melted into a puddle.

How do I function without a heart?

Chapter 33

Sometime in the afternoon, Morgan texted me. "Stayed and rode Knight. Mrs. B has no idea. Fed me lunch. Heading to train station. Did MapQuest. Text you when I'm there. Thanks."

Since I had no heart left, numbness took over. *What should I do?* If I told my parents, they would rush to go get her. But at least she'd be safe then.

What if I don't tell, and she gets hurt?

Mom stepped over and looked at me. "What's going on in that mind of yours? You have a strange look."

"I'm—" I rubbed my cheek. "—I'm worried about, um, Colton. He's not going to know why he's not with me."

Mom smiled and patted my shoulder. "I'm going to get you some chocolate chip ice cream. That will make you feel better."

By five o'clock, my nerves rattled in every limb. The ice cream churned into sour butter. I hadn't heard a word from Morgan. She had promised to let me know she was safe by five o'clock, or she knew I'd tell my parents. I'd give her a few more minutes. Evenings came earlier, and I'd have to get help before it grew dark. By five thirty, I sent a text to her. "Where are you? Will get help."

My phone vibrated just as mom walked in with a cup of tea. I hid the phone under the blanket and smiled up at her. "Thanks. I'll sip on this. And close my eyes for a little while."

"Good idea. Dinner in an hour."

As soon as she disappeared, I yanked my phone out and read her message. "Trees down. Can't get around. Got lost. Almost to hayloft."

I sighed. *Woo.* So far, she was okay. And I hadn't gone back on my promise.

Mom's phone chirped in the kitchen. She spoke in a friendly tone, and then her voice changed to a high pitch. "I don't know. Hold on, and I'll ask Trina."

Her conversation didn't sound like it was with Sarah. *Uh oh!* Mom took forceful, giant steps toward me. I pretended to be asleep. Her voice went to a whisper, and she walked back into the kitchen. "She's sleeping right now. As soon as she wakes, I'll call you back."

If that had been Sarah, Mom would have said, "Trina will call you back." My eyes stayed closed while I thought. Tomorrow was a teacher workday, no school for us, and then Morgan's parents would come home. I'd only miss the next two days of school, and they'd be excused.

After a few minutes, I needed to check the lightness out the window, but instead of seeing the view, Mom sat in the recliner, watching me.

"Okay, sleepy head. Do you want to tell me what's going on?"

I flinched. "What are you talking about?"

"Where's Morgan? Her parents came home early because of the storm. I guess they had a sitter scheduled, but no one's at the house. Turns out Morgan called and canceled the sitter. I know she's around because she helped you with barn chores."

Truth or consequences? I stared at her.

"Trina, I know why you want to protect Morgan. Convince me why I shouldn't say anything, and I won't mess up her plan. But please tell me, so I won't worry. I'll keep it hush-hush. I don't like her parents, and I'd like to give them a piece of my mind."

I lifted my head from the pillow and breathlessly asked. "You're not angry at me?"

"I understand why you didn't tell me about what's going on. But I'd like you to be honest with me now. I promise, I will help, not interfere. Does this have anything to do with your injury?"

"Um. In a way." I told Mom what happened.

She nodded. "I believe you've already suffered the consequences for not asking for help. Next time, I hope, you'll feel better talking things over with us. I agree with what you did. I'd have done the same thing."

My heart came back to life, thumping a cheerful beat.

Mom's skin wrinkled around her eyes. "But if she gets hurt on her way back, I'd feel responsible. Do you have any idea where she is?"

I shook my head. "No!" The sour butter bubbled up my throat. I made a sick face, and put my hand over my lips and swallowed. "She said she's on her way back to the barn. She's going to hide in the hayloft. It seems the roof didn't blow off."

"Doesn't it seem a little silly to have her hiding in the barn when she could be at our house, warm and safe?"

"Really?"

"Does Mrs. Brown know she's there?"

"Nope. Morgan told her she had something to do today and wouldn't be coming back. I'm not even sure if Heather went over to help. I feel terrible leaving Mrs. B stranded."

"Accidents happen. I'll call and see if she needs a hand. Now rest."

When Mom vanished, I texted Morgan again. If she was peddling down the street, she probably didn't hear the phone buzz. I waited. What if something bad's happened? I hope she's close by.

Mrs. Brown didn't expect to see Morgan. When she showed up at the barn she'd pretend she came to check on Knight. Oh no! Morgan doesn't know her parents are home. They'll drive over to the barn.

I texted Morgan again. "Your parents called. They're home looking for you."

Since I hadn't heard anything for almost an hour, I wanted to scream. And I couldn't move from the darn couch.

Mom slammed the back door and rushed over to me. Breathing fast, she mumbled incoherent things. "Honey. You were so right in helping Morgan. I'm almost tempted to call social services. Don't they know what they're doing to their daughter?" She rubbed her hands back and forth.

"What's going on? Tell me. Morgan never texted me. I'm on my last nerve from waiting."

Mom paced two steps away and returned with a scowl. "After I arrived at the barn, Morgan peddled her bike into the barn. Just as I started to speak to her, a car sped up the drive, raising dust. Two car doors slammed. I looked up, and Morgan's parents stood face to face with her. Furious doesn't begin to describe the scene. I understand why they'd be angry. And it wasn't my place to butt in. Words were said."

I nodded and only said, "Oh!" I shivered inside.

"Her dad placed her bike in the trunk. Morgan calmly walked to the car, climbed into the back seat, and crunched down while the tires screeched their goodbye."

Smiling, I relaxed. "I guess she got her parents attention."

Mom frowned. "If that's what you want to call it?"

"Well. I hope it works for Morgan. I'll know tomorrow." I looked down at my phone to see if it was charged. I sighed and shrugged. "She better be in touch."

Chapter 34

Awake most of the night on the couch, I fought sleep and fidgeted. The dark, empty room echoed loneliness. *Could Colton sleep without me? Was he eating? And what about Morgan?*

I pictured Morgan and her parents in the same house together. That brought a shudder. I hoped she told them how she felt and made them listen.

With the sunrise, catlike footsteps moved through the hallway. Mom leaned over me.

I smiled.

"Oh, you're awake. Can I help you to the bathroom?"

I nodded. "That'd be great."

Mom handed me my crutches and followed me to the bathroom. The room spun. I wobbled, but Mom caught me just before I threw up in the toilet.

She kept a steady hand on one arm and led me back to the couch. "Last night I called Sarah and told her what has happened. She wants to come over, but I've told her you are kind of out of it. She said she'd call today."

Next to the couch, a stack of books and Discovery Teen magazines lay on the end table along with my new phone and iPod. This was how I was supposed to pass my day. I looked out the sliding glass door and into the woods. Cardinals, wrens, doves, and bluebirds took turns flying from one bird feeder to the next.

Enjoy these days, birdies. Only five more days without Colton, which meant only five more days of free-flying room with no dog chasing them. I pictured Colton's waving tail, toothy grin, and dangling tongue.

After lunch and a nap, my phone buzzed. The caller ID said, "Morgan." My heart knocked on my chest in a staccato beat. I caught my breath. "Hello!"

"Hi, you! It's me. I survived last night's war. First, I need to know how you are."

"Oh!" I inhaled twice. "Thanks for calling." I crashed back into the cushion with a giant sigh. "You won't believe how my leg looks. It is so swollen and black and blue, the doctor had to put on a temporary cast almost up to my knee."

Morgan groaned. "Oh. I'm so sorry."

"It wasn't your fault." I spoke louder. "So don't go blaming yourself. I see the doctor again on Wednesday, and I'll get a purple cast." My voice squeaked. "For six weeks." Then I spoke in between crying. "And I don't have Colton right now. He had—had to go to my trainer's house."

"That's terrible." Morgan whined. "I said, I'd help you. Once I get things worked out here, I'll be over."

"That'd be great!" I drew in a long gulp of air. "Tell me what happened. I need to think about something else besides missing Colt."

After a long pause, Morgan started from where she left off. "I think I won the first battle. Thanks for all your help and suggestions. I didn't bark, but I spoke up."

I covered my mouth so she couldn't hear me snicker. "Oh, good for you! Tell me what happened. If you want to."

"You were right, Trina. They had no idea about the way they treated me." Morgan even made a small giggle. "Dad especially listened. He had no clue Mother stayed so busy and ignored me. He realized how much they did without me, but he thought I didn't want to be with them. I know where he got that idea." Morgan stopped talking for a few seconds.

I wasn't sure if she was crying or just catching her breath. I waited.

"And then Dad said he never knew I hadn't agreed to sell Melody or Sally. He glared at Mother, turned to me and asked, 'Did you want Knight?' I shook my head. Dad gasped. 'What is going on here?' He stared at Mother. She didn't say anything, so he stared back at me."

"I'm so proud of you." I couldn't stay quiet and found the energy to squeal. "You stood up to your parents, and now they know how you feel."

"I think Mother recognized her secret behavior glowed like a red flare. And I thought Dad was going to boil over like lava. He knew Mother wasn't thinking about me, but herself. I quickly told them, how I've gotten attached to Knight, and how I wanted to compete with him. The clincher was how I've found my something special." Morgan paused.

I waited her out.

"Okay. Here's my new idea." She snickered. "I plan to learn therapeutic skills with Knight and work with special needs people like you do with dogs."

"Wow! You never told me."

"I have other reasons I'll share later." Morgan's voice soared with excitement. "I've been watching you and Colton. I've heard the stories about Sydney and Logan at the beach from Sarah."

"Oh, I didn't know." I smiled and my heart swelled with warmth.

"Anyway, Dad nodded. His eyes were wet when he said, 'I always believed you were content if you were at the barn.' I looked him square in the face and told him, 'Part of that was right. I just didn't like being stranded for hours at a time, never knowing when someone was going to get me, or if I needed to call the taxi.' Then Dad choked and asked. 'What do you mean, call a taxi?'

"This is when I realized Dad had no clue about how my life played out when he traveled. He made me feel terrific when he raised his voice at Mother. Her face sagged. I couldn't tell if she was angry at me or Dad or maybe with herself. All I know is Dad asked her to follow him to their bedroom. Watching them leave made me want to set off fireworks.

"When Mother and Dad returned, she sat in front of me and looked at the floor. She took a long breath and lifted her chin. Her stern face showed no emotion at all as she began talking. 'Morgan, as I grew up, my mother—your grandmother, whom you never met—was overwhelmed with four kids and teaching school. Your grandfather was a doctor and gone all the time. Mother ignored me and badgered me to do well in school. Now, I see she wanted me to be different from her and to have a better future. I always thought it was because I could never be good enough for her. She pushed me into studying and setting goals, and I tried to do those things to gain her love. Which never happened.'"

As Morgan said this, I blinked to clear my eyes. The pain meds and her story caused an eruption of emotion and I lost all control. With my tears overflowing and dripping down my cheek, I moved my mouth away from the speaker.

Morgan sobbed on the other end of the phone and caught her breath. "Between Mother's waterworks she told me, 'Until now I never realized I was doing the same thing to you.' Shocked by her comment, I just stared at her. She held my chin, making sure I paid attention as she said. 'I'm going to get some counseling. And maybe we should all go.'"

I blurted. "Oh, Morgan, that's great. So you didn't get into a lot of trouble?"

"I guess I should say no," Morgan grumbled. "But now I have to check in with my parents, especially my Dad, and tell them where I am. I don't really mind. It's actually kind of nice that they're interested. Listen to this." Morgan's voice grew shriller. "Our next horse show is in Florida. And they're going to let me miss three days of school. And we'll stay with my Grands. They have a barn, and Knight can stay with us. And I can practice in their arena. Everyone is going to watch my events. I will practice hard now."

"Yay!" I bumped my shoulders to my ears. "Once I have a wheelchair, I'll have free hands and can video you on my new phone."

Morgan added a spark to her voice. "Sounds like a plan. Ugh. Got to go. Footsteps coming this way."

Chapter 35

Tuesday evening, I worried myself sick about Colton coming home. How long would this terrible pain last? Could I train Colton from a wheelchair? The moon slipped away as the sun rose. In a few hours, I'd get the real cast and start counting down the days until Colton was home.

Dr. Mack made me promise to stay down until all the pain had disappeared. He warned me, "The earliest you should return to school is one week from today, but it depends on how your ankle is healing. If it still hurts, you need to stay off your feet."

My brain lit. Anxious about getting Colton back home, I decided to fake it.

Six days later, Dad argued with Mom about letting me go back to school one day early.

She put her hands on her hip. "It hasn't been a whole week."

He lifted his head, smiled, "If Trina says she's doing well, we need to believe her." He grinned at me.

He didn't persuade Mom.

On Wednesday, Mom gave in. Dad drove Sarah and me to school. He pulled out my crutches from the backseat, and Sarah grabbed my book bag. For years, I had found quiet ways to help others and stay unnoticed. As I hauled myself down the hallway, friends and acquaintances noticed me in my purple cast and on crutches. In seconds, they surrounded me like an eager mob seeing a celebrity, and I had nowhere to hide.

"Trina!" Wesley yelled.

I recognized his voice before I saw his face, and wanted to turn the other direction. What in the world? I didn't know Wesley was at my school. We never talked about school or other things, only dog stuff.

He shoved through the crowd, pushing them out of his way. He reached his hand out to Sarah. "Here. Give me her book bag." And pulled the book bag from her hands.

Sarah scowled at Wesley, and then glanced at me.

I shrugged. I wanted to hide my blushing face, but I had no free hands. "Thanks, Sarah. I'll see you later." Not wanting to make a scene, I let him carry the backpack. "Okay. I'm heading to English on the next hallway."

He grinned from ear to ear. "I know. I'm in the same class."

I lifted my head. "You are?"

He snorted. "I'm behind you, three rows back. I saw your empty seat. Just transferred on Monday. Ms. Stevens mentioned to the class why you were absent."

My eyebrows spiked. "You never said anything about moving or changing schools at my birthday party."

"I had a feeling I'd scare you if I was around too much. But see? It worked out. Now you know. I took notes for you yesterday and gave them to your friend."

"Sarah?" I scrunched my face, thinking. "She never said anything last night about who gave her my homework. Thank you, Wesley. That was very nice. Are you in any other classes with me that I don't know about?"

"No." His smile dissolved, and then his eyes glimmered with hope. "But I could meet you at your other classes and help you get to the next ones."

This was getting to be a bit much. "That's very nice, but I don't think I'm going to need help from room to room. I have to learn to do things on my own so Colton can come home."

His head drooped, and he stared at his shoes. "Okay. But will you let me call you and check on you?"

"That'd be fine. When I get home, I won't be going anywhere."

He smiled and let me hop in front of him. Mrs. Stevens had me change seats with Freddy, who sat on the end of the row. She placed an extra chair next to my desk and propped my leg on it. As soon as I settled in my seat, I glanced back to where Wesley sat.

He waved. I cracked a small smile and the flush of warmth trickled up my neck.

Mrs. Stevens announced to the class. "It's nice to have you back, Trina."

Friends agreed. I smiled for second before I bent my head and twisted a loose curl.

Every time I glanced at the clock, it seemed to be stuck. My ankle throbbed and burned. I couldn't concentrate on what the teachers said nor take decent notes. I stared straight ahead, letting my thoughts worry on what Colton was doing. Two more days and he'd be home, unless Ms. Sue thought he wasn't up to par on his training skills.

In the last class of the day, Social Studies, I fell asleep sideways. My friend, Janie, sitting next to me, tapped my arm just before the bell blared. She had written down our homework and handed it to me.

"Thank you. I'm out of it today. This has been really difficult."

Janie smiled and said, "Ms. Lester knew how you felt and told the class to let you sleep."

I leaned on my elbows and covered my cheeks with my hands. Sarah walked over to help from the other side of the room. "Come on. Let's go home."

Clomping down the hall, I didn't make any eye contact and forced a smile as other students offered support. Seeing Mom parked in the handicap spot by the front door brought instant relief.

Poof! Wesley appeared. He shoved himself between Sarah and me. She backed away as he opened the front car door, helped me slide in, and placed my cast on the floor. He proceeded to place my crutches in the open trunk, and then waved goodbye. I tried not to grimace.

Sarah climbed in the backseat behind me, leaned forward, and rubbed my shoulder. "Wesley! He's too much!"

I shook my head in disbelief. "What is wrong with him?" And then I moaned. "Mom, please, take me home."

———

Just two days until Colton would return. I planned to not complain about hurting, but I secretly wondered how in the world I'd care for Colton or train him.

The next day, Mom studied me at the breakfast table. "Did you get any sleep, Trina? You don't look well."

My head hung low. I dripped some milk on my tongue and swallowed one Cheerio. My stomach didn't want it. I hadn't finished my homework and dreaded going back to school. But my motivation was to get Colton home. With me. If I couldn't do regular activities, no way they'd let him come back. I resisted looking up and spoke to my bowl. "I'm okay. I did wake-up a thousand times, but I'll be fine. I just have to make it two more days."

Mom pulled her chair closer to me. "Honey. Look up. I want to see your eyes."

I didn't move. She lifted my face to hers, and I twisted the other direction.

"Why are you hiding your face?"

"I miss Colton, and I'm scared." I glanced up for a second, not wanting her to see my blood-shot eyes.

"Trina, you have nothing to be frightened of. Ms. Jen wants you to get well and be his trainer. This is just a minor setback. You need to be honest with yourself. If you bring Colton home too soon, it may slow down his learning. I'd say, no more school this week. I want you to do your assignments here and rest. Then you'll have to decide if you're ready for Colton to come home. Ms. Sue is taking him on all kinds of outings, and he's with other puppies. He's happy and doing well. But he's still yours."

I raised my head and tears blurred my vision. "Can I go back to bed for a little while?"

"Yes. I'll wake you when Sarah comes to give you your homework."

Mom helped me to the guest room, and I collapsed into bed. As soon as she disappeared my chin trembled and my face puckered. My armpits and hands already ached as much as my leg. *Six weeks in this awful cast. And then I have to wear a walking boot for two more weeks.* After burying my face under the covers, I grumbled and pounded the mattress then cried until I ran out of tears. No one could hear me. After a few minutes, I opened my eyes. I couldn't spend any more time feeling sorry for myself. Maybe next week, I'd begin working with Colton in the wheelchair. I needed hands.

The pain was tolerable if I didn't move. Mom brought me a protein milkshake and some vitamins, and yesterday's homework. The minute I started to study, I fell back on my pillow, and slept another couple of hours.

Dreams filled my head with memories of Colton's first night, his first bath, his first walk on the grass. I remembered his face watching his first bird flying overhead, and his body quivering as his first squirrel darted in front of him and dashed up a tree. There were so many firsts, they ran on and on like a movie show. Someone rang the doorbell, and the movie fast-forwarded to Colton racing at the front door. But I woke to voices. One sounded like Sarah. I wanted to be alert and seem wide awake. I only had one more day until the verdict was decided on Colton coming home.

Footsteps headed my way. I heard Mom saying, "She's slept all day. It is time to wake her up and get her moving." Then I only heard whispers. I worried about what Mom wasn't saying out loud.

I sat up, stepped down on the floor with my good foot, and grabbed my crutches. They both jolted when they saw me approach. "Hi Sarah. I heard your voice. Let's go to the den."

Mom tossed her head up and smiled. "How about some chocolate chip cookies. I baked them while you slept."

"Yum. I smell them. I'm actually hungry.

"Oh, I love hearing that. I'll make you a grilled cheese sandwich. Sarah, do you want one?"

"No thanks, Mrs. R, but I'll have a cookie. I can't stay long. I have a ton of homework and soccer practice."

I made a quick trip to the restroom by myself. Wobbling made my leg throb. I hopped my way back to the kitchen exhausted but put on a happy face.

Sarah filled me in on school. "Poor Wesley. He waited for you to show up at school and refused to go to class when the bell rang. The principal came out and told him he had to go to class. He gave me this English assignment after school and said he was going to call you. So be prepared."

"He's too much." I snickered. "I'm not going back tomorrow. I need more time to recover and catch up on my work."

Sarah's eyes smiled. "How's that going?"

"Not well so far. Maybe this afternoon I'll make some headway."

We chatted, and I nibbled on my sandwich. I got one half of it down and broke a corner off of a cookie. I slumped in my chair and my chin fell to my chest. "I think, I need to lie down."

Sarah followed me to the bedroom and helped move my leg across the bed. "Give me your phone. I've found this new app to add a tune to the person's name. I'm putting in the lyrics, "Oh...I Won't Let You Down," on my name. Whenever you hear that tune, you'll know it's me. She poked around on my phone and then called me from her phone.

We listened to the words play twice.

"I won't let you down," and I hung up. "Oh, that's fun! Thanks."

"Here, hand me your phone again. Let's add one for Chase. What song do you want to use?"

"Umm. How about, "When I'm With You.""

Sarah giggled. "That's a good one. I guess you'll have to test it out when he calls." She leaned over and gave me a tiny hug. "I'll come see you after school tomorrow. I called Peyton and told him about your ankle. He's telling Chase."

My head flopped back on my pillow. "Did you two talk any?"

She wrinkled her nose. "Yeah. He's staying busy like I am. He's passed his learner's test and is practicing driving. Maybe once he has his license, we'll all be able to see each other."

"That'd be great." My eyes closed for a second, and then I forced them open. "Thanks for coming. But Sarah, please don't tell anyone at school how

I'm really doing. I don't need them feeling sorry for me. I have to prove I'm ready for Colton to come home."

She gave me a thumbs up and winked. "I won't let you down."

Chapter 36

On Saturday morning, Mom's phone rang. I hoped it was Chase, but he would have called my cell phone. I would have heard my tune. My heavy heart dropped to the pit of my stomach. It had to be Ms. Sue. Being honest with myself hurt. I was behind in my studies, and I couldn't stay up for more than a few minutes. My heart pounded so hard it was like hearing a constant drum beat inside my head.

Mom answered the phone. I flung myself into the kitchen, and in between my pulsating heartbeats, I listened to her side of the conversation.

Mom nodded and repeated, "That's wonderful...We sure miss him...Yes. I think so. Trina's right here. Let me get her on the phone. She'll be thrilled to hear all the good news."

My hands sweated, and I couldn't get any air into my lungs. My good leg shivered. I had to get a hold of myself. Mom continued to speak into the phone, giving me time to settle in a chair. As soon as she handed me her phone, I licked my lips and tried to speak, but nothing came out. I cleared my throat, and suddenly a whisper emerged. "Hi, Ms. Sue. Sorry, I'm having a hard time talking. I've missed Colton and I'm worried about him."

She answered, "There's no reason for you to be concerned. He's happy and doing well. You need to get yourself strong so you can take over."

Silence hung on the phone. I didn't know what to say. I knew I wasn't ready, but I needed him to be with me.

"Trina, I know your mom has said it's your decision, and it should be. Both of your parents are working, and you have to go to school. I know you miss him, but this is the tough decision. Are you ready to work with him?"

My stomach did a somersault. I stared at Mom through my tears. I shook my head, blotting my lips, making them disappear. Not able to say a word, I handed the phone to mom.

Mom's eyes leaked, and she leaned over to put her arm around my shoulders. "Sue, Trina knows she's not ready. I think one more week, and she'll be up and around."

I couldn't listen anymore and hauled myself back to bed. My heart ached like someone had drilled a hole right through it. I let myself cry for a few minutes and then made up my mind. I had to start pushing myself to get stronger, do my homework, and be ready for Colton next Saturday.

Over the weekend, I wiggled my toes, kept my cast high above my heart on a stack of pillows, and didn't take any meds. I forced myself to tackle my assignments and eat. I had to get my strength back.

Monday morning, Mom folded her arms and shook her head. "I'm going to have a say this time. And it's no. Let's see what tomorrow brings."

That evening, my cell phone rang with "When I'm With You." My hands flew to my chest. I wanted to squeal. *Chase!*

Frustration and excitement made my heart gallop. I had carried my phone in my pocket for days, getting more bothered with each day that passed. I let the short tune repeat twice, thought about not answering, and then answered in a perky voice. "Hey, Chase. What's up?"

"You don't need to pretend you're okay. Sarah called Wednesday and told Peyton about your accident. I feel terrible I haven't spoken to you. How's the ankle?"

He paused long enough for me to say, "Okay."

"Oh, that's good. I'm assuming you didn't call me because you felt so bad. I hope you're not mad at me? Will you tell me what happened?"

"I will, but first, I want to hear what you've been doing. It's been a while." I didn't mean to sound annoyed. Or maybe I did.

"Oh, just busy with stuff. Logan and Sydney keep me hopping. I've gotten involved with the art club at school. Did you know that Jessica—she said she knows you from PAALS—goes to my school? We're making posters and designs for tee shirts for their next fund raiser. My way of getting involved."

My body tensed. I lowered my voice and spoke slow to stay in control. "Aww. That's why I haven't heard from you." My eyes burned. Closing them, I clenched my jaw and told myself not to be jealous. But anger took over. I couldn't handle any more pain. "Chase, I'm not feeling well. Can we talk another time?"

There was a long silence. His voice softened and he whispered. "Please don't think I'm ignoring you. I think of you every day, but it is so hard being so far away. Just because I'm staying busy, doesn't make me miss you less. I'm going to hang up and call back tomorrow. Please answer the phone. I still want us to be, you know, friends."

And he hung up.

I crashed on the couch, irritated. He must have been, too. I hadn't answered him, and we left each other upset. That added a new pain to the list: a crumbled heart.

Boys! They were nothing but trouble.

Tuesday morning, I tried hard to look normal, but I didn't pass the test. That night Chase called, but I didn't answer. I needed time to figure out how to handle us being apart.

Wednesday, I moved a little better, but Mom firmly put her foot down.

Thursday, I woke early, dressed, and fixed my own cereal. When Mom entered the kitchen, I smiled up at her with a full mouth.

She tilted her head, looked at me sideways. "So you think you're ready?"

I nodded.

"You can handle school all day?"

I nodded, twice. Now, I'd prove to her I was ready.

Mom poured herself a cup of coffee, sat at the table, staring at me.

I had laid a plastic grocery bag on my lap. I put my spoon and empty bowl in the bag, slid my hand through the opening, and gripped the crutches. The bag hung from my wrist and flopped back and forth as I hobbled to the sink.

Mom laughed and stood. "Enough. You've proved your point. I'll get your book bag and take you to school."

At the front circle, Wesley rushed to my car. Mom snickered and pushed the button to pop open the trunk. He lifted the crutches, helped me stand, snatched my book bag from the back seat, and threw it over his left shoulder.

I shook my head in awe. "How'd you know I was coming back to school?"

He shrugged, grinning. "I've waited each day, knowing you'd eventually come back. I planned to be here when you returned."

Exasperation made me scowl, and then a smile slipped out. "Thanks, Wesley."

In each class, a friend guided me through the maze of chairs or desks to a side table where I could prop my leg. Wesley supplied a small pillow for me in English. I had never felt so pampered. Determined to be cheerful and pay attention, I breezed through the first two classes. Then the day started to wear me down.

By lunch time, I ached all over from the crutches and lost my appetite. After making myself eat half of my sandwich, I had a few minutes to stretch out on the cot in the nurse's office and waited for the next bell. Only two more classes to go.

After school, Sarah made sure I had all my books, carried my book bag, and rattled on in a whisper all the way home. Mom dropped her at home. I napped in the recliner with my phone timed for one hour. Before starting homework, I sipped a protein drink. I had work to do. One day down, and only one more to go.

Morgan surprised me by coming over to visit and filled me in about the barn, Mrs. B, Chancy, and Knight. "The only thing I can't do are the horse treats at night. Mom and Dad expect me to be home. I'm still checking in with them even if they're not around. Dad is having an easier time juggling his schedule, but Mother forgets. Or gets tied up, so I still call the taxi. Dad is involved in everything that is happening. Once you're up and around, the horses will be happy to have you back. This Saturday?" Morgan paused, and wiggled her nose. "You're getting Colton back, right?"

"That's the plan." I smiled a giant grin. "I'm not babying myself any more. I have to get with it."

She clapped. "If he comes back on Saturday, I—"

I held the palm of my hand in front of her face. "There's no if. Colton will be back on Saturday."

"Super! I'll be over to help." Her eyes lit up. "Remember, I promised you when you helped me. You'll have to show me what you need me to do. Okay?"

"That'd be great. How are you with writing? Math? I'm really falling behind in math, and making a ton of mistakes in my writing. Maybe it's the meds."

Morgan smiled. "Trina, I have played down my academic skills. If my parents knew how easy things were for me, they'd demand more. I purposely bring home unfinished work, so they think I'm not doing well. Instead of attention, I used to get left behind so I'd work harder. It was a vicious circle, but it's definitely getting better now."

"That's terrible." I reached out toward her and grimaced "Morgan, I'm getting sore and stiff. I need to move around. Would you mind getting my crutches? I'm not getting stronger sitting here." I took my phone out of my pocket and checked to see if I had missed any calls. No messages, so I left it on the side table."

Morgan followed me outside, and we sat on the porch. She helped raise my leg onto a pillow. "What's happening with you and Knight? Are you ready for your next show?"

"I'm working hard, and Knight is fantastic. We'll leave next Wednesday. I'll have a couple days with my grandparents before the show. Everyone plans to watch each event. I hope I place, so they'll want to watch again."

I shook my head. "It shouldn't matter if you win, but you're trying your best and having fun."

"Right." Morgan whined and then gave a small chuckle. "Well, my family isn't like yours. I'm taking this one step at a time."

"Probably a good idea. Hang in there. I'm pulling for you to work this out."

I had mastered staying awake and doing all of my assignments, just not as carefully as I should. At night, I lay awake, figuring out what I really wanted to do. In my spare time, I spent hours researching agility training on the computer. Colton was too young to jump. He had to be at least a year old, but there were many obstacles we could do with me in a wheelchair.

The computer spelled out the directions on how to teach a puppy to go through the tunnel, navigate the weave poles, and walk on a flat board. Kids younger than me were running their dogs through courses and competing. Puppy agility was encouraged for mischievous and energetic dogs, and it was cheaper than competing with a horse.

Friday afternoon, I struggled to make the trip to the barn with my crutches over bumps and around holes in the dirt path. When I got close, I called out to Chancy. Hearing my voice, she neighed from her stall. My heart raced with delight and anxiety. Life was getting back to normal, but I was limited on choices.

As I stood in the barn, Chancy swung her head sideways, interrupting Heather's task at tacking up. My stomach knotted, and I couldn't catch my breath. Heather's long brown hair was clipped with a barrette under her riding hat. Curious to see why Chancy reacted, she peeked my way.

Her shoulders fell and in a halfhearted voice, she said, "Hi, Trina. Welcome back."

"Hey, Heather. Thanks for taking such good care of Chancy. I'll watch you two ride."

Her hazel eyes widened. "Really?"

"I won't be riding for a long while." I looked down at my cast, inhaled through my nose, and whooshed it slowly threw my lips. "I'm glad you two are getting along. I'll still come and see Chancy and do treats at night. You can keep her in shape."

Morgan walked over and stood next to Heather.

I glanced at Morgan. "I can still help with a few things at the barn. Then my eyes fell to the floor. "It will be months before my ankle is healed." I braved looking up and caught Heather's face.

Heather stared at me. "So, it would be okay if I ride Chancy every day?"

"Yep." A boulder crashed into the pit of my stomach. Squirming to hide my ache, I nodded in Heather's direction, and said what she wanted to hear. "That'd be good for her."

And then I turned away.

Chapter 37
October

Saturday was like having Christmas morning during the second week of October. Butterfly wings tickled the inside of my stomach. My legs and arms tingled with anticipation. Dad surprised me first thing in the morning with a wheelchair.

And Morgan waited with me for Colton to arrive. I sat in my wheelchair rolling back and forth, back and forth, until she fussed. "Stop moving. You're making me crazy!"

I maneuvered the chair by the front window. "What time is it? How much longer before they're here?"

"They'll get here." Morgan made a face at me. "You never know how much traffic is on the road."

I stared at the driveway. "What if they were in a car accident?"

"Trina. Stop that." Morgan shook her finger in my face. "They're just running behind."

Just as Morgan finished her sentence, I spotted a car through the branches of red, orange and yellow leaves on the street. I screamed. "They're here!" I turned the wheels as fast as my arms could push, but I still didn't get there fast enough.

Mom and Dad faked not being excited. They let Morgan help me over the threshold. I waited outside on the porch, all jittery inside. When I saw my boy bouncing in his harness on the backseat, every part of me buzzed.

Dad opened the back door, unharnessed Colton, and lifted him in his arms. I wanted to run to him, but I had to wait until Dad set him on my lap. Colton licked each tear dripping down my cheek as I held him tightly. He seemed to have doubled in size during his missing three weeks.

His warm eyes stared into mine, tilting his head, as if questioning me. *Where did you go? How come you gave me away?*

I squeezed his body closer, and whispered in his ear, "I've missed you so much, and we'll never be separated." I choked and swallowed the words. Even though he didn't know what they meant, I couldn't go there. So I added. "Just wait until you see what fun I've planned for you.

I started to roll us into the house, and Colton sat upright looking at the wheels and back at me. My body tingled with happiness. Having a broken ankle had given me a new opportunity with Colton's training. We'd learn new tricks together.

Morgan volunteered to walk Colton to the barn until I needed help getting the chair over bumps on the path. She handed me Colton's leash, and for the first time in weeks, I gained control of my boy. Morgan chattered as she pushed me forward. I inhaled the cool, crisp air with a scent of burning leaves.

Grinning, I finally had to ask. "So are you really allergic to dogs?"

She leaned her head over my shoulder. "I had to have an excuse not to get close."

"And that would be because...?"

"Now that you know about my family, you know I could never have a dog." She snickered. "And if I liked Colton, which you know I do, I'd have trouble not wishing I had one."

"That makes sense." I turned as around as far as I could in the chair and smiled at her. "I didn't really believe you were allergic, anyway."

Chancy neighed as we headed toward the barn. Heather was already there. She smiled at us and removed Chancy's bridle. Colton flopped across my lap, panting. I spoke to Chancy but didn't rub her nose. It was Heather's time with Chancy.

I wrapped Colton's leash around my wrist and had him Look, Sit, and Wait while Morgan tacked up. Then we followed her to the stadium. Colton lay next to my chair as she warmed-up. "Okay, Trina I'm ready. I'll do my dressage routine."

I pulled out my fancy phone, and noticed I had two missed calls from Chase. How had I missed his song? I turned up the volume and made sure the sound was on.

After staring at his name, the adrenaline hissed through my arms, and I clicked video. Trying to keep my hands steady, I got most of Morgan's test. Instead of watching her test recording, my mind drifted to Chase. Guilt made me blush. I really had messed things up. We both were in the same spot, wanting to be together with no way of conquering the distance. And I wasn't making it any easier on either one of us.

She walked Knight to the fence. "Okay, Trina. Let me see what I need to do."

My thoughts of Chase interfered. I only caught snatches of her comments.

"Oh, I need to work on my...I went too far before I saluted. Umm. What else?" She stared at the video and moaned. "Knight...we're supposed to be walking. And, I see my posture isn't right....and my hands...Okay, Trina, let me try again."

My head popped up, and I pretended to be in step with her. "Ready?" I asked with feigned enthusiasm. We repeated the process, me filming and Morgan correcting those sections until my leg screamed. I was at my limit, and waved to Morgan, "We're out of here. I've had enough. Come over for lunch."

Morgan waved back, hoped off Knight, and set up more jumps. "Will do."

At home, I lifted myself on my good leg, scrambled butt first into the recliner, and texted Chase, apologizing for being so stubborn. Colt curled under his paws next to the chair, and I dozed off until my phone played "When I'm With You."

I didn't let the song play long. "Hey, Stranger!"

Chase said a sad, "Hey!"

"I probably shouldn't call you a stranger. It's my fault, not yours. I was jealous. My leg ached, and my feelings hurt. I was a mess and not thinking straight. I'm sorry for not talking. Can we try again to be friends?"

Chase made a mournful sigh. "That would make me really happy. I'm not sleeping and not able to focus on anything. If I could make the miles go away, I'd be at your front door."

"I know. I feel the same way. Let's promise to share everything. We can pretend we're in front of each other and talk. Maybe one day we'll be back together, but for now, it's okay if you're with other girls. Just don't like them too much. Okay?"

He chuckled and made crazy promises.

"I'm so busy with training Colton, I don't have time for anything else, but it's nice to know we'll still be good friends."

"Whew! I feel better already." His voice cracked and a deeper twang came out. I had to smile. "One more thing we need to get straight. If we don't have time to talk, neither one of us will get upset."

"Yes, I agree. With my new phone, I have unlimited texting now!" We talked for another thirty minutes catching up. I was wired, but enjoyed stretching out, day-dreaming about the days we had shared together.

Morgan's high pitched voice roused me from the kitchen, discussing her upcoming horse show with Mom. Not quite ready to move, I listened to Morgan's conversation and her dreams spilling out. I hoped she'd be happy now.

What about my dreams? Was I meant to train dogs? I'd been riding for years, but I hadn't gotten very far. If I continued working at the barn, I could afford dog shows and the entry forms. But how could I be around the horses and not feel the call to ride? My stomach ached those first few days of ignoring Chancy, and a rush of sadness started at my neck and tingled down my back. I pretended not to care as Heather became her friend, and by Wednesday I pushed myself to compliment her. Chancy would understand soon. I was not her caretaker right now.

Morgan practiced for her last time before going off to her show. I stayed away until the weekend. I could call Chase anytime now, and that helped.

Colton learned new commands, Tug and Drop. Once he grasped those skills, I'd tie ropes on door handles and let him learn to pull open doors, the refrigerator, and the dryer. He needed to learn to fetch things for me and turn on lights. My heart bubbled with eagerness. We had a lot of work ahead.

Morgan called Wednesday evening and Thursday afternoon. For the first time, she talked like an excited child on her first excursion to Disney World. She babbled about her grandparents' house and their barn, and how Knight loved their arena. She carried on about how she and Knight had become a team. I listened since getting a word in edgewise was impossible. She didn't slow down until she told me about each of the activities they did together. After a short pause, she promised to call Friday evening after she had organized her tack room and walked the cross country course.

Late Friday afternoon, I put my phone on the end table, propped my leg on pillows, and dozed. It seemed like only seconds since I had stretched out, but Mom patted my shoulder.

"Time for dinner, Hon."

Colton hadn't budged nor begged for dinner. He waited patiently for me to care for him. I glanced outside. The days were growing shorter and it was getting dark earlier. I checked my phone. No messages or calls. Every muscle in my stomach tightened and twisted. Maybe Morgan had forgotten me. Maybe she was too busy to call. I sighed and hoped everything was going as planned.

I sent her a text. "Have fun! Good luck tomorrow. Call when you can." I turned up the volume on my phone and put it in my pocket.

Chapter 38

By Saturday evening, my insides grew numb with worry. Morgan had to have completed Dressage and Cross Country, but she hadn't called. I told myself I'd hear about her performance when she returned home. Sunday afternoon, I rolled to the barn, only to find Heather riding Chancy. Colt and I sat in the shade of a brilliant tomato-red maple tree to watch.

Envious, I inspected Chancy's movements and realized she had improved with her daily workouts and seemed happy. Seeing them together gave me a chill that I wasn't the one out there on her back.

Colton and I visited with all the horses in their paddocks. I broke tradition and brought an afternoon treat; one dog biscuit for each horse. I needed to feel their affection.

There was a board laying on the sand inside the stadium. All the horses were either in their paddocks or in the barn. I rolled to the spot and pulled out Colton's treats. I had watched enough You Tube videos to know how to begin. I unleashed Colt, turned my chair sideways, looked and pointed my hand over the board. "Touch." He tapped the board and got a piece of apple. Then I said, "Walk." He took a step, I clicked, and he received another piece. His ears perked, his eyes blinked and widened. He understood what I wanted him to do and took three steps.

"Yes!" I clicked, and we repeated this all the way to the end. As I wheeled my chair the other direction, Colt walked the entire board. I leaned over sideways and hugged him before I gave him a handful of tiny apple pieces.

He panted with pride, as he heeled next to my chair, all the way into the barn. I rolled into the tack room and put myself to work cleaning leathers.

I dropped my polishing rag and told Colt, "Get It."

He looked at the cloth, and back at me, squinting.

He lifted the corner of the material.

"Yes!"

That was a start. He raced around, shaking the cloth like he was instinctively killing an animal.

I patted my lap. "Bring."

He crinkled his eyes, thinking.

I patted my lap again. "Bring."

He stood in front of me, and chewed on the rag. I patted my knee, "Drop." He took a couple of seconds to process the word before recognition set in. As he dropped the soggy cloth on my lap and I patted his head and smiled. "Yes."

I worked longer, continued to drop objects, and commanded, "Get It."

During our training session, a loud, rumbling diesel engine approached. My heart galloped as I rushed to the open area. There it was. The gray truck and its beautiful trailer. Seeing them drive up reminded me of the day when Morgan first arrived—but this time, her dad helped and Morgan spoke to him in a loving tone.

They worked together.

Morgan glanced over at me, gave me a half-hearted smile, and called, "Hi, Trina. Finally back home. That was a long trip."

Knight backed off the trailer like a pro and pranced into his stall.

As they passed me, I told Morgan. "Hurry and get Knight settled in his stall. I'll visit with him while you unload. I can't wait to hear all about your trip."

Morgan looked to her father. "Dad, this is Trina."

He stopped what he was doing, walked over, and shook my hand. "I've heard a lot about you while we were in Florida. So nice to finally meet you." He glanced at my chair, "I was sorry to hear about your injury. How are you doing?" His eyes shined as he smiled.

"I'm surviving." I grinned back. "It's great to meet you, too. Did you have a good trip?"

He looked at Morgan, examining her expression. "I think so. Have a few things to work out, but overall it was a wonderful trip." He looked over at me and exhaled. "We can't really stay long. I'm going out of town tomorrow and must get back to repack."

Morgan and I glanced at each other. Her shoulders slumped. "I'll call you as soon as I get home."

"Okay, that'll work." I wiggled my pointy finger at myself. She leaned closer, and I whispered in her ear. "I'm dying to hear. Promise to call?"

She pulled back, "I do." She gave me a look of—what? Regret? Resignation? It wasn't exactly excited or happy.

I squinted. "All right. Tell me what I can do so you can get home." I smiled and hissed. "You better call."

Morgan shared a teeny smile and gave me a short list of things I would be able to manage with Colton's help.

"Yep, I can do all those things. Head on out. I've got it under control."

Morgan filled Knight's bucket with fresh water and added a flake of hay.

I hung her leathers over my arm, and her supply bucket on the arm of my wheelchair and rolled into the tack room. "Bye!"

Cleaning leathers relaxed my brain. I rubbed the oil back and forth, and watched the leather shine. With the radio on, I hummed to the country music and sang the lyrics I had memorized. Colton had passed out in his stall, which left me free of worries. Instead I thought back to the agility videos and daydreamed.

My phone chirped in my pocket and I pulled it out. A new message from Chase.

I texted, "Morgan's home. Talk tonight."

Mrs. Brown drove the golf cart into the barn and started scooping dinners. I pushed myself out of the tack room. "Oh my, Trina. I didn't know you were here. This is a nice surprise. How did Morgan's trip go?"

I shrugged. "We didn't have time to chat. Her dad couldn't stay. I could help you pour dinners in their buckets. I can maneuver one bucket at a time."

"Super, duper! I'll get finished faster. Did Morgan seem in good spirits?"

"I'm not really sure." I wrinkled my nose. "I'd say it wasn't what I expected."

Colton heard the food clinking or smelled the aroma. He woke up and whined. All the horses were in their stall, so I let him walk around. He saw Mrs. B and nudged her with his nose. She found a treat in her pocket, bent down face to face, and handed him the goodie.

"See you later, Mrs. B. Need to get home before it gets any darker. Let's go, Mr. Colt."

Before I headed out the door, Mrs. B called. "Trina, let me know what's going on with Morgan, when you hear."

"I will. I only hope I don't have to wait too long. I hate the not knowing."

Chapter 39

I attacked the last bits of homework but hoped Morgan would find time to check my writing assignment before I had to turn it in. She was proving to be an excellent editor. Sighing, I stretched out on the recliner to read a new edition of *Discovery Teen* magazine. I wanted to read, "How to Be True to Yourself." I scanned the pictures on each page, read their captions, and then returned to the article. After reading one paragraph, the sound of neighing blared from my phone.

My back straightened, adrenaline surged through my veins. I grabbed my phone and hit the green button. "Hey, it's you!"

There was a pause, and then Morgan giggled. "It's me all right. What are you doing?"

"Not much. I'm kind of like a prisoner in this body. All I can do is read, wait for dinner, and hope to hear from you." I waited for her to comment. But I only caught her rapid breathing in my ear. "Okay, Morgan, enough suspense. Are you going to tell me about your trip, or are we ignoring you've been gone?"

She laughed. "Dad actually offered to bring me back to the barn to check on Knight. He knows I need to talk with you. Can you go to the barn after dinner?"

"Morgan, come over for dinner. If you like Mexican, we're having tacos and beans. It's too hard to roll over there in the dark. And I bet my Dad would drive you home."

"Hold on. Let me ask. Dad's packing for his business trip." In seconds, Morgan came to the phone, panting. "He said that would be fine. See you in twenty."

I got myself into the kitchen and mentioned I had invited Morgan for dinner.

Mom smiled. "Okay. I'll cook more ground beef, and you need to do extra shredded cheese, chopped tomatoes, and lettuce."

Mom laid the package of cheese and the vegetables on the table. I put the chopping board across my lap and wheeled myself to the table. As I finished slicing and shredding, Mom scooped the items into bowls. We finished up just as Morgan's dad dropped her off.

After dinner, Morgan and I went into the guest bedroom and closed the door. The only place to sit was on the bed. Colton leaped up, I stretched out, and Morgan sat crossed-legged at the end. We stared at each other.

"Okay. I'm waiting."

She sighed. "I'm—I'm trying to think where to begin."

"Start with driving from the barn and heading down the road. I'm all ears."

Morgan tucked a pillow under my ankle, and I slid back into another pillow. "All right. I'm skipping the long boring drive. It was exciting arriving at my grandparents' house and getting Knight settled. That was Wednesday night, and Gram had a special dinner prepared and an awesome cake. We sat at the table and talked."

She paused and her face beamed. "At home we never have family dinners. Dad even told some funny jokes. After dinner, my grandparents walked out to the barn with me. Knight seemed relaxed. When we went back into the house, Mother and Dad had gone to bed. Gram made hot chocolate, and we stayed up talking. I told her about Knight, and how I had to learn everything to do for him. And that you showed me how to be his friend."

"Wow!" A warm, fuzzy feeling made me grin. "That's nice. Did she want to know why?"

She made a quirky face. "Dad had already told them about me running away. And why we came down to do this horse show."

"Oh, that's good."

Morgan's hands trembled and she took short quick breaths. She uncrossed her legs and stood. Her expression tightened.

My eyebrows lifted. "Isn't it?"

"Yeah, it turned out to be good." Morgan paced the room. "Want me to do your hair like mine? It's called a Two-Strand Twist. It'll give me something to do while I'm telling you all this."

"I'd love that." Another clue. She was hurting.

Morgan reached inside her purse and grabbed clips and a comb. "I guess I need you at the side of the bed or back in your chair."

"I'd probably be more comfortable in the chair."

She helped me move.

I smiled up at her. "Would you please put the pillow under my ankle? Oh, that feels better. Thanks."

At the bottom of my neck, she pulled down a small section of hair, separated the hair into two thin locks like you do for braids, and crossed one on top of the other. As she worked her breathing slowed, and she restarted her story. "Mother showed her true self, and my Grands decided to be there for me. Dad was, too."

I frowned. "Oh, Morgan. What happened?" I fidgeted in the chair, twisted my shoulders back and forth.

"Hold still. This is going to take a while." And then Morgan spilled everything.

"Saturday morning, I warmed up with Knight. We were brilliant and ready for dressage. There were ten riders and I was number four. Knight and I practiced halting and me saluting, stopping trot and walking, all the things you videoed. We clicked. It was so awesome, Trina."

"Oh, I'm so glad. So—?"

"My name was called. I squared my shoulders and entered the ring, halted in the right spot, and did my salute. My elbows stayed straight and lined up. I didn't make one mistake. But—" Morgan started to cry and dropped my braid.

I slouched closer to her. "What in the world?"

"Oh, Trina. It was so stupid. I was so excited about how we were clicking, I forgot to drop my whip at the fence before we entered. I got disqualified."

A loud gasp flew from my mouth. "What?"

Her face sagged. "It's against the rules to test with a dressage whip in your hand. You can practice with it, warm up with it, but you must drop it outside the ring when you test."

I let out my worried breath. "So, did you still do cross country and stadium?"

"Yes." She huffed and finished the braid in progress. "But I couldn't place. I was disqualified. Do you want to hear the worst part?"

"Okay."

"I won the dressage test. My score was the highest I've ever had. But the whole weekend I couldn't compete."

"Oh. My. Gawd! That had to be so maddening. But, Morgan you should have been so proud of what you accomplished. You performed perfectly. Right? Didn't someone point that out to you?"

"Nope. That's what you would have said if you had been there. But you weren't and..."

Morgan started laughing, kind-of-a-fake-laugh. "I tried to feel that way. Of course, Mother had a stroke. She had taken the time off to come and watch.

And I screwed up! You know that's not allowed. She didn't want to watch me do cross country because there was no reason when I couldn't win. And she had reports to do."

Morgan was on a roll now, braiding faster, so I didn't say anything.

"Dad was furious at Mother. I heard later from Gram, he had made Mother stay. Gram now knew why I was so upset before we came. She understands I'm not causing trouble but trying to hide from it."

I blurted out. "Sounds like you have everyone else on your side."

"Yep. But it sure hurts that my mother can never be there for me. She didn't watch stadium. She had a migraine. Anyway, I survived. I had a perfect cross country with only one penalty for being one second late. On Sunday, I was in first place standing, but not in the competition. I had to do stadium first, since I was disqualified. But for the first time, I had a clear course. We didn't knock one fence, and I raced to the end on time. Trina, I would have won with my scores. It made me realize Knight and I are a great team. It was a thrill and such a disappointment."

"But you have to see how good you did. You made a silly mistake, and I bet you'll never do that again."

"I sure hope not. Anyway, Gram and Gramps want me to come and stay with them when I'm on Christmas vacation. Dad's been supper nice and supportive. I think we're starting counseling next week." Morgan moaned, drawing out each word. "That should be fun."

Trying to be encouraging, I spoke in a higher pitch. "Well, maybe it'll help."

Morgan kept her eyes low, and inhaled. "Dad said to call when I was ready to come home. It's nice he understands and let me come talk with you."

"There's no need to call your dad. Remember, mine offered to drive you home, and Colton and I will go with you. When you finish my hair." I giggled until my eyes filled.

Morgan stopped braiding. "This must be funny for you to get all choked-up. I need to hear something funny."

"It's nothing. Just a silly memory with Sarah from our beach trip."

"Come on, Trina. It's your turn to tell me a story."

I bent my head and a gush of silly laughter poured out. "Sarah noticed I hadn't shaved my legs."

Morgan leaned over my shoulder. "Really?"

"Yep, I'm a little slow on some things, but I'm catching up." I giggled again. "After dinner we snuck into the bathroom. Sarah handed me a new pink razor and showed me how to shave. We laughed every time I nicked myself. Mom stood at the door, asking what we were doing. I blurted, 'Sarah's fixing my hair.' So, after we covered my cuts with band aids, Sarah had to do my hair in a French braid."

Morgan cackled, and I shushed her.

Then Mom knocked on the door. "You guys okay in there?"

In between laughs, I called out to her. "Yep. Morgan is giving me a new hair style. I'll be out in a few minutes, and you can see my new do." I snorted and spoke softer. "We're doing the same thing, Morgan. This is too funny."

When Morgan quieted, she finished my hair and handed me a hand mirror. I admired my new look. "Wow! How long will this last?"

"It depends on your hair. Since yours is softer than mine, yours may come undone easier. But, I bet it will last a couple days."

She squatted to my head level with her phone. "Okay, selfie. Smile."

After taking a couple selfies, Morgan and I modeled our hairdo together before Dad drove her home.

For the first time, I saw where Morgan lived. Her gorgeous brick house with a manicured front yard didn't look very inviting. All the windows had closed blinds or curtains. No flower pots on the front porch. No autumn wreath on the door. A rock path lead to the solid brown wooden door with no side windows. I turned to Morgan. "So, I'll see you tomorrow at the barn?"

"Yes, and Mother plans to pick me up. She's apologized and wants to make it up to me. Who knows what that could be? Or if she'll even remember tomorrow."

Before Morgan opened the car door, she grabbed my hand and squeezed. "Thanks for having me for dinner. And, thanks for being my friend."

I squeezed her hand back.

Chapter 40

Monday morning, Mom drove Sarah and me to school. Sarah couldn't stop touching the braids.

"I can't wait to show them off." I touched them, too. "They are so different."

I started to open my door and moaned. "Ugh, there's Wesley. Why hasn't he given up on helping me?"

Mom frowned and used her soft, drawn-out voice. "Well, bless his heart. Trina, he's just trying to be nice. That's very sweet. Why don't you invite him over after school one day?"

I looked at her as if she'd lost her mind, and shook my head. "Nope. This is more than enough. Come on, Sarah. We're going to be late."

Wesley barged over and retrieved my crutches. Then, once I stood up, he handed them to me. He took my book bag from Sarah without saying a word.

She smiled at him this time. "Trina, I'll come over tonight, and we'll fix your problem."

Wesley froze. "I can help, Trina. If you have another problem, I'm at your service."

"Thanks, Wesley." I pouted and squeezed the rubber handles on my crutches. "But this is a problem for Sarah and me."

All afternoon, instead of listening to the teacher, I practiced what I'd say. And then I'd decide that wasn't what I wanted to say at all. *How do you tell a boy not to like you?*

When Sarah arrived at my house, my nerves jangled as if I'd been thrown into a snake pit. Every part of me quivered. I had always helped people, not told them to stay away. Sarah followed me to the guest room. Once again, I climbed on the bed and scooted back against the pillows. Colton leaped up and examined me.

I stroked his head and smiled at him. "It's a good thing you can't talk. You'd tell everyone what I've said, and I'd never have any secrets."

He blinked.

Sarah pulled a chair from the kitchen, flipped it around, and straddled the seat. "Okay, Trina, this is what you have to do."

My stare widened. She had my full attention.

"You need to call Wesley and explain."

"Explain? What? That I want him to leave me alone. That I don't have time for a boyfriend. I have other interests."

"No, silly. You do it nicely. Compliment him on how nice he's been to you. And how he's been a huge help, but now that you're well, you have to get back to being busy. Tell him you don't want him to feel bad when you don't have time to hang out or talk on the phone."

"Stop!" I put my hand in front of her face and almost shouted, "I have never called him or encouraged him."

"*We* know that. He doesn't. He'll argue with you that he'll wait for you. But then you tell him, you've seen other girls look at him. They'd love his attention. Tell him you'd feel better knowing he had another girlfriend who had time to be with him."

"Really?" I scrunched-up my face. "You think he'll buy that?"

Sarah sucked in her cheek. "It may take a few times saying it, but he'll eventually figure out you're not interested."

My eyes bulged. "And I do this over the phone?"

"It's a lot easier than face to face." She stared at me. "Want to do it now? I'll stay right here and keep your spirits up."

I took a long breath. "All right. The sooner the better." I lifted my cell phone and dialed. "Hi, Mrs. Cooper. This is Trina Ryan. Is Wesley there?" I smiled at Sarah and made an okay sign with my finger and thumb. Just as Sarah started to speak to me, Wesley's voice came over the phone. My words caught in my throat. I gagged and sputtered. "Hold on." I swallowed, and waited. "Okay. Sorry about that."

Before I could start into my speech, he apologized for being so persistent.

"Well, that's kind of why I called."

He broke my train of thought, telling me how much he liked me, and why I was so special.

I listened. Inch by inch my back slid down the pillow as I shook my head in disbelief.

Sarah waved her hand in front of my face, silently moving her mouth saying, "Do it. Come on. Do it."

I had to turn away from her. She moved around in front of me, jerking my free arm. There was no way I could talk. I needed to tell him my way without Sarah. "Um, Wesley. Can I call you back? My mom is calling."

I hung up and looked at Sarah. "I can't say those things to him. You should have heard how he complimented me. It's *sooo* embarrassing. I'll make him a card. And mail it."

"Hmm. That's not a bad idea. Do you want me to help?"

"Nah, I'll do it later. Let's go outside and let Colton run. I need some exercise, too." I grabbed the crutches, and we headed for the porch swing.

Swaying in the cool breeze, Sarah jabbered about the boys she had liked, and how after a couple weeks they bored her. "It works out perfect with Peyton in Columbia. We can talk on the phone and not feel obligated to be together all the time."

"I guess that's the problem with me. I'm more comfortable with Chase. He isn't bossy, and he's easy to get along with. If he was closer, I'd be happy being special friends."

"Uh-huh. That's your problem with Wesley. You like Chase."

I looked at my cast and the new striped purple and white sock covering my toes. "Yeah, I do. I did. He's different. My first boy crush, but being so far away is hard. Nope. I'm done with boyfriends. We agreed to be just friends from a distance."

"Really? Are you two not talking?"

"We had an argument. He has another girlfriend. Because we're so far apart, we decided we'd not be jealous of other friends. And I was free to have another boyfriend."

Sarah glared at me. "What? All this time and you never told me."

I wiped a loose tear. "I needed time to figure out my crazy life. So many changes are happening, and he's just complicating things."

Sarah leaned closer, questioning me with her look. "All my friends make a big deal out of having a boyfriend, because it makes them feel special—but it *does* get tiresome. That's why we change boys so often. I understand how you feel, but I never expected you to break it off with Chase."

I shrugged. "We missed each other, so we agreed to talk or text any time. That's working. We don't talk about other people, only what we're doing. I do miss him, but I'm more interested in Colton and being at the barn. Maybe one day being with a boy will be more important, but right now I'd rather not worry about one more thing. I want to be free. Free to do what I want to do. Which reminds me. Mom got a call yesterday from school. I've gotten permission to take Colton on the school bus, starting tomorrow. He's going to my first period class, and then Mom'll pick him up. Do you want to ride on the bus tomorrow?"

Sarah frowned. "How are you going to do that with crutches?"

"Umm, I hadn't thought about that. Look. My arms have gotten stronger." I flexed my muscle in my right bicep and poked at the round muscle.

Sarah rolled her eyes. "Impressive!" And then she glared. "How early?"

"Seven o'clock. Before the sun comes up."

Sarah groaned. "Yuck! That's usually when I'm waking."

I smiled my best smile. "One morning. Come on. Do your hair tonight and have your clothes ready."

She tilted her head. "I guess I can try getting up that early, one time, just for you."

I squeezed her hand. "Thanks, Sarah. You are the best."

Chapter 41

In the dusky, damp morning, Sarah's flashlight glared straight ahead. She met me in front of my house, complaining. "This is way too early. I don't like getting up in the dark."

Colton happily wagged and bounced from one leg to the other as I swung myself forward.

As the sun slowly peeked over the trees, I called, "Come."

Sarah leashed him and put on his cape.

In a few minutes, the rest of the bus riders joined us. Excited to have a dog riding on the bus, they teased Colton.

Because he reacted while wearing his vest, I gave the command, "Down."

The bus slowed to a stop, and the brakes squealed. Colt's ears perked at the whine. We waited, and Colton stayed in his Down position. I let the others climb aboard. Sarah held my crutches. I grabbed each side handle, took one step with my good foot, and lugged my cast up. Colton waited for me to move up one step. Then he bounced behind me with Sarah. I scooted across the first bench seat and collapsed. Colton lay by my feet, and Sarah slid in next to me.

Once we drove off, my panting slowed. Sarah whispered in my ear, "Did you make a card for Wesley?"

"Nope. Totally forgot." I faced her. "Another day."

She crossed her arms, and smirked. "You're going to be sorry. He's going to embarrass you, again."

"Nah, he'll be bored with all that by now."

Sarah circled her head like she was loosening her neck muscles and gave me a sideways glare. "Oh, this is going to be good."

"Yep, it should be. The plan is at 9:05 a.m. I walk Colt outside. Mom will take him to her office for a playtime with the dogs boarding at the clinic. And after, he'll practice sitting under her desk. One of the rules for fostering a service dog is: Puppies can't be alone for more than four hours."

At lunch time, Mom will bring Colton home, and he'll nap until I get home. If all goes well, he'll go with me each day this week. Then on Friday, Dad has a half-day off, and he plans to pick me up after school. We'll take Colton downtown to walk around the beautiful park and across the Reedy River Bridge high above the waterfall. I bet the leaves will be gorgeous this time of year."

Sarah leaned back and relaxed. "Are you going to ride the trolley up and down Main Street? Now that he knows how to ride a bus, he'll enjoy the ride."

"Yep. Would you like to join us?"

"I would, but I've got a soccer practice that afternoon." She looked down at her sneakers. "I want you to know I'm not getting up this early again. Can you get Colton on the bus without me?"

I hiked my shoulders. "I guess I'll find out."

Monday's school day went well. But Tuesday started off rough. I made it to the bus stop with Colton loose. I called him to me as the other riders showed up, but he expected to repeat yesterday's free-for-all and didn't listen. Not able to get his attention, my pulse speeded, and my good leg shook. Wincing from discomfort, I gripped my crutch handles. Colton had transformed into a slippery fish.

My ears heated, and I pleaded with the others running and chasing Colton. "Please stop. He needs to stand here."

They halted. A younger neighbor boy approached me and asked if I had a treat. I breathed a sigh of relief, reached into my pocket, and handed him a piece of cheese. He took my leash, called and baited Colton. He hooked him and reeled him in as the bus rumbled toward us.

My face cooled, and I managed a smile long enough to thank the boy. I pulled myself up the steps and he followed. Colton proved I had expected too much too soon.

I hobbled into English, only to find Wesley had brought Kaiser. I maneuvered to my desk, and Colton lay next to my good leg. Our dogs knew each other and challenged us to keep them at our desks.

Melissa who sat behind me, tapped my shoulder, and handed me a folded piece of paper with my name on it. When I noticed Wesley's handwriting, my mouth puckered and exasperation whooshed through my nose. I didn't want to open the note during class and set it inside my English book.

A few minutes later, I had another tap on the shoulder and another note appeared. This time the writing said, "Open Now!" I swiveled around, and glared at Wesley, shaking my head, NO!

Colton watched my reaction. He sensed when I was upset or stressed, and without a command, he threw his front legs on my lap, putting pressure on my thighs. This skill, called a Hug, helps relax people with Autism or PTSD. I stroked his head, and let my anxiety stream out of my fingers. The teacher never missed a beat about formatting essays.

Finally, the bell rang and my legs had fallen asleep, so had Colton. I tickled inside his ear and he raised his head.

"Off."

He had all four paws on the floor.

I responded with a, "Yes!"

Since I was in front of Wesley, he waited for us to move to the door. I had planned to shuffle out and ignore him, but that didn't happen. Our dogs nosed each other and wiggled.

Mrs. Stevens approached. "Wesley, I didn't know you were bringing your dog. We can't have both dogs here together. Please wait until next week, and then you can have a turn."

His face pinked and his few freckles popped up across his cheeks. His sky-blue eyes shined, and I thought to myself. He really is cute. Too bad he's such a klutz. He nodded to the teacher.

I blurted, "Wait. Mrs. Stevens, let Wesley bring his dog back. I can't handle Colton with crutches another morning. It's too much. I'll bring him back when I can walk."

"Are you sure, Trina?"

I smiled, relieved.

Wesley stood next to me, staring. "Thanks for that. Did you read my note?"

I shook my head. "NO, Wesley. I was listening to Mrs. Stevens." I screwed my face. "What's so important?"

"Um, I didn't want to ask you in person." He hemmed and hawed. "But I will now. Do you want to go to the dance Friday? I can pick you up, or I can meet you there?"

My stomach churned, but I smiled. Here's my chance to be honest. But all of the other classmates stood around, listening. The longer I didn't say anything, the closer they squeezed in. I didn't want to embarrass him. I leaned in to whisper in his ear. He leaned in, too, and pulled me closer with one arm. I instinctively backed away and almost lost my balance.

I glared at him. "Please don't do that. Can I talk with you after school? Got to go. Mom's picking up Colton out front."

"I'll walk with you. Kaiser's going home, too. So see, you can tell me out front. I'll hold Colton's leash."

A volcano erupted in my stomach, making me sick with worry. *What do I say?* I walked slower than usual, shaking with fury. The minute we stepped outside, but before he had time to look into my face, I said, "Wesley, thanks for the invitation. I can't dance on one leg, and I really don't have time for boys right now. Do you understand?"

"Yes. But we could spend time together with our dogs. They like each other, and that would make it even more fun. They could be like brothers, and we'd be like a happy family."

I laughed hysterically and slowly gained some control. "You are too funny! Wesley, we're only going to have these dogs for another year, and then they'll be gone. By then you'll have found another girl, one who likes you, with or without a dog." I paused. The words were falling out before I knew what I was saying. "One hint for you to think about. Don't be so pushy." I looked away. "Oh, here's my mom. Bye Wesley. Thanks for holding Colton. I'll see you at another dog class. Please ask someone else to the dance. Come, Colton." I floated to mom's car, light as air. I had told Wesley the truth, as nice as I could, and I was free!

Mom buckled Colton in, and asked me how the morning went.

I put my hand up and smiled. "Too much to tell."

She gave me a funny look and hugged me. "Okay. Later it is. Have a good rest of the day."

At the end of my very long day, Sarah rode home with me on the bus. I turned to her with a giant grin. "Sarah, it's done! Problem taken care of."

She gave me a High-Five and whispered. "Way to go! How?"

"Tell ya', later."

She leaned in, beaming. "Now, we'll have to find you another boy that is more likable."

I shook my head. "Nah, I'm good without. I'll stick with horses and dogs. Staying on this subject, do you want to go to the barn after doing some homework? I'm going to use my wheelchair. I'm exhausted."

Sarah hiked her book bag onto her lap. "Let's go home, have a snack, and then go before homework. I need a break from thinking."

The bus stopped at our spot. "Sarah, text me when you're ready. Meet you at the tree."

Inside the barn, Morgan spoke to Knight. He threw his head high and whinnied as if he was giggling at her.

My heart floated like a hot air balloon. I bit down on my bottom lip and stopped rolling my chair. "Sarah, let her have a few alone minutes with Knight, and then we'll go in. They're so happy together."

Sarah put her chin down and gave me a wrinkled face. "What's gotten into you?"

"I haven't told you about her vacation with her grandparents and her show. She needs this happy time."

"I hear you out there." Morgan hollered. "Come on in. Knight's waiting for his pats from you, Trina."

I rubbed Knight's soft nose and patted his satiny round belly. "Hey, Morgan. How long are you here?"

"The plan is for me to wait until Mother shows up. And then we're going out to dinner." She pursed her lips and shook her head side to side. "This will be a first. I'm not really expecting her to be on time or even remember. If it gets too late, I'll have dinner with Mrs. B, and then she's offered to drive me home."

I put my hand on her arm. "That sounds like a good plan. You know, you're always welcome at my house."

Sarah stood next to me, listening.

Morgan walked Knight to his stall. "I know. One way or another we're going to work out our problems. My grandparents have a Plan B that I like, and maybe we'll move toward that direction. I'll have to wait to see, but I'm doing research."

Sarah started to walk away.

Morgan touched her elbow. "You don't have to run away. It's okay if you hear. No secrets any more. I'm going to be happy with the people who care. Do you guys want to hear what my grandparents are working on?"

"Well, yah." I stared at Sarah.

She nodded. "I'm in. Tell."

"I researched boarding schools before we left for Florida. I haven't told you everything about my older brother, but I will." She bowed her head and stared at the straw floor. In a moment, she lifted her wet eyes and smiled. "I found three fabulous schools with riding programs near my Grands. We stayed up late, talking about me living closer to them. There's a military hospital close by."

My head shot up. I opened my mouth to interrupt, but Morgan put her hand up. "I promise I'll tell you about Quintin. Just not right now." Tears flowed again, and she wiped her nose on one of Knight's cleaning rags. "Okay?"

Sarah straightened.

I squinted for a moment. Did I say anything to Sarah about Morgan having brothers?

Morgan pouted. "Dad travels all the time so he could make trips to visit. Mom loves where she's working right now. But who knows how long that'll last."

"So when would you leave?" My face puckered. "I'm happy for you, but I'll miss you and Knight."

"If we decide this is what I want and if I get accepted, I'd start the new semester in January. They teach riding classes to help with special needs. I'd never be able to have a dog like you, but I can help people with mobility problems get their balance and feel the freedom of movement on a horse."

She stared at me, and her chest heaved as she sucked in all the air around us. "Ummm." She lifted her chin. "I need to tell you the bad stuff. My older brother has lost his left leg above the knee and has PTSD, Post Traumatic Stress Disorder. He needs psychological help, and he loves horses. This would be a great solution to make both of us happy."

I caught myself before I showed alarm or sadness. "Yah. That sounds like a wonderful way for him to get help, and you'd be together."

As I started to ask more questions, gravel popped under tires. We stiffened. No one moved. Morgan's mother's heels clicked toward our trio. Her head turned sideways, inspecting the barn and us.

I moved forward and put my hand out. "Hey, Mrs. Hart. I'm Trina."

She looked at my hand as if to see if it was clean, and then patted my hand with the tips of her red-painted fingernails. I didn't try pretending to be nice. I pulled my hand back and introduced Sarah.

Sarah didn't reach out to shake her hand and said in a monotone voice, "Nice to meet you, Mrs. Hart."

She blinked, nodded, and turned to Morgan. "Are you ready to go?"

Morgan smirked at us and said, "Yep, let me get my book bag."

I moved my lips. "Good luck!"

Watching them leave the barn, neither Sarah nor I said a word. Car doors slammed, the engine roared, and then the car rattled down the gravel drive. We hadn't shifted a muscle. I sensed Colton at my side and looked down. He glued his eyes on Sarah and me.

Sarah spoke first. "Well, that was something, wasn't it?"

"Oh. My. Gawd! No wonder Morgan is like she is, or was. I hope she gets to go to Florida and have normal people around her."

Sarah grabbed my arm. "Okay, Trina. Tell me about Morgan's trip."

Heading home to start our homework, I told her everything I'd been told. I didn't know any more about her brother than Sarah.

A smile spread across her face. "Morgan's dad likes dogs, so maybe her brother could have a service dog, too, if he's living with his grandparents."

"That's true, Sarah. And Morgan confessed she's always wanted a dog. I'm going to encourage her to apply to those schools."

Sarah took hold of Colton's leash. "So how about you? What will you do when Morgan's gone? Heather has pretty much adopted Chancy."

"Well. That's temporary."

She stopped and stared at me. "Is it?"

Chapter 42

Sitting at my desk with Colton next to my cast, I slogged through homework until my phone neighed. I smiled and answered. "Hey, Morgan. How was dinner?"

Her heavy breathing gave me a cause for alarm, and I waited for her to speak. "Surprising. Are you ready for some good news?"

All of my fears whooshed out, and my body crumpled like I had deflated. I sort of screamed, "Yah. What? Tell?"

"It's a lot. Can you roll to the barn? Dad said he'd take me and come back and when he finishes his errands."

"Absolutely. I need thirty minutes to finish one assignment. I'll do the rest later." I rushed to get Colton's cape and leash. "Want to go to the barn one more time?"

He wiggled into a U-shape and wagged. Filling my backpack with yummy treats, Colt's tongue swiped his lips and his eyes flashed on my pouch.

I chuckled. "You always act like you're starving."

He nodded in agreement and jogged up the path on alert for something to chase. I had decided to use my crutches and enjoyed the evening air. We heard squawking, and over the trees a flock of geese flew in a V formation like the pelicans had done at the beach. Soon the leader fell back and they changed formation.

I arrived panting.

Morgan greeted us. "Let's sit over here." She patted the hay bale. "I'm shaking with news. Okay, here I go. If you need a break, let me know."

I flopped on the bale and chewed on a loose piece of hay, but didn't budge. "I'm good. Just start."

Morgan inhaled and blew it out quickly. "Yesterday, Mother took me to the clubhouse. You saw how I was dressed."

I nodded but didn't interrupt.

"Not to her terms, to say the least, but she didn't say a word. Actually, after so many times of her being angry about the way I looked, I was embarrassed for the first time." Morgan hunched her shoulders. "I waited for Mother to make me feel small and unimportant, but she actually asked me questions about my day, and whether I had homework."

I pulled out another piece of straw to twiddle while I listened.

Morgan straightened. "It was stressful having her act this way, and I wasn't comfortable talking to her. After I told her a few things, I asked about her day. She smiled and showed the same discomfort. We both carefully chose safe subjects to talk about. Finally, I blurted out, 'Are you as uncomfortable as I am?'"

Morgan stopped talking to catch her breath.

I raised my head. "What did she say?"

"Mother's eyes widened and she stiffened. Finally she moaned. 'Umm. I'm your mother! You should be able to tell me what's on your mind.' Then Mother slumped, and her fake smile went away. She muttered, 'I know I haven't been around much, but I'd like to try and change that. It's my fault we feel this way right now. I promised to get some counseling, but it's going to take some time for me to change. You have to know I'm going try.'"

"Wow! Morgan that's super!"

"It gets better." As Morgan told her story, she acted out each of her mother's actions. "Mother shifted her shoulders backward and smiled a real smile at me. I—I honestly didn't know if I should stare back. She frightened me. I sat stiff in my chair, waiting for her to continue, and the waiter showed up.

"She told me to order whatever I wanted, and then she ordered a salad and a glass of wine. As soon as the waiter turned, Mom perked up. 'I have some news I'm dying to share.'"

Now I sat up and my pulse speeded. What could be so exciting? I patted the bale of hay, inviting Colton to hop up.

Morgan paced while Colton settled. "Mom said, 'Morgan, I know you have been unhappy for a long time, and I haven't bothered to help. But after being at your grandparents' house and seeing you relaxed and happy, I see what I've been doing to you. I can't make those years go away, but I can make your next ones better. While I was acting like a jerk at the horse show, scouts from different boarding schools were watching all the riders.'"

Morgan pressed her hands together. "Trina, my heart galloped so fast, I almost choked!"

Now, I was hooked. I couldn't move or look away.

"Mother reached across the table and grabbed one of my hands. Two Scouts from two of the schools I liked may offer me a scholarship for the rest of the year. It will depend on how I place during a show in November and one in December. If I do get accepted, and do well academically next semester, and continue winning at the shows, I could have a scholarship through my senior year." Morgan's hand went to her heart. "Knight has turned out to be my man in shining armor."

"Oh. My. Gawd! How awesome is that! Oh, Morgan. Is she okay with you going away?"

"Mother is thrilled at the idea. That I'd be doing what I want to do, and she could get some counseling while I'm being happy and productive. But now I have a ton of pressure to place in the next shows."

I stood for a moment, wiggled my bottom, and sat back down. "Wow! That's really wonderful! But what will I do without you at the barn or helping me with homework?"

Morgan sat next to me and grabbed my hand. "I can still help you online. You just send me your questions. And I'll be coming back and forth to see my parents. I'll expect you to come and visit with Colton."

Colton, hearing his name, leaped off the bale. The tops of his ears lifted.

I patted his head and then looked at Morgan. "Have you chosen which school you want to go to?"

"I can't. Not until I hear about their offers, but I really want to go to the one closest to my Grands and Quintin."

"Which is?"

"Tallahassee Riding Academy. You should see the grounds and the barns. Knight will miss you, but he'll love it there. I'd share a room with another girl. Trina, now that I've met you." She shook her finger at me. "I'm determined not to be afraid of making new friends. Anyway, I'll go to the dining room for meals. And there's every kind of activity I'd ever want to try."

Morgan's phone chirped. "Oh, Dad's calling. He's on his way. Let me go see Knight. Don't tell Mrs. B. I'll surprise her tomorrow."

I watched her dart away. *She might actually get the chance to follow her dream, and here I am still trying to figure out mine.*

Chapter 43

After hugging Morgan goodbye, I spent minutes breathing in the aroma of the barn while Colton checked out each corner. I needed to see Chancy, feel her attention, and tell her what was on my mind. Although I didn't want to be in the barn when Mrs. B arrived to feed the horses, it turned out I didn't have a choice.

She hurried in, turned on her favorite country music station, and hummed while she filled buckets. Colton whined and raced to her legs. I followed.

Mrs. B. backed up, and her voice squeaked. "Well, hey hon. What are you doing here?"

"Morgan came over to check on Knight while her Dad ran some errands, and then he drove back to pick her up. Her parents are really trying to get their act together."

"That's wonderful to hear." She scrunched her face. "How about you? Are you figuring out what you want to do?"

I halted, and raised my eyebrows. "What do you mean?"

"Honey, I promised I would keep Chancy for you as long as you wanted to ride her. Follow me while I feed everyone." She went in and out of stalls, changing empty buckets with full ones.

My brain made a screeching noise like a DJ scratching a record. *Do I tell her what's on my mind?*

Mrs. B put the lid on the grain container, and guided me to the tack room. "Do you want to tell me what's going on? I feel like I might be the last one to know."

I gave her a puzzled look. "The last to know about what?"

"Heather asked me if she could take lessons on Chancy. I almost choked. I didn't know you had given her permission to ride her. Heather's getting awfully attached, and I think Chancy is enjoying her, too."

"Oh!" I sucked in a breath. "I'm probably the last one to know. I'm not sure what I'm going to do. It will be another month or six weeks before I can ride again. Chancy needed to be worked, and Heather loves her." Tears slipped out. "The last time I rode I realized I hadn't improved very much. I don't have time to practice, and I am really enjoying training Colton. I'm so confused. I know I'll be sad when he has to be returned, but I have a long time before that happens. There are so many things I can do with him, and still work at the barn, see the horses, and earn money for dog classes."

Mrs. B put a hand on each of my shoulders and kept eye contact.

"I haven't made up my mind for certain, but I guess I'd tell Heather to go ahead and take lessons on Chancy. It won't hurt either one of us, and if I decide to ride again, Chancy will be that much better, and she can teach me. Mrs. B, when I know for sure what I'm doing, you'll be the first to know. Mom and Dad have no clue what I've been thinking. They'll be surprised, too."

She hugged me. "Scoot home. You have time to figure it out. I just want you to make the best decision you can. I'm always here for you."

"Thanks. Mrs. Brown. I'll be back tomorrow."

At dinner, Mom and Dad asked why I was so quiet. I tucked my chin and mumbled. "I have a lot on my mind. I'm taking Colton outside and then going to bed." Outside, I called Chase instead of texting. He knew my code for urgent.

He answered. "What's going on?"

I filled him in on my newest problem.

He listened until I finished. "You need to listen to your heart. We've found out it's okay to change our minds. You chose to train another pup." He paused. "And aren't you happy that you did?"

He couldn't see me, but I nodded.

"You did what felt right. If I was with you now, I'd be more than just your distant friend. I'd be giving you a hug, encouraging you to do what comes naturally. Pretend I'm there. Okay?"

I closed my eyes and sensed his arms go around me. "I am. Thanks, Chase. I miss you. I'll call you tomorrow. Now you pretend."

"Thanks, I pretend every day. Talk tomorrow."

I tossed and turned. Finally, I gave up sleeping, switched on my light, and read another article in *Discovery Teen* magazine about setting goals. I had always been a goal setter but now those goals were changing and confusing my life.

Mom questioned me on why I looked so tired at breakfast. I gave her a weak smile. "I had to study late last night." I don't think she believed me, but she let it slide.

At lunch time, Sarah stared at me. In her knowing way, she cross-examined me. "What's bothering you?"

"I'm okay. Just didn't sleep last night. Any chance you could come over after school, just for a little while?"

She tilted her head. She knew me too well. "I have a soccer game at seven-thirty. Let me see how much homework I have. If I can put off doing my homework until after our game, I'll rush right over."

"That'd be perfect. Thanks."

———

While outside with Mr. Colton, Sarah joined me in the back yard. "Hi, mystery girl?"

I smiled, and Colton barked. "Hey, to you! I really needed your company."

The brisk wind picked up, and goosebumps grew on our arms. Neither of us had a jacket.

I lifted my shoulders to warm my neck. "Before we shiver to death, let's go inside. We can fix hot chocolate, and I'll tell you what's going on."

Sarah bounced from foot to foot, eager to hear secrets, or get involved in someone else's problems. She pretended to throw a branch for Colton. When he ran ahead looking, she giggled and waved it in the air. He wagged his tail and she tossed it to him. Her lively voice grew intense as I followed her to the house.

She spun around and faced me. "You have been a little secretive lately. I know I'm not around as much for you to confide in, but we promised we'd always find time to tell each other our thoughts. Right?"

"I hope so, Sarah. We have a lot of history together. We just have to take the time to stay in touch, and never stop sharing what's going on."

We tore open our hot chocolate packets, filled our giant mugs with water, and set them in the microwave. Colton had plopped on his foam bed, stretched out, and hung his head over the edge.

I snickered. "Look at him! I guess he likes the blood rushing to his brain."

Sarah found the Oreo cookies in the pantry and filled a plate.

I smiled and settled on a chair. "Perfect. I need energy to say my ideas out loud."

Sarah grinned like Cheshire cat. "Oooh, this is going to be fun. She peeled apart the cookie, and with her teeth, scraped off the frosting from each chocolate cookie, and then put it back together, and ate it."

I watched each step of her procedure. "I've always wondered. Why don't you eat it together?"

She shrugged. "My dad eats it this way, and I've always copied him. Have you ever tried it this way? It's more chocolatey."

"Nope. But I'll try it your way if you'll try it my way."

Sarah snickered. "Okay, on three. One, two, three." Sarah took two bites of a whole cookie, and it was gone. I licked the frosting off and swallowed before I bit into the chocolate cookie. Sarah waited until mine was gone. "So what do you think?"

"I need a sip of hot chocolate." I smiled and took one more sip. "It takes longer to eat the pieces separately, and I can taste the cookie more, but I like them together. What about you?"

"I like my way. I love the frosting. But see, we can do it differently and still be friends. Now will you stop stalling?" She pulled out another cookie and spilt it apart, staring at me, waiting.

"Okay. Okay. I'm not sure, but this is what I've been thinking about. And I haven't told this to Mom and Dad yet, but I'm coming close to making a decision." I hesitated for a long moment.

Sarah blurted out. "All right. Get to the meat of what you're going to say. At this rate, you'll still be telling me what you don't know when I need to leave."

"Oh, Sarah. I'm trying. Let me get my thoughts organized." I started to speak, but sighed instead. I exhaled one more time, and then let the words rush out. "I'll never be a good enough rider to compete with Chancy or join a college team."

Sarah sealed her lips, and stared.

For a long moment, I looked at Sarah. "I love being at the barn, helping with the horses, and maybe doing trail rides." I smiled and shook my head. "But, no more crazy dreams of riding in the Olympics." My voice softened to a whisper. "Heather wants to take lessons on Chancy and will probably want to show her. She's already a better rider than I'll ever be. And Chancy would be a great show horse." I squeezed my eyes, not wanting them to leak, and worried saying those words out loud might make it all true.

Sarah gave me a startled wide-eyed look. "Wow! That's not anything I thought I'd ever hear you say." As she drew in a long, lungful of air, she hiked her shoulders to her ears. "So, what's your new plan?"

Bubbles floated in my stomach. I bent my head, and pictured training Colton as a mobility dog and for fun doing Rally competitions and running courses in Agility trials. When I looked into Sarah's face, I knew what I was going to say was right on.

My excitement rose to my chest, and I had to let it slip out. "I'm not only going to train dogs, but I want to compete in dog sports. I have it all figured out. I did Rally with Sydney, and we were just getting the swing of things, before—" I inhaled as a sharp pain stabbed me in my gut. For a moment, I stared off into space.

Sarah didn't say a word and waited.

I gasped. "I was saying, before he went back." I smiled. "Now I have Colton. I can still work for Mrs. Brown, and earn money for lessons and the entry fees. All I need is a car and a driver, which I have. And no special clothes. I've researched how to make jumps and other obstacles. And Dad loves to make things, so I know he'd help."

Sarah didn't even blink as I spoke. "Just a couple of questions. After you return Colton, then what do you do?"

I grinned, and grasped my left fist. "I was ready for that question. I've spent a lot of time thinking this through. I will already know how to do Agility and Rally, and I'll have all the obstacles made, and the next puppy will learn, too. I can keep doing it with each service dog until one day. Are you ready for this?"

With huge enthusiastic eye, Sarah nodded.

"Until one day, I'll have my own dog."

Sarah jolted upward, leaned forward, and slapped her hands on the kitchen table. "You're really thinking of having your own dog? To keep?"

My head bobbled up and down. "Yep. I'm getting closer to wanting my own dog." I paused and peered straight at Sarah. "I know it will grow old and leave me. But now I know I can handle being sad, and start over with each new dog that comes my way."

Sarah nodded and smiled. "You really *have* thought this through, haven't you?" As Sarah finished her sentence, the back door opened, and Mom buzzed into the kitchen. Startled, our heads snapped toward her. Sarah glanced back at me. I put my finger to my mouth and shook my head.

"Well, hello to you two. You look like you just got caught in the cookie jar."

Sarah and I cracked up. "That's just what we've been doing, Mrs. Ryan."

Laughing, Mom stashed her belongings on the counter. As she heated water for a cup of tea, she chatted about her emergencies at the vet clinic. Then joined us at the table. "Yum. Any cookies left?" She peeked into the box. "Oh, my! You two have made serious dent in this package."

Sarah and I waited to see how she'd eat hers. Without knowing we were watching, she pulled out a cookie, and split it apart. Sarah winked at me and smirked. Then Mom ate the one half with frosting, and then the other plain cookie.

I laughed out loud. "Now there are three ways to eat an Oreo."

Realizing what we were doing, Mom smiled and said, "I bet there are even more ways than three."

Then we experimented with new ideas on eating Oreo cookies.

Sarah leaned back in her chair, rubbed her stomach, and groaned. "I've had too much sugar. I need to go home. Thanks Mrs. R. that was fun."

Mom moved to the sink, filled her teapot once more, and busied herself waiting for it to whistle.

Sarah glanced at me with shining eyes. She did a thumbs-up. I grabbed my crutches, and we stepped outside.

She hugged me and whispered in my ear. "You've got to tell your parents tonight. They'll be happy with whatever you decide to do, but you can't keep it inside."

Chapter 44

Throughout dinner, I never said a word and shoved the food around, rearranging their places on my plate. Mom cleared the table, and I never realized both parents sat, staring, until Dad cleared his throat.

"Okay, T. Something's bothering you, and we need to know what's going on in that mind of yours."

My eyes welled, and I wiped both of them at the same time. I repeated what I had told Sarah.

Their expressions went from worried, to confused, to maybe sad; but they listened. After a long conversation about why I was giving up my dream of riding on a college team, both parents nodded.

Mom sighed. "You have made a well-thought-out decision. And it seems as if you've chosen something you're very talented at. But I hope you keep experimenting with lots of different activities. Some you'll choose to never do again, but others will grab you and won't let you go." Mom cackled. "Do you remember when you begged to take ballet lessons?"

I crinkled my nose. "I was around six and after the first class I cried, stomped my feet, and fought going to class. You made me continue my lessons because you had already paid for the month. I remember not knowing one step of the routine and watching everyone else dance in the mirror."

Mom shook her head slowly and giggled. "Ooo. You were never going to be a ballet dancer."

Breaking up with laughter, I blubbered, "I was so terrible! Thank goodness you let me quit. I've always just wanted to be around animals. Then Mrs. B invited me to help at the barn, and of course, I wanted to be an expert rider. I pretended Gretchel was my horse, and taught her to follow commands and jump over bushes."

All of a sudden, a bright light flicked on in my brain. My hands went straight to my face and covered my nose and mouth. I slowly twisted my head back and forth. "Oh. My. Gawd."

Each parent stared back at me as my thoughts jelled in the silence.

"It's taken me a long time to figure this out." Blinking, my grin grew and grew. "Do you realize I've been training dogs since I was six years old? This is what I'm meant to do."

Dad popped up out of his chair. "Be right back." He wandered into the den and returned with a dog magazine. He flipped to the folded pages and laid the magazine in front of my damp face. "Look T. I had planned to make some obstacles for Colton to keep him busy. See? Great minds think alike."

I glanced at the agility pictures, and Dad began describing how he'd make the teeter-totter and the table as he turned the pages.

My heart raced, listening. I stood and forgot about my crutches. Dad put his hand under my bent elbow, and balanced me as I hopped to the computer and sat. "I have to show you something."

My fingers danced across the keyboard. "There's a dog agility competition in Asheville, North Carolina, the first week of November. It's only an hour and a half away. Colton can come inside the arena and watch the event. Look, these are videos of last year's trials. Can we go?"

Mom's eyes glowed. "Sounds like fun and another learning experience for Colton. Let's take him on his first trip, stay in a hotel, let him wander around at the dog show, and go out for dinner. We haven't been on a vacation in a while."

I blinked back tears and felt the hundred-pound bag of sand fall from my shoulders. I would tell Mrs. Brown my decision. Chancy needed someone who would be better for her.

Even though I was losing another best friend, I had a sense of relief.

I drew in a slow long breath and let it out with determination. I'd be free to find my true self and blaze a new trail.

I could now put all of my energy into being the best dog trainer ever.

Saturday morning, I flung myself into the barn, ready to do my chores. My eyes zoomed clear through the barn and caught Mr. Simon standing in the middle of the stadium, coaching Heather. "Push your heels down. That's it. Now keep them there. Steady your hands. Elbows in. Pretend there's a pin in your head and someone is pulling you up."

Hearing those familiar words punched me in the gut and robbed my breath. I continued observing. Chancy moved with amazing precision. Heather did her dressage test, and Mr. Simon strolled to the fence to sit on the top rail and sip his coffee. *So, Heather is going to a horse show with Chancy.* I hyperventilated and wobbled to a bale of hay where I sat and hid my face under my hands. I gulped air, trying to calm my body. I had made my decision, but I wasn't sure my heart would follow through.

Colton stood next to me, staring out through the same door. He pawed my knee, plopped his front legs across my thighs and stretched his neck to lick the tears dribbling down my cheeks. I stroked his soft fur and looked into his caring eyes. His ears flopped forward and the tip of his pink tongue stuck out. I smiled at his loveable face, his blinking brown eyes, and gave him a giant bear hug. As soon as I released him, he stared into my eyes.

"Yes, Mr. Colton. We have a lot of work ahead, but we'll be a great team."

Colton woofed.

I stole one more peek through the barn opening. Heather maneuvered Chancy like a ballet dancer. I stood and wobbled away from the barn. Happiness swelled inside my mind and body. I glided down a new dirt path filled with golden orange, rusty-red, and brown leaves, all in different stages of colors and designs. They layered the ground like a colorful patchwork quilt, growing thicker with the wind.

I unhooked Colton and we headed home. His eyes sparkled with mischief as speckled leaves drifted down. He followed one leaf at a time, swirling back and forth. He caught it, spit it out, and caught another and another. Growing bored with catching leaves, he concentrated on a fallen tree trunk blocking our way. He never missed a step and bounced over the log. I halted, and called him back with hand signal. He repeated another small leap, lifting his face to me with a silly dog grin.

Bending from my waist, I held his face to mine. "You are so smart! You already know what's ahead, don't you?" He never looked away. "And you're showing off to make me feel better. Aren't you?"

He popped up, circled, and sat, wagging his tail across the leaves and pine needles. "Mr. Colton, I can't wait to see what you and I will accomplish in our next year together." I tucked my right crutch into my arm pit, and threw my right hand forward. "Come on. Let's go home and play."

He jumped over the trunk one more time, twirled around, and waited to see what I was going to do. I flung one crutch at a time over the log, leaned forward, balanced, and then flung my legs across.

Grinning, I looked him straight in his eyes. "See, I can do it, too. We're going to make a super team, and we'll have months of fun ahead."

Also from Sheri S. Levy

Seven Days to Goodbye: A Trina Ryan Novel

Coming Soon from Sheri S. Levy

For Keeps: A Trina Ryan Novel

---

www.SheriSLevy.com

Acknowledgements

First, I want to thank my readers and my SCBWI friends for investing their time in reading *Seven Days to Goodbye* and *Starting Over.* I appreciate your support, your comments, and your reviews. And to my critique group; Caroline Eschenberg, Jo Hackl, Landra Jenkins, Marica Pugh, and Carol Baldwin. I treasure our years together.

My stories developed because of finding PAALS. Jennifer Rodgers has helped me with research, and her volunteers and service dog owners have been gracious in sharing their experiences. It is often said, 'Be careful what you say or how you act in front of an author. You never know when you will be used in one of their stories. Mrs. Brown is based on a real person. Because of her devotion to my daughter when she rode horses, I wanted to show my love and gratitude by including her in *Starting Over.*

Thank you, Sue Conklin, affectionately called the Puppy Nanny. You helped me grow as a dog trainer and enabled me to write about dogs. And a big thank you to Dr. C J McCormack, for your medical advice on Trina's injury.

Cindy Koepp, my editor, deserves a standing ovation. She waves her magic mouse around the sentences and makes the words sing. Thanks Cindy, for all of your hard work and sharp eyes. My talented web designer, Sue Goetcheus, amazes me with her creative skills as she highlights my events, school visits, and writing life. I also want to send a big cheer to Sara Gracia, who designed my adorable cover. How can you not fall in love with Colton?

And to my publisher, Barking Rain Press, I appreciate your support and efforts in creating each novel. This has been a wonderful adventure for me, and I feel privileged to be working with you.

A big thank you goes to my children and grands who eagerly help me with ideas. And to my husband, Murphy, I am so lucky to have you beside me, allowing me to spend hours in my own world and pecking away at the computer. I did promise to take time to enjoy our next adventure!

Kayaks, here we come.

ABOUT SHERI S. LEVY

Sheri S. Levy is the award-winning author of the *Trina Ryan* series. The debut book in the series, *Seven Days to Goodbye,* won in the Special Interest category: Service Dog Award in 2015 from the Dog Writers Association (DWA). Her magazine article, *Scent with Love,* won a DWA award in 2011.

Sheri is an active member of SCBWI and SIBA. After a twenty-five-year teaching career in special needs, she has remained active with tutoring teens in reading and writing. PAALS, (Palmetto Animal Assisted Living Services), has helped with her research on writing about service dogs and how they change lives. Sheri, in turn, shares her book proceeds to support PAALS.org. It is a special pleasure for Sheri to do author visits and teach writing workshops. When she is not writing, she reads, plays with her two dogs, listens to music, and hangs out with her husband and family. You can find more information on her website, on her Facebook page, and on Twitter.

WWW.SHERISLEVY.COM

About Barking Rain Press

Did you know that five media conglomerates publish eighty percent of the books in the United States? As the publishing industry continues to contract, opportunities for emerging and mid-career authors are drying up. Who will write the literature of the twenty-first century if just a handful of profit-focused corporations are left to decide who—and what—is worthy of publication?

Barking Rain Press is dedicated to the creation and promotion of thoughtful and imaginative contemporary literature, which we believe is essential to a vital and diverse culture. As a nonprofit organization, Barking Rain Press is an independent publisher that seeks to cultivate relationships with new and mid-career writers over time, to be thorough in the editorial process, and to make the publishing process an experience that will add to an author's development—and ultimately enhance our literary heritage.

In selecting new titles for publication, Barking Rain Press considers authors at all points in their careers. Our goal is to support the development of emerging and mid-career authors—not just single books—as we know from experience that a writer's audience is cultivated over the course of several books.

Support for these efforts comes primarily from the sale of our publications; we also hope to attract grant funding and private donations. Whether you are a reader or a writer, we invite you to take a stand for independent publishing and become more involved with Barking Rain Press. With your support, we can make sure that talented writers thrive, and that their books reach the hands of spirited, curious readers. Find out more at our website.

WWW.BARKINGRAINPRESS.ORG

Barking Rain Press

ALSO FROM BARKING RAIN PRESS

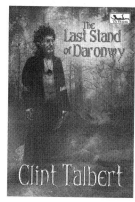

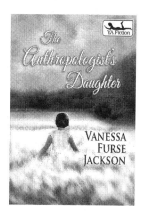

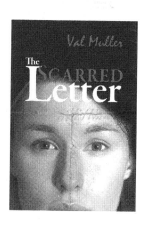